ROGUE HEART

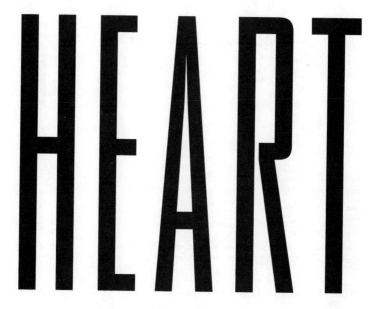

HEART

a companion novel to Rebel Seoul

AXIE OH

TU BOOKS
AN IMPRINT OF LEE & LOW BOOKS INC.
NEW YORK

BOOKS BY AXIE OH

Rebel Seoul

TU BOOKS, an imprint of LEE & LOW BOOKS Inc., 95 Madison Avenue, New York, NY 10016

leeandlow.com

Manufactured in the United States of America

MIX
Paper from responsible sources
FSC® C002589

Book design by Sheila Smallwood
Edited by Stacy Whitman
Typesetting by ElfElm Publishing
Book production by The Kids at Our House

The text is set in Granjon

10 9 8 7 6 5 4 3 2 1

First Edition
Cataloging-in-Publication Data is on file with the Library of Congress

FOR MY FATHER, JOHN,
MY MOTHER, JANE, AND
MY SISTER, CAMILLE

ACT 1

01

NEO BEIJING

The dreamers gather in Neo Beijing's starlight district. The wanderers and the thrill-seekers. Those with poems in their souls and secrets in their hearts. All those racing toward the bright, unknowable future.

All those running from pasts painful and unforgiven.

If you listen carefully, you can hear the song of the city. It's in the sharp, raucous laughter of the kids barreling down the crowded streets, in the heavy electronic beats erupting like great beasts from basement clubs, in the wind whistling through dark alleys, and in the rain as it drops onto the city like so many falling stars.

Two years ago, I stumbled into the city, half starved and afraid, and I couldn't hear the song. My heart beat louder than the music.

Memories rise unbidden—of pain, of loss, of a handsome face so beloved yet turned from me. I place a hand against my throat until the rapid pulse steadies. The past is in the mind, as Dr. Koga used to say. Let it go. Let it be.

The future is in the heart.

Tonight, the song is a light patter of droplets on the windowpane. I listen for a moment more before turning back to the café, broom in hand. The Alchemy of Dreams lies in the labyrinth of shops surrounding the Moon Court. The proprietors run the shop with their university-bound daughter, TingTing.

I believe at first they hired me out of pity—a girl, just sixteen, who couldn't understand their language, let alone speak it, who had but the clothes on her back and—according to TingTing—a haunting in her eyes. But after these two years I've wedged my way into their hearts. They undoubtedly have in mine.

A few patrons linger at the small, round tables dotting the dim interior, lit with strands of fairy lights. At the back of the café is the counter, beside which stands a small glass case of desserts. The familiar sense of peace settles over me, of being *here*, alive and safe.

TingTing approaches with a broom of her own. We've been sweeping along the perimeter of the café. Now we meet in the middle by the display of lychee rose cupcakes. TingTing grips her broom tightly, her pretty face flushed, her eyes beseeching. As she speaks, Tour Guide, my translation app, whirs the music of her voice into language in my head.

"Anmei?" she begins, calling me by the name I'd given her when we first met. It was the name of the heroine of the most popular Chinese drama at the time. "Do you mind if I leave early tonight? My boyfriend wants to take me out for our anniversary." She wrinkles her nose. "Can you believe I've been in love with the same person for two years?"

She doesn't expect a verbal answer from me—as a native Mandarin speaker, she never downloaded Tour Guide. Still, I attempt a little brokenly, "I don't mind. I'm happy for you. I—"

I can believe it.

Exuberant, she throws her arms around me. "What would I do without you?" Stepping from the embrace, she smoothly extracts the broom from my grip. "No more of this. Take it easy until closing. I'll set the bots to roam." She slips through the beaded curtain to the kitchen, presumably to hang up her apron and apply a sweep of cherry gloss across her lips. A few minutes later, I'm met with the steady drone of the dust bots as they awaken and shift listlessly through the curtain. They're old models, mid-twenty-second century, that TingTing bought at a junk auction last fall and restored by watching instructional videos on the Net. One bumps into my toe before careening off into a cake stand. We usually don't take them out. TingTing's parents, Ms. Chen and Auntie, are traditionalists and prefer lowTech amenities. Still, it's a constant war these days against the dust that sweeps across the city limits, piling worst in dead ends and cul-de-sacs, like the one that shelters The Alchemy of Dreams.

I perch on the stool behind the counter and reach beneath to where I keep a basket of books—a Mandarin language book, a romance novel in Korean, and an outdated encyclopedia. In theory, I could read any of the articles or light novels that pop up for free on the Net through my interface, a highTech operating system activated through a refurbished chip that I'd purchased after saving up for a year, and that TingTing's bioengineering-major boyfriend had installed last fall, but I prefer physical books. Having spent most of my life as if caught in a waking dream, it's a relief to hold something real.

I whisper the shortcut verbal command that I'd preprogrammed, and Tour Guide switches from Listening mode to Reading mode. I remove the small crêpe rose bookmarking the place I last read in the encyclopedia. The app translates each page as I turn it, interposing words in holographic Korean over the Chinese characters.

I'm so engrossed in a scholarly discourse on the principal reasons for the Great War that I almost miss the tap on my shoulder.

"Taking off now," TingTing says. Her hair is in a loose bun, and she wears a pale gray blouse and slacks. She looks elegant and mature. The phone in her pocket chirps, and she slips it out to laugh at a text. She looks happy. Not for the first time, I wonder what my life would have been like had I grown up the same as TingTing, with parents who loved me, in a city much like this one. Would I even now be hurrying out the door, on my way to meet a boy waiting for me in the rain?

I push the book aside, no longer able to concentrate. As I move to stand, a sharp pain penetrates my skull. I grip the counter to keep from falling.

It lasts for less than a second. When it's over, I search the café, but only a few patrons remain at this late hour—two middle-aged women gossiping while finishing off a pot of tea, and a sleeping boy, head tucked against his arms.

"Anmei?" TingTing asks, looking up from her phone. "Are you all right?"

I take a deep breath.

She chides, "You've been reading too much."

That must be it. People have headaches for all kinds of normal reasons. Why shouldn't I? And I've been careful, moving only between this shop and my apartment, routine being the second most effective way of controlling the pain. The first—keeping an emotional and physical distance from people—I've stuck to faithfully. Sometimes I catch an expression of hurt flicker across TingTing's features when I decline an invitation to a picnic at the park or to see a movie at the cinema, but it's better this way.

TingTing grabs her clutch off the counter, then hesitates. "I can stay if—"

I shake my head. "Go."

"All right, all right." She raises her hands in surrender. "I'll text you the work schedule tomorrow."

As she pushes open the door, she almost bumps into a girl entering the shop. *Welcome, Customer*, the automated message plays overhead along with the tinkling of the shop bells. I stand

and smooth down the apron of my skirt. The girl approaches the counter. She wears a baseball cap, the bill pulled low to cover her eyes. The pain rushes back, stronger than before. It intensifies with every step the girl takes until I can almost hear it, a rhythmic thumping in my head.

I inhale and exhale slowly, going through the exercises Dr. Koga taught me all those years ago. I close the door in my mind. Lock it with the silver key. Bury the key in the grass beneath the tree with leaves the color of autumn.

The pain is in your mind.

The girl reaches the counter, muttering in a low voice, "Is it a trick? Like one of those placebo things?" Smoke billows through the crack beneath the door. Before I can respond, she continues, bitterly, "As if it matters. At this point, I'd do about anything."

She turns to the glass case. In profile, her face is lovely. And young, about my own age. Within the shadows beneath her cap, I can see her eyes, hungry and bright like stars.

Most people's thoughts are like a summer wind, fleeting and inconsequential, whether to eat a lunch box from the convenience store or hot pork buns from a food cart, what film to see with friends once cram school lets out, whether to take the train or the bus home. Most thoughts are harmless. It hurts no one to think them, least of all yourself.

Then there are the thoughts Dr. Koga used to call "second-level" thoughts, those tied to emotions like shame, embarrassment, and fear. Hope, desire, and loss. These thoughts have colors to them, flavors and sounds. Even earlier tonight, I knew

TingTing had plans to see her boyfriend. Her anticipation had sounded like a flute in the wind.

And last are what I consider "third-level" thoughts, those thoughts people keep behind closed doors. Their secrets. These are the thoughts that manifest within me as debilitating headaches. I'm not sure why. Maybe it's instinctive on the thinkers' part, a sort of defense mechanism. They know somehow that for every door they lock, I hold the key.

Dr. Koga insisted that my theory of "third-level" thoughts was impossible. *Their thoughts are not your own. Your capacity for empathy inhibits your abilities. Remember . . . the pain is in your mind.*

With trembling hands, I pull gloves from the purification container, sliding them past my wrists. If I can only serve her quickly, she'll leave, and with distance, the pain will recede.

"This one." She taps the glass with the tip of her finger.

She's chosen a lemon berry éclair with pink glaze. It's one of the Alchemy's most popular items. After she consumes the treat, she'll have a dream of flying. We stock this particular dream in several flavors.

"And this."

A black bean brownie. A dream of nothing, also popular.

Carefully, I take each item and place it in a small, recyclable case. The pain seems to be lessening. If I can just hold on—

"And this." The girl's finger presses so hard against the glass it leaves a smudge. Her last choice is a round pastry with an intricate design of a lotus in bloom. Out of all the desserts in The Alchemy of Dreams, this is the only one I haven't tried.

A mooncake. For a dream of someone you once loved.

I place the cake beside the other two pieces, securing the lid over the top. Then I take off my gloves and dispose of them in the sanitation container. The cash register beeps and lights up green. She's transferred the necessary funds through her interface. The transaction is complete. My head thumps wildly. She reaches for the box. Her finger, still cool from pressing against the glass, slides across my knuckles.

I should never have taken off my gloves.

There's a storm inside her. Rough wind in all directions. Thunder, roaring and deep. A chaos of colors—blue, black, orange, and red. And at the eye of it, silence.

Slowly the door opens to a memory. A white hospital room, sunlight streaming through an open window. On the sill is a small vase with a single white chrysanthemum peeking over the rim. Beside it is a neatly folded soldier's uniform. The only piece of furniture in the room is an empty bed. The girl, dressed in black, stands at the foot of the bed. She holds the baseball cap in one clenched fist. "I love you," she says. "Come find me in my dreams."

I'm snapped out of the memory as the girl takes the case, frowning at my sudden stillness. My headache has vanished. She turns and walks out the door.

The pain is in my heart.

■ ■ ■

It's 23:00 by the time I close up shop. The rain has stopped.

The streets are slick and gleaming. Carefully, I step over neon-colored puddles and potholes reflecting the bright signs of cafés and restaurants.

Curfew is not for another hour, but the main square of the Court is crowded with people, clusters of uniformed day workers and off-duty soldiers. I pass a group of schoolgirls outside an arcade, sucking matching lollipops, their otherwise plain uniforms brightened with colorful accessories, baubles in their hair and brooches on their collars projecting holograms of stars, cats, and moons. These are the newest fad to come out of the highTech companies: holojewels, holopets, holomasks, attachments to "Enhance and Collect!" I pass through the glowing phosphorescent wings of a man, momentarily stunned by the static.

A pack of schoolboys fast approaches, heading toward one of the many simulation rooms in the Court. I move to step out of the way, but the crowd hems me in. The boys break around me like a school of fish. One, slouching with his hands in his pockets, catches my eye and winks, his thoughts tinged red with admiration. Blushing, I quickly move to the edge of the avenue.

You'd think with all these people, it would be difficult to keep everyone's thoughts at a distance. But it's actually easier to block in crowds. Not many people are thinking third- or even second-level thoughts when they're walking and laughing, talking and playing. And no one besides the occasional shopkeeper or glancing stranger is thinking of me.

A great airship passes overhead; its haunting drone settles

deep in my bones. Through the tide of people, I catch sight of a police bot, its red scanner sweeping over the crowd. Quickly I turn a corner and slip down a narrow alley.

My destination lies in Jazz Alley at the very edge of the starlight district, beside a great drop-off where Neo Beijing's Dome closes over the city. The massive barrier, a staple in every Neo city, solidifies at midnight, decorporealizing six hours later in time for the day workers' commute.

In the sunlight, the Dome is translucent. But as midnight approaches, it begins to glow, an aurora of vibrant colors. Before I came to the city, I'd spent six months in a small village where most of the elderly villagers preferred lowTech devices, if any. I'd had to flee when a man came through asking about a girl with strange powers. The village elder had pointed him to the east and me to the west to a city where, he said, I could become anyone I wanted. When I saw the Dome for the first time, that visible sign of the highest technology, I knew I'd come to the right place. I could feel the raw energy pulsing from it, a constant hum in my mind.

A loud clatter jolts me from my thoughts.

On instinct my hand reaches for the Taser in the pocket of my coat, a gift from TingTing. But the street, one of mostly lounge bars and speakeasies, is experiencing a rare lull of activity. The only movement is a stray cat lapping water from a broken drainpipe.

I slowly release the gun. Two years ago, fear would have driven me back to my one-room apartment. But routine and relative safety have given me courage. No one is looking for me, not anymore. And even if they were, they'd never find me. The person I was no longer exists.

I turn to the last building on the street, its fluorescent sign blinking: LIVE MUSIC. The low sound of a piano drifts from the smoke below. I hurry down the steps.

Ren, the bartender, glances up when I enter. "You look like you're in need of a drink."

I sigh and shake my head. I could never get used to the taste of alcohol.

"You look like you're in need of a song," a low-pitched voice interjects.

The piano man, a weathered-looking gentleman, sweeps a scale in F minor over the keys.

I walk over and place a hand on the piano, cool beneath my fingertips. "Every night, Jimmy." I speak in Korean, but Jimmy, a foreigner like myself, has downloaded Tour Guide.

With a grin, he responds in English, "What'll it be tonight? A song for the restless, the bereaved, the listless, the lost . . . ?" He catches the expression on my face. "Ah, a song for the broken-hearted."

I move slowly toward the stage, the microphone and stand illuminated by a lone spotlight.

"Your admirer is back," Ren calls from the bar, and I glance to the corner seat where a figure sits in shadow. "Your soldier in the corner." He chuckles at his own jest.

The soldier first appeared three months ago, and since then, he's shown up every last night of the month, occupying the same corner seat. I've never seen his face—he wears a cowl that conceals his features—but Ren and the others call him "the soldier" because of the way he carries himself, stiff and straight backed, a gun visibly holstered at his side.

I slip the coat from my shoulders and place it over the back of a chair. I give the verbal command to shut down my interface, and the ever-present miniscule whir disappears. In the silence, I take a breath.

The piano begins. I take the microphone from the stand and raise it to my lips. The words are in Korean, but it doesn't matter; music is universal.

Can they feel it—the way I feel now?

With the spotlight on me, I can't see the people in the room, but I can see their minds like spots of light in the darkness.

An old woman worries about her grandchildren, off fighting at the battlefront. A man wonders if he'll make rent this month, and if he's watered the daisy on his windowsill. The bartender dreams of blue skies. I see myself in someone's gaze. Hair bobbed at the chin, wearing a dress of pale silk. *Lovely girl. A voice like forgiveness.*

The mind in the corner is silent as always, right outside the reach of my powers.

I sing for them—for every one of them is a dreamer. Every one of them holds a secret in their heart. They've all come to the starlight district in search, in *want*, of something. And to this bar for a song.

The night is coming to an end. Last call was an hour ago. Soon the fear of midnight will drive them home, and another day will begin just like the last. The song reaches its final refrain.

There are many reasons I come to this bar—a respite from anonymity, to temper loneliness, for a moment in time. I sing for myself because sometimes I *feel* the secrets inside me burning like stars.

I have many secrets. My real name is Ama. I was a subject in a government experiment creating weapons out of children. Two years ago, the ship meant to transport me to a new facility crashed into the Bohai Sea. In the official reports, there were no survivors.

Far and away across a starlit sea, a friend once told me that freedom is a song. I still believe so, and yet . . .

There's a restlessness in my soul, a longing for things and people I cannot have. And after everything—the painful experiments, the losses and betrayals, freedom is not enough for me.

Why can't I be satisfied?

The song ends. I grab my coat and hurry home.

It's not far. Up the stairs and into my small one-room apartment above the bar. Through the neon-tinted window, I watch the rest of the patrons leave as high above the Dome crystallizes, cloaking the city in midnight.

02

THE AMATERASU PROJECT

After a night of fitful dreams, I wake at daybreak and slip into the shower, letting the cool water sluice over my heated skin. Afterward, wrapped in my favorite robe, I drop a tea bag into hot water, ladling in a healthy dose of honey to soothe my throat, sore from last night's smoky room. Mug in hand, I face my wardrobe—a single clothing rack drooping with a collection of shirts, slacks, and dresses, including a red slip dress that I bought on a whim last month on my birthday, the tag still attached. With no occasion to wear it, the dress's sole purpose has been to collect dust and remain on the rack, untouched and unloved.

Not unlike me.

I reach for an oversized sweater. Though spring, the air still holds the chill of winter. Properly dressed, I pull from beneath the clothing rack a hatbox containing my stockings.

The alarm on my phone goes off just as my interface flashes ⬚6:⬚⬚, the two synced together. Like most interfaces, mine is controlled through my phone, where I can download apps and program them into my interface with voice commands. Most people have a variety of different apps—music, social media, text messaging—but I prefer to limit mine to Tour Guide and a few reading apps. There's already enough noise in my mind.

The Alchemy of Dreams doesn't open until 10:00. Usually I spend my mornings practicing Mandarin or helping with cleanup at the bar. Sometimes I take a book and walk along the river, where the only people out are joggers, their thoughts hidden by the music blasting through their interfaces.

I close the lid of the hatbox and shimmy it back into place. It catches on something, refusing to budge even when I push it with force.

I retrieve a dust mask and begin to remove items—the hatbox of stockings, another hatbox with an actual hat inside, a plastic box full of miscellaneous accessories for lowTech gadgets, a dusty sweatshirt that must have fallen from its hanger, and lastly, a lowTech tablet, released from its hidden place beneath the sweatshirt. For a moment, I just stare at the dark screen, dust motes caught in the thick cracks that spider out from the center. I had forgotten about this tablet in my struggle to build a new life, in my desire to forget the old one.

From the plastic box of gadget accessories, I take out a universal charger and plug it into the wall, and then, with a separate cord, I connect the charger to the tablet. After a couple of minutes, the screen lights up. A photo of three children stares back at me. The caption at the top reads: Year 2194, The Amaterasu Project, Trial 03.

And there we are, the three of us wearing the same drab gray uniforms and identical expressions of discomfort, though admittedly, the other two more so than me. I stand in the middle of the photo, a cherry-cheeked eleven-year-old. Beside me, taller by an inch, stands Tera, age twelve. I remember the way her fierce gaze made the scientist snapping the photo fumble with his camera. On my other side is Su, though later he would go by the name Tsuko; at age ten, he was the youngest of us.

I was happy to finally stand beside them after being locked up in our individual rooms for so long. The scientists wanted to keep us separated so that we wouldn't form attachments to one another. I'd always thought that was a futile effort. Our friendship was inevitable.

I trail my fingers across their faces. It's been seven years since this photo was taken, two since I last saw them. My fellow experiments. My comrades. My friends.

The doorbell of my apartment trills. For half a heartbeat, I hope. But then my interface connects with the CCTV outside my door, projecting the feedback of a petite young woman with caramel-colored hair pulled back in a ballerina bun. TingTing. The clock on my interface reads 06:15. For as long as I've known her, I've never seen her make an appearance until well past 09:00.

I slip the tablet beneath my bedspread. Then, with a cursory glance around the apartment for details that might reveal my past, I head toward the door. I wince as I'm hit with a loud clamoring sound in my mind, a discordant group of bells ringing at once.

"TingTing!" I reach for the door and wrench it open.

She stands on the stairwell, tear stricken. I check her for visible signs of injury, but other than her obvious distress, her appearance is immaculate. Her blouse and skirt are freshly laundered, and her makeup is rosy and light. Instinctively, I probe her mind for a glimpse of her recent memories, but the anguish of her thoughts conceals the actual event that provoked them.

I have a sudden, awful misgiving. Are Mrs. Chen and Auntie in trouble? But no, TingTing would have never left them. A fight with her boyfriend, then?

I start to probe once more, then stop myself. Just because I *can* read her mind doesn't mean I should. The best way to learn what troubles a person is simply to ask them.

I usher TingTing inside to my small kitchen table before placing a warm cup of tea in her hands. As she stares around my room, the clamor of the bells in my head lessens, replaced with the chime of curiosity. I fidget, nervous, unused to having someone in my apartment.

I wait for TingTing's gaze to come full circle. "What happened?" I ask in Korean, raising my shoulders to express a question.

She reaches into her clutch and pulls out her phone, turning the screen toward me.

I don't have to read further than the subject line: Notice to Report for Armed Services Physical Examination.

"I thought my status as a university student would exempt me." She slides her thumb along the rim of the teacup. "Danzhu was exempt. But the difference is that he's studying engineering while I'm studying poetry." She leans back in the chair, sighing heavily. Though morbid, her thoughts hold the sunny tinge of humor. "Maybe I'll write him poems from the war front. At least that'll be romantic. And maybe one day they'll be published. Of course, they won't be famous unless they're published posthumously."

Abruptly she sits up. "Will you come with me?"

I startle, thinking she means "to war."

Then she continues, "The examination is near the financial district. Danzhu said he'd skip his morning classes, but I don't want to give the government an excuse to draft him too."

Normally I wouldn't hesitate to help TingTing or her parents—they've done so much for me—but my stomach sinks at the thought of going into the inner city.

"I forgot!" TingTing presses a hand to her mouth. "I'm so sorry. I know you don't like going out." She stands. "I can be so thoughtless. Please forget I even asked."

The bells in her head start to ring.

"Wait!" I grab her arm. To let fear stop me from helping someone I care about is to let the people who instilled that fear win. "We'll go together."

She opens her mouth to protest, but then bites her lip, her wide eyes hopeful. "Are you sure?"

I grab my coat. She doesn't argue, and soon we're catching a bus into the inner city.

We sit side by side on the cushioned seats, TingTing throwing me anxious glances until I reach over and squeeze her clasped hands. As always with skin-to-skin contact, I get a strong onslaught of her thoughts, but I endure the rush of worries and fear and concentrate on the feel of her hands against my own. I need this as much as she does.

Leaving the starlight district behind, we enter downtown Beijing, the blue-lit streets of the Grid widening to accommodate the numerous cars zooming by, most driverless, controlled by the Grid's electromagnetic core beneath the city. On either side of the streets are giant skyscrapers and massive billboards with ads in constant motion, displaying commercials ranging from toothpaste to video games to cosmetic injections. Scrolling across the buildings' sides is a constant stream of war propaganda.

> Apart we are broken; together we are mighty. Join the Alliance army and uphold the Neo Charter.
>
> Upcoming battles scheduled for 18 February, 25 June, and 1 September. Don't miss your chance to bring glory home for Neo Beijing!

I turn from the window. A few months ago, the Alliance forces and rebel factions signed a treaty to schedule battles, an unprecedented change in an ongoing war. For months there were roundtable discussions and think pieces on the event, though I deliberately chose not to watch or read any of them. The war isn't my concern, not anymore.

Turning to TingTing, I ask, "How was your anniversary?" I hold up two fingers to indicate *two-year anniversary*.

"Really great! We went skating. And . . ." She grins widely. "Danzhu bought me Tour Guide for an anniversary gift! I've already installed it." She taps her brow. "I know you've been learning Mandarin, but I thought how wonderful it would be if we could express our thoughts to each other in our native languages. Danzhu knows how much you mean to me."

"TingTing—" I'm at a loss for words, now that I have words to express myself.

"Don't cry or I'll cry! Anyway, it worked out well because it'll help me when I'm in the army. I hear the divisions are made up of people from all the different Neo states."

The bus stops at a shopping mall, and several passengers disembark.

As the bus moves back onto the Grid, the windows frost over and an ad begins to play across the newly formed screen. C'est La Vie's lead singer belts out a fast-tempo song accompanied by her bandmates, banging on drums and wildly flinging their guitars about. It's the theme song for the upcoming battle, "Flowers that Bloom in Winter."

C'est La Vie performs on a war-torn battlefield, with God Machines fighting overhead. It's obvious that most of the footage is CGI, yet the battle is still impressive, giant humanoid machines the size of small buildings speeding through the air and shooting one another with massive artillery that causes vibrant explosions—all to the backdrop of electro-pop music.

During the song's bridge, the screen switches to show some of the ace pilots in the upcoming battle. They stand in the foreground with their names, ages, and hometowns displayed at the bottom. Wing Kan, age 19, born in Neo Hong Kong, representing Neo Hong Kong. Fujii Hiyori, age 22, born in Okinawa, representing Neo Tokyo. Lee Byul, age 17, born in Gwangju, representing Neo Seoul. In the background are their respective God Machines, rotating on platforms like cakes on display.

Which reminds me. I turn to TingTing. "What about the café?"

"Oh! My twin cousins actually just moved to the city from the countryside. They'll help out until they find jobs of their own."

I nod, biting my lip. I've never worked in close quarters with anyone but TingTing. It'll take some time adjusting to new individuals with their own thoughts.

The ad ends with a message of recruitment and the words: Heroes will be made on the battlefield.

Then the windows clear, revealing our location.

I gasp. Coming up fast on our right is Neo Beijing's Tower.

In order for a city to be ratified as "Neo" and gain a representative seat on the Neo Council, it needs to have three things: a

Dome, a Grid, and a Tower. The Dome protects the city from outside attacks as well as having self-sustaining components, like antipollution technology. The Grid acts as traffic control and an almost-foolproof security measure. Lastly, the Tower is a place designated for the advancement of weapons technology.

I was raised in Neo Seoul's Tower, a subject in a secret weapons project. Had my transport carrier not crashed, it would have taken me to Neo Beijing's Tower, where the scientists had specific orders: to rehabilitate me—or if they couldn't manage that, to have me exterminated.

"Anmei?" TingTing motions to the door. "This is our stop."

I remain frozen, staring at the gargantuan structure of the Tower beyond the window. It's exactly like Neo Seoul's Tower, well over eight hundred meters in height, taking up half a hundred acres, a symbol of total power.

"Anmei? Are you all right? Anmei!"

I drag my gaze away, only to notice that the other disembarking passengers have stopped to stare, curious at what's caught my attention. I search each of their faces, but of course I recognize none of them. "Sorry," I say, "I get dizzy sometimes when the windows do that."

TingTing grabs my arm, and we exit down the ramp together. "I know what you mean," she says. As she speaks, I study the people exiting the bus and heading toward the shiny silver doors of the Tower—mostly office and maintenance workers, by their uniforms. No white-coated scientists. "One moment you're at your local stop, and then a shampoo ad plays, and you're so distracted by the glossiness of the model's hair that before you know it the windows clear and you're halfway across the city!"

The physical examination is held in a large gray edifice opposite the Tower. A queue is already forming outside the door marked NEW RECRUITS. As I hold our spot at the back of the line, TingTing hurries over to a food truck vendor selling hot buns and coffee at the edge of the Grid street. It's still early in the morning, and the truck has a line to rival our own.

As I wait, my gaze keeps wandering across the street, searching every individual who walks in and out those silver doors. My hands tremble so hard I have to slip them behind my back, cradling one fist in the other.

"Ay," a low male voice groans from behind me, "what's the point of advertising for recruits if they're gonna make us wait? Lines are the quickest way to get someone to give up."

I know the words aren't directed at me, muttered beneath the breath, yet my interest is sparked. He spoke in Korean.

Slowly I turn toward the speaker, wanting to take a peek without being seen. My caution is needless. He's looking down at his hands. He twists a wide band around his finger in a counterclockwise motion. Something about the movement is mesmerizing. Around and around he turns the ring until he stops, slipping it over the first knuckle to reveal a tattoo beneath. A red circle—the symbol of the most powerful crime syndicate in East Asia.

I gasp.

He jams the ring back in place. "You weren't supposed to see that."

"You're a member of Red Moon," I say in Korean.

"Hey, don't speak so loud!" He glances around, but no one is paying attention to us. "They're not exactly the most popular group around. And I'm an ex-member."

"It's difficult to leave a gang." I've only met one other person who's ever managed it.

He sighs, sweeping his ringed hand through thick black hair. "It wasn't easy."

"How did you do it?" I ask, surprising myself with my boldness. It feels good, almost liberating, to speak in a language I know all the rules to, all the subtle rhythms and nuances.

The boy arches a brow, clearly surprised himself. I can see him making his own calculations about me. Young. Ethnically Chinese, but able to speak Korean like a native. I don't have to read his mind to know that he's curious.

Finally he shrugs. "I was in Red Moon from ages eight to fifteen, when I was 'volunteered' to take the fall for one of the underbosses. Served three years in a Busan penitentiary. When I got out, I'd had enough. Fled the state. And now I'm here." He gestures widely. "In the longest line known to humankind. You'd think I'd have more patience after prison. You can move up."

I turn to see the line has shortened. I take a few steps closer to the door.

"What about you?" he asks. "What's your life story?"

"Nothing as interesting. I work at a bakery with my friend TingTing." I point at TingTing, who's successfully reached the window of the food truck, encouraging the worker as he stuffs pork buns into a paper bag. "I'm here to support her. She received her notice of draft this morning."

When he doesn't respond, I glance behind me to see he's looking over my shoulder, a small crease between his brows. "Hey now," he says softly, "I was honest with you."

I blush. That's the problem with noticing people; they tend to notice you back. "It's the truth. I'm very boring."

"I . . . see. Tell me, are those friends of yours too? They've been staring at you the whole time we've been talking."

I whip my head around to look across the street, where two figures in civilian clothing stand outside the Tower. Though they wear caps with bills lowered over their eyes, it's clear their gazes are trained on me. "I've never seen them before."

At least, I don't think I have. There were countless scientists and Tower personnel working on the Amaterasu Project at Neo Seoul's Tower. When the Tower was destroyed two years ago in the Battle of Neo Seoul, it's logical that many would have been transferred to Neo Beijing's Tower.

I count the beats of my heart, but neither of them—the woman or the man—approaches.

From behind me, the boy drawls, "And you said you were boring."

TingTing returns, handing me a pork bun and ushering me into the recruitment building. I wait for her in the small waiting area, unable to eat. I lose track of the ex-Red Moon member, whose name I never did find out. When TingTing finishes the examination, I follow her cautiously outside, but the man and woman are gone.

It's 23:00 by the time I leave the café, having stayed past my shift to help TingTing close for the night. After the examination, she'd been talkative, even cheerful, but as the afternoon hours waned, she'd become more reserved. I offered to stay with her until Danzhu finished with his part-time job, but she insisted I leave. And though I saw tears in her eyes, I forced myself to turn away, swallowing my need to give comfort over her need to be alone.

A few blocks from my apartment, it begins to rain. I duck beneath the awning of a chicken shop, the rich, salty smells blending with the smoke. Droplets patter on the plastic tarp roof. Raucous laughter erupts from within the shop, colleagues enjoying a meal after hours. I close my eyes and let my mind find solace in the rain. Soon the bright light of a police bot washes red across my eyelids. Leaving the cover of the awning, I slip into an alley.

I wonder if TingTing feels resentment toward me. Since I technically don't exist in Neo Beijing's citizen database, I can't be drafted. I can live in this city, walk its streets, and enjoy its food and music, yet I cannot fight for it. I cannot bleed for its people.

An old man sits on a lawn chair on the balcony of his second-floor apartment, smoking a pipe. A woman pulls a cart, the wheels clattering against the rough pavement. Inside the cart a small boy crouches, clutching a plastic robot.

I think of TingTing as I left her, beneath the fairy lights, her arms curled around her shoulders as if to keep from falling apart.

If the Amaterasu Project had been a success, she wouldn't have to fight. Instead it would have been Tera and Su. It would have been me.

I stop in the alley, the rain soaking my hair and clothes.

Should it have been me?

I remember Tera's words the last time all three of us were together, before the battle of Neo Seoul: *I am not a weapon to be wielded. I am my own person. To fight or not to fight, that is* my *decision to make.*

And Tsuko, his black eyes bloodshot and furious: *There is no decision to make. This war was never about your* feelings. *You will fight, because if you don't, hundreds of innocent people will die!*

And me, silent and torn between the two people I loved most in the world.

Where is the war fought? On a battlefield of thousands or in the heart of one individual?

Thunder rumbles overhead. The alley is mostly deserted, just a man at the end smoking a cigarette. I pull my coat closer around my shoulders.

The memories this day has dredged up feel like reopened wounds. It began with finding the tablet with the photo of Tera, Tsuko, and me, the ever-present ache of their loss, then Ting-Ting's draft notice, the guilt of wanting to keep myself safe, and then that man and woman outside the Tower, the fear that all of this was for nothing, and that I'll be brought back to the place where it all started, turned into the monster I was meant to be.

Painful memories open the door for even more painful ones, and soon I see a face, breathtakingly beautiful, and feel the ghostlike trail of fingers along the edge of my neck, so gentle it breaks me.

No! I shake my head and concentrate on the sound of my boots as they hit the pavement. To remember *him* would be unbearable.

Even at the beginning, when I made the choice to forge a new identity, I never thought I'd stay in one place. The threat of discovery was—*is*—ever-present. Peace and safety are just an illusion.

Maybe it's finally time to leave this city. I could go to Neo Taipei or Neo Hong Kong. Start over. Again and again, if I must. Until there's nothing left of the old me but a song in a smoke-filled basement bar, the only listeners a grandmother, a bartender, and a soldier in the corner.

Stepping over a pothole, I chide myself. Tera and Su always teased me for my dramatics. I'm almost at the end of the alley. The man has stopped smoking and is looking down at his phone, the light from the screen casting a low, eerie glow across his face. Though it's dark and the street deserted, I keep a slow and steady pace so as not to draw attention to myself. I pass him with my gaze averted.

I turn down another alley. In the night, they all look the same. I pull my coat tighter, longing to be under the covers of my warm bed, the portable heater tucked in snug against my feet. I'm turning down the last street to my apartment when a vision enters my mind, moving like a silent film.

A dark alley.

Rain slick on the pavement.

A girl walking alone, her back to the watcher.

A chill steals into my bones, and I pick up my speed. In the vision, the girl starts to walk faster. And then I can *hear* footsteps, heavy on the pavement behind me. My heart races. In the vision, the killer is almost upon her, he almost has her. The vision turns red as he nears, narrowing in. His hand reaches out. The air behind me shifts, a heaviness, a weight like the world falling down on me. With a shout, he lunges.

Abruptly, I turn and sprint down a side street, screaming for help. But there's no one out at this hour, not that they could hear me if they were, not in the rain that begins to pour even harder, thundering onto the streets.

As I run, the vision of his mind overlaps with the streets in front of me, and I can't tell who I am, let alone where I'm going. Every street looks the same. My head throbs painfully, battered from the inside. I try to block his thoughts, but they tear through with cruel, horrible images. A knife in the dark. Blood. Me, on the ground, my throat slit. And it's like it's already true. Is it the future? Is it the past? I can no longer tell the difference. I'm running through a maze in my mind. And there is no escape. Then . . .

Silence.

So sudden that I trip and fall into a puddle, drenching my already-soaked clothes. Quickly I stand and turn. There's no one there, just an empty street lit by one bent lamppost. My mind probes into the dark. There's nothing, only emptiness where there had been chaos and noise. Is this a trick? But how? Very few people can block their thoughts from me, and never someone whose mind was open to begin with.

I take a step back in the direction I'd fled from. It's foolish, I know, but I need to make sense of what happened. Have I lost my abilities? In my fear, I'd forgotten TingTing's Taser, and I grip it tightly now.

Slowly I round the corner and immediately stumble over an arm. I press a hand to my mouth, too shocked to scream.

My pursuer lies facedown on the ground. A horrid thought hits me—did I do this? In my panic, did I kill him with my *mind*? But then I hear the soft tread of feet. I look up to see a figure separate from the shadows of the alley.

It's the soldier from the bar, his cowl pulled back to reveal his face.

I recognize him immediately.

Tsuko.

03

TWO GHOSTS

Blood trickles from the man's head, swirling pink in the rainwater rushing toward the gutter.

I look up. "Did you . . . ?"

"He's unconscious," Tsuko says in a clipped voice. "I'm not a monster, however others might thrust that role upon me."

His words echo my own thoughts from earlier. *The monster I was meant to be.* He and I were always so similar, though he would argue that he and Tera were more alike. With their physical enhancements, they're ten times stronger and faster than the average human. But in truth, their similarities end there. Tsuko, the only one of us with both physical and mental enhancements, shares the same telepathic abilities as me. And like me, he's always accepted that his powers make him different, dangerous, a *monster.*

Yet his words imply that perhaps his views have changed in the years we've been apart.

"You look different," I say. His hair, which he always kept shorn close to the skull, is long now, dark strands clinging wetly to his forehead. He'd always been the shortest of the three of us, but now he stands a head taller than me. At seventeen, he's no longer the child I once knew.

"You don't," he says evenly, holding my gaze for a moment before looking away. The rain, which had lessened for a spell, picks up once more, and he motions to a dry spot beneath a small overhang. Leaning against the wall, he busies himself wringing water out of his coat. In this small space, we should stand close enough to touch, but he keeps his distance, with one shoulder in the rain.

For so long, I had thought him dead, perished in the battle of Neo Seoul. Now that he's here beside me, it takes everything within me not to reach out and hold him close.

I have so many questions I want to ask him. *How did you survive the attack on the Tower? What have you been doing these past two years? When did you discover that I was alive, that I'd survived the transport carrier crash? How did you find me?*

Instead I fall back into old habits. "I cried for you when I thought you had died. Did you cry for me?"

He stops fidgeting with his shirt, letting it drop. He meets my gaze with a frown, his eyes wary. "I forgot what you were like. Please, let us disregard all societal norms of conversation."

"*I* might not have known you were alive and in this city,

but you knew I was. Why did you never say anything?"

He doesn't respond, his expression unreadable.

"You're not with the Neo Council anymore, are you? You're in hiding like me." If he were still loyal to the council, he would have returned to wherever the Neo State of Korea's military had set up its base of operations after the destruction of the Tower. The fact that he hasn't shows that his beliefs, at least where the Alliance is concerned, have changed.

Shivering, I glance at the man on the ground. "If it weren't for him, would you ever have spoken to me?"

"No."

Pain stabs me at his words. If this hadn't happened, he would have never spoken to me. He would have passed me by, a ship in the night.

"Do you know him?" Crouching over the body, Tsuko pats down the man's jacket.

I think back to that moment in the alley, the light of his phone illuminating his face. "No, I've never seen him before."

Finding the phone, Tsuko picks up the man's limp hand and presses it to the biometric lock. The phone lights up. "He knows you."

On the screen is an image of a younger me, my hair shoulder-length, my cheeks flushed. I'm gazing not at the camera, but off to the side. I remember the day this photo was taken. Dr. Koga had wanted individual photos of all three of us for the archives. Tera had taken her photo with her usual dour expression. Tsuko hadn't shown up for his. Every year I managed an obedient, tight-lipped smile for Dr. Koga's benefit, but that day, we'd had two more people in the room—Lee Jaewon and Alex Kim, soldiers from Apgujeong's military academy.

I wasn't looking at the camera because I was looking at them—at Jaewon, who was making silly faces in a heroic attempt to get Tera to smile.

And at Alex, who was looking at me.

"You're still in love with him." Tsuko's dispassionate voice breaks through my memories. It's not a question. I fight to contain a blush, having forgotten what it felt like to be on the receiving end of his telepathic scrutiny. "He thinks you're dead."

I wince. Tsuko never was one to mince words.

The urge to ask questions this time is almost unbearable. *Have you seen Alex? Is he safe? Where is he? What is he—?*

Tsuko glances up, the light of the phone reflected silver in his eyes, and I realize he can *hear* all my questions, all my thoughts and emotions. He always has, just as I can—

I frown. Since we've been together, I've heard nothing of his thoughts. In the bar, I'd assumed his physical distance and mental walls blocked them from me—but here, standing beside me, my mental strength should have overpowered his. Though both physically and mentally Enhanced, Tsuko was always weaker than Tera and me when it came to the individual abilities. What's changed in the past two years?

If he notices the turn of my thoughts, he doesn't show it, breaking our gaze to hold up the phone, still illuminated with my photograph. "The problem is, someone knows your lie for what it is, and would kill to make it a truth."

"The Neo Council?" I ask. *Have they finally found me?*

Tsuko shakes his head. "No, I don't think so. If it were them, they wouldn't hire an assassin to kill you quietly in an alley. They'd send a team to get you back. You're worth trillions in investments."

"Then who?"

"I don't know." He glances at the man on the ground. "I'll have to ask him when he wakes. But he's not the only reason I wanted to speak with you tonight. Ama, you need to listen carefully to what I'm about to say."

I nod, though it's hard to concentrate with my heart leaping at the sound of my name. It's been two years since anyone has called me by it.

"Have you heard of a group called P-H-N-X, more commonly known as Phoenix?"

I frown, unfamiliar with the English word.

"It's an international organization of resistance fighters. PHNX stands for Protectors of Humanity and Nations—X Division."

"No, I've never heard of them." In order to keep a low profile, I've avoided searching up or reading articles about the ongoing war, since the government tracks keywords and topics of interest. I only know the basic facts: that the war, fought in three Acts, is on its third and final one, and that between the two combatants—the states under the control of the Neo Council and the seceded nation of South China and its rebel allies—the Neo Council is poised to win.

"Why?" I ask. If PHNX is a resistance group, then it must be allied with the South Chinese forces.

"The Neo Council might not have discovered that you survived the crash, but according to one of my sources, PHNX *has*, or at least suspects that you might have. They've sent out operatives in search of you."

I glance nervously at the man on the ground. "Maybe PHNX sent the assassin."

But Tsuko's already shaking his head. "I don't think they want to kill you." He pauses, watching me carefully. "I believe they want to recruit you."

"Me?" I blink, surprised. "Why me?"

Tsuko arches a brow. "You're the result of a very expensive and lucrative super soldier program. Why do you *think* they want to recruit you?"

"They would use me for their own agenda, just like the Tower. I won't go back to being a weapon to be wielded by others."

Tsuko nods, as if this were the reaction he expected from me. "What will you do?"

"I'll leave the city." The events of the night have revealed that I'm no longer safe here.

"Where will you go?" Leaning once more against the wall, Tsuko looks down at his hands.

"Somewhere far away from here. I refuse to stay and be forced to join the resistance or be murdered by an assassin." Everything I need for my escape is in my apartment: money, my forged citizen papers. If I'm careful, I should be untraceable.

"There's a third option." Tsuko says the words casually. As we've been speaking, he's been focused on the movement of his hands, and I realize he's tracing a scar that runs diagonal across his lifeline. Unlike me, he doesn't scar easily, his enhancements allowing his body to regenerate at an accelerated rate. To leave a scar like that, the wound must have cut deep. "You could come with me."

I'm too shocked to reply. The thought never occurred to me. According to his mindset, it would be a "tactical disadvantage" to bring me with him, as I lack physical enhancements and have little to no combat experience. I'm also apparently wanted dead or alive by a few outside forces.

Unlike Tera and me, who were as close as sisters, Tsuko always kept himself at a distance. He believed attachments weakened the will of a soldier.

Even so, the offer is tempting. Going with him would mean he would shoulder the burden of so many of my fears. But more than that, going with him would mean I'd no longer be alone.

"This assassin should have never been a threat to you." Tsuko faces me fully. "With your powers, you should have been able to stop him, muddle his thoughts or cause him to hallucinate. You're strong enough that you could have even knocked him unconscious. Have you forgotten all your training?"

I grimace. "I don't want to hurt anyone."

"He was trying to kill you, Ama!"

"It doesn't matter."

"You weren't upset when *I* knocked him unconscious, though I used my hand and not my mind. The execution is fine as long as you're not the executioner."

"Stop! I don't want to argue with you." I wrap my arms around myself. I'd forgotten how cold it was, warmed by the presence of him beside me, but now I feel the ache of it again, the rain-slicked chill.

"If you come with me, I can help you control your powers. These past two years, I've been testing the reach of my abilities, learning how to build walls in my mind, how to break down walls in others' minds."

So that's why I can't pick up on any of his thoughts or emotions. He's been *practicing*. He's been sharpening his powers . . .

"For what purpose?" I ask softly.

I don't have to read his mind to know that *he* knows I won't like the answer he's about to give. His jaw muscle ticks. "You know I can't stand by and let this futile war go on."

"You would only help me," I say slowly, "so that I could help you. But I know you. Do you still believe the end justifies the means?"

His answer is immediate. "Always."

I start to turn away, but Tsuko grabs me by the wrist and pulls me toward him. "You don't know how incredibly powerful you could be." His voice is thick with emotion. "More than me. More than Tera, even. You could single-handedly turn the tide of this war. You could bring peace to the world, Ama. If you would only—"

"You would use me!" I shout. "Just like the Tower. Just like the rebels. You would make me a murderer for your own agenda. Killing doesn't stop the killing!"

My voice echoes hollowly, ricocheting off the alley walls. Tsuko drops my wrist, his eyes shadowed. For a moment, there's silence.

Then he says, "Not everyone can be a saint like you, Ama."

I want to cry. Why has it come to this? After so long apart, why do we have to fight?

"If you're going to leave the city," he adds quietly, "you should leave tonight."

"I'm sorry, Tsuko. I don't want to part with bad feelings."

He says nothing. Instead, he steps from beneath the over-hang. He lifts his hand, palm up. "The rain's stopped." He then nods, indicating the man on the ground. "I'll take care of him. Discover who he reports to. Cut out the source if I can. You don't have to worry anymore."

"Su . . ."

"Do you remember what you said to me, that last night before the battle, after Tera had left, and it was just you and me?" He turns his face so that I can't read his expression. "I . . . liked it, when it was just you and me."

And now I am crying. For everything we once were, for everything we can never be again.

"Is this what you really want, Ama? Running? Hiding? Is this the future you saw for yourself that night?"

I say nothing. The words are choked up inside me. Even my mind is a chaos of thoughts and colors.

"Go," Tsuko says. "It's almost curfew."

I head in the direction of my apartment, turning back after a few steps. "For three months you showed up at the bar. You never spoke to me, but you still came. Why?"

In the alley, he's encased in shadows, but then he lifts his head, and the moonlight washes over his face—a little older, but still very young, with a proud, sullen mouth and eyes wary and haunted.

But then he smiles, a small quirk of the lips. It feels like forgiveness. "I wanted to hear you sing."

04

PHNX

When I arrive at my apartment, the door is slightly ajar. After the events of the night, I shouldn't be surprised. A quick probe shows that the two individuals inside already know I'm here, having seen my approach through the window. Their thoughts are the calm blue of an ocean with a tinge of pink on the horizon—anticipation for my arrival. No thoughts of violence or ill intention.

I push open the door.

A stylish young woman turns from the window beside my bed. She's dressed in a dark green bomber jacket over a thin, slitted black sheath. At the kitchen table, a boy wearing jeans and a hoodie jacket quickly stands, pulling a cap off his head and running a hand through wavy, reddish-brown hair. Immediately I recognize them as the woman and man outside the Tower.

"Excuse us for the intrusion," the woman says, her voice earthy and full. "We're trying to keep a low profile. Otherwise we'd have waited for you outside."

It's a reasonable excuse for breaking and entering, and after my conversation with Tsuko, I have an idea of who they might be. I close the door behind me, wary of eavesdropping neighbors.

"I'm in a hurry," I say, moving to my bed and reaching underneath for the carpetbag. "You can talk while I pack." Usually I'm not a rude hostess, but I *am* in a hurry, and they *are* intruders. Unlike the man in the alley, I sense no hostility from them, just cautious optimism from the woman and curiosity from the boy.

"My name is Helen Li," the woman begins. "I'm the leader of a small, elite group that reports to an organization called PHNX."

"I've heard of PHNX," I say, grabbing clothing at random off the rack and stuffing it into the bag. I hesitate over the red slip dress, and then finally decide to throw it in with the rest. If anything, I can sell it for cash.

"Then you'll know we're part of the resistance working to bring an end to the tyranny of the Neo Council, though our tactics differ from our brothers and sisters who take up arms. We specialize in espionage and covert missions. You can imagine a talent such as yours would be invaluable."

I was right. They want to use me just as the Tower would have, weaponizing my mind for their own agenda. "What makes you think the resistance is any better than the Alliance?

To my understanding, they both force individuals into situations not of their own making."

Helen doesn't immediately respond, which gives me the impression that she doesn't have an answer. I continue stuffing the last of my socks into the bag.

"I don't."

I stop to look at her. She sits at the edge of my bed, with one long leg casually crossed over the other. "I don't know which side is more right than the other. If it were easy, no one would ever fight. There would be no such thing as choices. But as life would have it, there *are* choices. I make them with every mission I accept and with every step I take to complete that mission. The consequences, both positive *and* negative, I live with." Her low, patient voice is mesmerizing. I can see how she became a leader.

"There is no wrong. There is no right. There is only the choice you make because of who you are, the events of your life that have shaped and guided you to the very moment when the choice must be made. The question is"—she leans forward slightly—"what choice will you make?"

I zip up the carpetbag and place it by the door. I then head into the small kitchenette and open the cabinet. My emergency banknotes are stashed in the small tin box on the top shelf. Standing on my tiptoes, I attempt to grab it. My fingers only nudge it back farther. I hear the scrape of the kitchen chair being pushed back, and soon an arm reaches up and grabs the tin. I meet warm, hazel-colored eyes set in a handsome, friendly face.

"So, it's true then?" the boy asks, holding the tin out to me. "You can read minds?"

"Shun," Helen warns.

I glance between them, noting the similarities in their features, though the boy's hair is dyed. They must be related—siblings, if I were to guess.

I take the tin from him and slip it into the coat of my pocket. "I can."

"Incredible," he says, then proceeds to *think*, loudly, that I'm a fraud. *I believe in science, not magic.*

He flashes a dimpled smile. If I couldn't read his thoughts, I would find it charming. Instead, I find it very annoying.

As he stares at me, his thoughts turn contemplative. A memory from last night stirs in his mind, when he'd been staking out my apartment and saw me outside the bar. I'd been gazing up at the Dome. In the memory, he speaks into a comm device. "I found her. She's kind of tragic, isn't she? Like a songbird caught in a cage." He moves and accidentally kicks a metal can that goes clattering onto the road. He backs up against the wall as, startled by the noise, I turn my head in his direction.

I blink, and the memory dissipates.

"You're wrong about me," I say, and Shun frowns. "I am not trapped." His eyes widen slightly. "I am not waiting for someone to save me. I save myself every day. Watch me, and I'll show you."

I grab my bag off the floor and turn to the door.

Helen is waiting with an envelope in her hand. "What if *you* could save others? In Beijing's Tower, they're experimenting on children, orphans just like you. At 04:00 tomorrow morning, the

Tower is relocating a group of them to a facility outside the city limits. A separate team will intercept the transport and release the children to safe houses for recovery and rehabilitation."

"They'll just steal more orphans," I say. "In war, there are plenty."

"That's where our team comes in. We have a plan to detonate explosives in select parts of the lab. We don't mean to bring down the Tower in its entirety, just cause a distraction from the team picking up the children."

"And blow up their expensive-as-hell equipment," Shun adds with a savage grin.

"We could really use your help," Helen says. "Use this as an opportunity to face the ghosts of your past and overcome them. You should help us, if only for that."

"I'm sorry," I say, and strangely, I am.

Helen holds my gaze a moment before nodding. "I can't say I'm not disappointed, but I respect your decision." She hands over the envelope. Inside are a train ticket and a new set of identification papers.

"Why?" I look up, surprised. Why would they help me now after I refused their offer?

"We're about to enter into a very dangerous situation to save girls just like you. To be honest, the probability of our success is low even with your help. At least I can ensure that you get away safely."

"Thank you." I hesitate, then take her hand.

Helen's grip is firm. Releasing me, she opens the door. "Good luck."

It's after midnight. The streets are deserted. Being caught after hours means a hefty fine and jail without bail for a twenty-four-hour period. Of course some people are exceptions to the rule—government officials, the military, those with connections to either the government or the military.

Adjusting my carpetbag on my shoulder, I reach into the envelope. The train ticket is for the first outgoing train at 04:00, en route to Neo Shanghai. Curfew ends at 06:00, which means this train must be limited to that select group of individuals. Which means, through my new identification papers, *I'm* a part of that group.

I'm impressed. PHNX must have an extensive network to acquire these papers. I quickly skim them and memorize the key components. I'm the second daughter of the chairman of a joint Chinese-Korean tech company, attending university in Neo Beijing, but returning home to Neo Shanghai for Lunar New Year.

Soon I'm passing the alley where I left Tsuko and the assassin. There's no evidence of either of them, no blood on the pavement. I wonder where Tsuko's taken him and what he'll do to get the information he wants.

The execution is fine as long as you're not the executioner. While Dr. Koga and Tera used to coddle me, Tsuko never did. Maybe it was because I was older than him and he expected more from me, or maybe it was because of his personality—he expected more from us all.

It's several hours to the train station by foot. I take a detour to visit The Alchemy of Dreams one last time. On the counter,

I leave TingTing's favorite of my dresses and a small folded note: *Write a poem for me.*

At the station, the clerk barely glances at my papers before passing me through.

I follow the directions on my ticket to a business-class cabin at the center of the train, where I store my carpetbag in the overhead compartment and take a seat by the window.

Thirty minutes until departure.

There are five seats in the cabin, but only the single seat across the aisle is occupied, by an elderly gentleman in a black coat. I can hear the gentle murmur of his snores. I lean my head against the heated window and watch the other passengers move across the train platform. It's still dark out, and in the dim lighting, they look like faceless shadows.

At the front of the car, a screen digitally displays the time. 03:35.

Twenty-five minutes until departure.

A commercial begins to play, advertising the upcoming battle scheduled in two weeks' time. The tagline: A battle to ring in the New Year. Similar to the ad I saw playing over the Grid yesterday, the commercial breaks down time: 09:00, place: the East China Sea, and several key players to look out for: Wing Kan, Fuji Hiyori, and Lee Byul.

"Though we're getting some more information from our ground correspondents at the barracks . . ." I tune the newscaster out and refocus on the activity on the train platform. I'm not clear of danger yet. *" . . . informing us to look out for some new, raw talent in next week's battle, a hot-shot transfer from the American Neo*

States and a handsome young pilot from Neo Seoul . . ."

The train car door opens, and two women enter. Bypassing the snoring man and me, they take the two seats together positioned at the front right side of the car. While one woman settles by the window, the other places their luggage in the overhead compartment. A name tag slips from around her neck, falling to her chest. *Dr. Irene Yu, Department of Genetic Engineering and Biological Weapons, Employee #0987, The Tower.* I curse my luck to end up in a train car with Tower employees. Glancing around the cabin car, she tucks the name tag back into her blouse. I'm careful not to be seen watching her, feigning bored disinterest as I gaze out the window, a privileged teenager on her way home for the weekend.

"Are you sure we shouldn't go back?" the first woman asks. She presses a panel on the wall, and a drawer opens. From inside she removes a pair of complimentary indoor slippers.

"There's nothing we can do," Dr. Yu answers.

The first woman drops the slippers on the floor in front of Dr. Yu. "Here, take these. We have a long trip. Didn't you say you had to use the restroom?"

"It's better to let the guards take care of these things anyway."

The first woman nods. "Is it true they caught him breaking into the labs?"

I sit up in my seat.

"Lower your voice," Dr. Yu hisses.

"Do they know why?" The first woman has pitched her voice low, but I reach into my pocket and increase Tour Guide's audio pickup. Her words become as clear as if they were spoken into my ear.

"They'll find out soon," Dr. Yu answers. "The man—boy, really—is undergoing interrogation as we speak. He won't last long. They'll determine whatever foolish plan he'd been a part of and put an end to it. Where are the restrooms again?" She stands and exits through the front door of the train car.

It's 03:50.

I feel sick.

Ten minutes until departure.

I'd only met the rebels briefly. Had these scientists not entered the car, I would have never known their fate. It shouldn't matter what happens to them. It *doesn't* matter. And yet I can't help thinking of Helen's calm, steady voice, her quiet eyes like still pools at night. And Shun, who might have doubted my abilities, but never doubted their decision to help me.

Then suddenly I'm thinking of Tsuko, and the way he kept his mind closed to me throughout our entire reunion, and yet I feel like I knew at every moment what he was thinking.

"Do you remember what you said to me?"

That last night before the battle, we'd stood together on top of the Tower and looked down upon the city. Tsuko had caught my gaze, an almost pleading look in his eyes, as if in my answer, he could find his own. *"What do you* want, *Ama?"*

I didn't have an answer then. I just knew what I *didn't* want.

"I don't want to sleep to see my dreams."

"I don't want to close my eyes to feel like I'm alive."

Why is it that to do nothing feels like dying?

Standing, I grab my carpetbag and exit through the front of the car. The washroom in the short hallway shows the red OCCUPIED sign. I flick my head to the left, releasing the lock. A spell of dizziness hits me. I haven't deliberately used my powers in two years.

Inside, Dr. Yu is applying a coat of lipstick. She stops mid-sweep. "How did you get in here?" I notice the moment she sees my eyes. They glow green when I use the telekinetic end of my powers. "Who are you?" she demands.

"I'm no one," I say. "You never saw me."

I break through the natural walls in her mind. Her eyes lose focus. Her expression turns dreamy, distant.

"Where are they keeping the boy for interrogation?" I ask.

"On the third basement level outside the labs where they caught him."

"How many guards are stationed in the room and on the floors?"

"In the room I'm not sure, though I would guess five or more. Each floor has one guard making rounds at all times."

"How do you get in and out of the building?"

She lifts her name tag. "With this, through most of the scanners. The laboratory has biometric locks."

"Give that to me." I take the name tag. "How did you get to the train station?"

"My car."

"Describe it."

"It's a white sports car," she elaborates, "parked outside the main terminal."

"Is there a car key?"

"A passcode."

"What is it?"

"'Nothing will come of nothing.'"

"When you return to your seat," I tell her, "you won't remember what transpired here. You'll have a headache and sleep the rest of the train ride. If someone asks you where your ID went, you'll say you lost it."

I'm halfway across the platform before I release my hold on Dr. Yu's mind.

04:00.

05

THE TOWER

"Nothing will come of nothing."

The car whirs to life with the voice activation. I find the Tower as the first entry in the address book and plug it in. As expected, Dr. Yu has twenty-four-hour access to the Grid, and the car zooms down the street uninhibited.

What am I doing? By now the train would have already departed. I have no plan. My head throbs as if there's a hammer incessantly drumming at the inner edge of my skull. It's been so long since I actively used my powers on another human being.

I need to find Helen. But how do I know where she is or if she's even still at the Tower?

It's quiet outside when I arrive, no evidence that a rebel plan has been foiled. For a few minutes, I idle in the car, taking long, steadying breaths. The last time I was in a Tower, I'd been a prisoner in mind and body. I'd only escaped because those who were searching for me had thought me dead. And I'm about to step inside another, of my own free will. I take one last deep breath, slip Dr. Yu's name tag over my head, and exit the car.

I approach the double doors of the Tower, sensing the minds of two individuals on the other side.

I picture Dr. Yu, her hair in a simple chignon. Her height, half a dozen centimeters taller than me in heels. Her clothing, a brown coat over an A-line dress. I hold my badge to the doors and they open. The guards inside turn at my entrance, hands on their automatics. In training, this was the moment Dr. Koga called the "smoke," when I throw a veil across their thoughts. When the smoke clears, they'll see what I want them to see—in theory. It's been a long time since I've used my powers like this.

For a moment, no one moves. They both blink slowly, as if disoriented. I hold my breath. I wish I'd had more time to prepare. Heels would have at least put me at Dr. Yu's height. I'm forcing their brains to accept that an eighteen-year-old girl is a forty-year-old woman. Our differences might be too vast for their brains to comprehend.

The one on the right lowers his gun. "Excuse our rudeness, Dr. Yu. We're on high alert with the security breach."

Tour Guide whirs to life, translating his words in my head. I blanch, realizing I'll have to respond as Dr. Yu would, in Mandarin. I don't think I have the capability of forcing them to believe my Mandarin is unaccented or that my Korean *is* Mandarin.

My nerves make the illusion of Dr. Yu flicker. The pounding in my skull doesn't help.

The guard on the left frowns. "Are you here to oversee the interrogation?"

Should I risk an answer? Desperately I probe the guards' minds. An impression of Dr. Yu emerges—built from memories of the scientist's routine—always in a hurry, her attention focused inward as she conversed with remote individuals through her interface.

Keeping to their expectations of Dr. Yu, I ignore them completely and walk by. Neither shouts for me to stop.

In the elevator, I back up against the far wall. What next? Dr. Yu said they were holding Shun on the third basement level outside the labs. I step forward and press the button labeled *3B*. Then, turning, I look directly up at a security camera.

I curse inwardly. This isn't good.

I can change an individual's perception of me if they're standing nearby, but not through an optical system. Whoever is monitoring the CCTV system sees me as I am, a teenager with a stolen name tag. Why haven't they sounded the alarm? Maybe they've already gathered to ambush me on the third level. The elevator stops on 2B instead. The doors open.

"Helen!" I say as I catch sight of her standing on the other side.

Immediately I realize my mistake. A man who'd had his gun pressed to the back of Helen's head shifts to point it at me.

It all happens in a moment. I jerk my mind to the right. The gun goes flying from his hand. Helen elbows him in the stomach, then grabs him by his collar and throws him against the cement wall, knocking him unconscious. We drag his body onto the elevator, and she presses the emergency STOP button.

"Ama, how did you—?" she begins, breathing heavily, then shakes her head. "Never mind. I'm so glad to see you. Shun's been caught."

"I know," I say, trying to focus on her face to offset the dizziness from the telekinesis. "Two scientists from the Tower were in my train car. I overheard what happened."

"I see," she says. "Then I owe you my thanks. I'll show my proper gratitude when this is over."

"We have an immediate problem." I point to the security camera in the corner. "My powers are limited to my proximity."

"We should be fine," Helen says. "Shiori set the feed on a loop." *Shiori.* Presumably another member of PHNX. "The explosives are already in place in key parts of the lab. If Shun hadn't insisted on doing one more sweep of the area, we'd have already completed our mission. But my little brother has always been a bleeding heart."

I think back to what Helen told me of their mission. They were to cause a distraction at the Tower so that a separate team could rescue those children being transported to another facility. "If the children are gone, why not attempt something more than a distraction? Why not destroy the Tower itself?"

Helen, who'd been reaching down to pick the guard's gun off the floor, slips the sidearm into a holster at the side of her chest. "Three reasons. First, we don't have the firepower. Second, it's too dangerous. The results would be catastrophic and uncontrolled, the loss of civilian life inevitable. I understand you came from Neo Seoul's Tower . . ."

It was obliterated in the Battle of Neo Seoul, the tallest building in the city now a pile of rubble with a blast radius of three kilometers.

"Not every battle has to be big to win a war. By destroying the equipment contained within the lab, we'll be putting the Tower back trillions, for which they don't have replacement funds—not with the focus on the upcoming battles. And even as we speak, Shiori is hacking into the security system's history in order to export the files. Releasing them to the public will reveal the extreme human rights violations happening here. And third"—a shadow passes over her face—"we were only able to rescue the children who were being transported. There are still more being held in the dormitories."

Of course. When I was in Neo Seoul's Tower, I never left it the whole time I was there. Not until the end.

"We have to go," Helen says urgently. She turns to the security camera and makes a sign with her hand, presumably a signal to Shiori. "The explosives are remote activated so we just need to get Shun and make our escape. How did you get past the guards at the front door?"

I hold up Dr. Yu's pass. "I changed their perception so they believed me to be this scientist."

She lifts a brow. "Impressive. Maybe we can use—"

A loud electronic ringing interrupts her. On the elevator

monitor, an upward-pointing green arrow appears. The system overrides the emergency STOP command, and the car begins to descend.

Helen curses. "They must have discovered my escape." We have about half a second before we reach the floor below. "I have a plan. Read my mind."

The door opens.

"Drop your weapons," Helen says. I feel the cold press of the barrel of a gun against the side of my temple. "Or I'll shoot."

Three guards and two scientists stand outside the elevator. I throw the mental smoke, but there are too many of them. It misses one guard in the back. She raises her gun.

"Stand down!" One of the scientists blocks her with his body. "That's Dr. Yu." The guard hesitates long enough for me to throw the smoke over her too, though the deception won't have a prolonged effect. Her mind has already made an impression of my face.

"Do as she says," Dr. Yu's colleague tells the others. The guard at the back shakes her head, as if dispelling a fog. Still, she places her gun on the ground.

"The guards should carry electro-braces on their persons," Helen says to me. "Find them." I don't have to look hard. Their thoughts shout the location of the braces. "Back to back," she barks. "Scientist to guard." They rush to follow her instructions. Between the guards, there are only three pairs of braces. "Shackle them together. Hurry."

I lock one strand around a scientist's wrist, the other

around the wrist of a guard. I use the final brace for the last guard, who blinks at me slowly, breaking free of the illusion. I hurriedly shackle her hands behind her back.

Helen ushers them into the elevator we've just vacated, forcing them to their knees. She presses the button to take them to the one-hundred-and-first floor, then shoots the operation panel so they can't override the system.

Once in the hall, I lean against the wall and take slow, steady breaths. Two years ago, an excessive use of my powers always came with side effects. Today it's even worse. I'm experiencing a massive headache, dizziness, and tunnel vision.

"Ama! Are you all right?" Helen's voice travels as if from a distance.

"Yes." I have to be.

There's a scream down the hallway. *Shun.*

"Don't move," Helen says. "I'll be right back." Grabbing Dr. Yu's badge, she rushes ahead. Soon I hear shouting and gunshots.

I limp after her, my mind in a haze. I round the door to see one guard on the floor, unconscious, and a bot in the corner smoking with bullet holes. Helen's helping a barely conscious Shun to stand.

"There are stairs down the hall past the labs," she says, dragging her brother from the room.

I stumble behind. At the end of the hall is the exit door. On either side are windows through which I can see dimly lit laboratories. They appear so much like the labs in Neo Seoul's Tower that for a moment, I'm unable to look away. Perhaps it's my overworked brain, but as I stare at the room beyond the glass, the world seems to dim around me. A buzzing sound starts in my ear. Familiar. A sound I used to hear every day, every night, since I was first brought to the Tower at eight years old.

It's the hum of the fluorescent lights in the ceiling. As I stare at the room, I begin to see a ghostly image of myself inside, projected over the metal examination tables where I used to lie, the cold metal sinking into my skin as scientists in white coats injected me, first with Enhancers, and later with tranquilizers when I showed signs of instability. Unlike Tera and Tsuko, my gene manipulation never resulted in accelerated recovery. I have mottled Enhancer scars all along my inner elbows. Through my dress, I touch them now.

I see myself projected over the simulation pods, where I used to receive lessons in battle tactics, espionage, and the history of the war. I see myself walking through the labs and the doors at the back that led to the small holding chambers, the buzzing of the lights following me. I can *feel* them, the children in their cells, those who remain—their pain and fear and anger and sorrow.

"Ama!"

But worse than their pain is the emptiness, their souls having fled them or destroyed, the only thing left a shell, a weapon, a monster.

"Ama!"

Helen's beside me, lifting my arm and placing it around her neck. On my other side is a young teenager with rainbow-colored hair.

"What's wrong with her?" Rainbow Girl asks.

"I think she's hallucinating. Neo Seoul's Tower was not a place that was kind to her."

I want to argue. I found some peace there. In Tera. In Tsuko. In Dr. Koga.

In Alex.

"What about the other kids?" Rainbow Girl again.

Save them.

"We don't have time. The dorms are apart from the labs. They won't be harmed. We have to go. Shiori, grab on to her. Run!"

Save me.

06

MEMORIES

The truth is, the first time I laid eyes on Neo Seoul's Tower, I thought it was the most beautiful sight I'd ever seen.

Later, I would come to realize it was a vision that was never supposed to be shared with me. After all, to know the shape of your prison is to dream of an escape.

I'd woken up on the transport bus ahead of our arrival. It was still a few hours before dawn. I could tell because of the pinkish-gray light that slipped through the small breaks in the blinds to fall gently onto the sleeping faces of the bus's other occupants—a few caretakers and the other seven- and eight-year-olds from Incheon's Children's Institute. The night before, we'd been given sedatives and instructed that when we woke, we would be in our new "home." Should we obey all orders given to us and cause no trouble, in a few years' time, we would be released as citizens of society. I'd swallowed the pill with ease.

Upon waking, I realized what had happened. Ever since I was little, my body had resisted mind-altering substances. "An anomaly," the institute's physician had called it. The expected thing to do was alert one of the caretakers so they could administer another sedative, but my curiosity overpowered my fear.

Beside me, Caretaker Sohn was snoring lightly. With slow, careful movements, I turned and pushed back the blinds.

Though the sky over the city was pink and gray, the buildings along the street were dark. Neo Seoul, like every other Neo city in the Alliance, kept a strict curfew from midnight to six A.M. I learned this from the previous year's lessons on "postwar city development," and I was proud of myself for remembering. I tried to count the windows, but there were too many—hundreds, thousands, hundreds of thousands. I imagined that behind each window was a person fast asleep.

What were they dreaming of? Warm, delicious pancakes. A hug from a friend. Rainbows. Blue-and-pink penguins.

I started to doze, dreaming of their dreams.

Soon the bus passed a large edifice with smooth, sleek black windows like a gigantic computer. At the center, a light appeared. Just one window out of thousands, like a candle in the dark. I shifted closer, my nose pressed against the glass. I wondered who was inside and if, like me, they were gazing out at the city, dreaming while awake.

The bus rounded a bend and the Tower appeared, so tall I

wondered if it could touch the heavens. And maybe because I had just been imagining all those dreaming people, I wondered how many dreams it would take to create such a colossal building—not just one, but thousands. With so many people striving toward one purpose, one goal, it must be good. It must be great. In that moment, I wanted so much to go there.

I didn't know at eight years old how soon this dream would become a nightmare.

■ ■ ■

My life in the Tower wasn't always awful. Though we were separated into smaller groups upon arrival, I still saw the other kids from the institute during our daily fitness activities held in the large underground gymnasium. There were kids from other institutes as well, from Daegu and Ulsan. My dorm had three fast-talking kids from Jeolla province. We never gathered all together at once, but I later learned there were a hundred and twenty of us total, twelve kids per ten dorms, all of us orphans. Since we were all born in the same year, 2183, our class was called the Year of the Goat, and since I was born approximately in the summer, I was placed in Dorm Eight.

At the institute, I'd been called Jangmi because I'd arrived at the facility at the age of two, covered in dust but with a single yellow rose clipped to my jumper. At the Tower, I was given a new identity: Subject 808.

I didn't mourn the loss of my name; after all, everyone was assigned a similar number—my bunkmate, a girl with ash-brown hair and a gap-toothed smile, was 805.

For the first few months, life at the Tower was new and exciting. The adults were interested in every part of our day: what we ate for breakfast, lunch, and dinner; how fast we could run on the indoor track; how quickly we finished our test worksheets on our tablets. We were enamored of their attention, which, if not parental in nature, still gave us a feeling of being noticed, as if we mattered.

When they gave us meds, we took them, even as our bodies became violently ill. When they introduced "lessons" through simulations, we complied readily, though simulations compressed time so that three hours in the simulation were only one hour in reality, leading to exhaustion of the mind.

Soon the days seemed to blur together. What was first a novelty became an unshakable routine.

Still, through it all, a memory stirred inside me.

At the institute, there was a girl who was kept in an isolated room separate from the rest of us due to her "violent nature" and "resistance to authority."

I used to visit this girl whose room walls were comprised of transparent glass, drawing pictures on a tablet and holding them up for her to see. For the most part she ignored me, but once in a while, I'd catch a change in her sullen expression, a quirk of the lips so fast the if I blinked I'd miss it. I don't know what drew me to her—away from the playrooms with the other children to the quiet space of the isolation room. I don't think it was pity—though our caretakers praised my "kind heart."

I think it was envy. She wasn't content. She wanted something, and she would fight to have it. Her fierceness of spirit was intoxicating. If I couldn't be her, I wanted to be near her, to feel a fraction of what she felt, a burning in the soul.

She'd been sent to the Tower a year before me. So though it was hard every day, I knew that she was somewhere nearby, perhaps on the floor above or below, existing alongside her own class, just the same as me. That's how I went on, fanning the flame of that memory with a hope that I might see her again.

■ ■ ■

In our eleventh year, we began the first trial stage of the Amaterasu Project: Enhancer injection.

To this day, my memories of that time are hazy, perhaps the mind's defense against irreconcilable pain. My life was a bit like that Western fairy tale. What was it called again?

Sleeping Beauty.

We were all sleeping beauties, sleeping to ward off an evil illness, waking one by one, only to close our eyes forever.

All I know is, when I surfaced from that nightmarish dream, I was the only one left awake.

It was a lonely time.

I was transferred to my own room with white walls and a one-sided mirror through which I was under constant supervision from Dr. Koga, the lead scientist on the project, and his team. By then I understood what I was—an experiment, property of the government, my worth determined by whether

I lived or died. And if I lived, whether the Enhancer had taken effect in my body. The second trial, Enhancer stabilization, had begun.

I knew the moment I woke from the dream that there was a change in me. When a nurse brought in my regulated meal, I could see her thoughts; I could *taste* them. She'd eaten blueberry pancakes for breakfast that morning with cinnamon and powdered sugar. She'd eaten them while watching a news report on the progress of the war, the number of casualties now estimated to triple that of the last world war. *But we're making a difference here*, she thought. I looked up to see her eyes on me. *Though I don't see how this poor little girl can save the world.*

In the labs, the nurse who took my blood was having an affair with the machine technician, Dr. Chung. This was a rather graphic and fascinating introduction to sexual intimacies. And when Dr. Koga visited me at the end of the day, his thoughts were clouded with worry for someone named Tera. I thought at first she was his child, but as I read his emotions, the most predominant feelings seemed to be a mixture of love and guilt, similar to how he felt about me.

Tera was on the minds of most of the people I came in contact with, though no one seemed to think about what she looked like, to my frustration. Just how they felt about her— fear, frustration, anger, and pity. One night, as I was returning to my room after an exhaustive day of testing in the labs, I heard screams and pounding coming from the room directly beside mine. My escort, a Tower guard, told me not to worry. After a while, the sounds ceased. The next night, they started again. I mustered up the courage to ask Dr. Koga who was kept in the next-door room.

Tera, his thoughts immediately revealed.

"No one to concern yourself about," he answered.

That night, I slept on the floor. In my white room, there were only a few pieces of furniture, all bolted to the floor—a white circular bed at the center of the room and a small desk and chair at the right side wall. The bathroom was a small closet that opened when you pressed a panel in the wall. I had no dresser, as my change of clothing—the same drab gray uniform—was delivered to me, neatly pressed and folded, every morning.

"Why did you sleep on the floor?" Dr. Koga asked when I saw him next.

"My bed is too soft. I was feeling restless."

In the following days, I slept on the floor in different parts of the room, outside the bathroom closet, beside the bed, right beneath the one-sided mirror. The lens on the security cameras zoomed in and out, studying my movements. After two weeks, my restlessness had become routine. So no one suspected when I slept on the floor beside the wall that I shared with Tera.

I knew by now that proximity to the person mattered in accessing their mind. At first when I reached out, I felt and heard nothing, and I feared that either Tera was too far removed in distance or she'd been relocated. Or worse, she'd succumbed to the Enhancers, like all the others.

But then, *Who are you?* The voice in my mind was strong and clear.

My name is Ama. It was the name given to me at the start of the second trials. *I'm your . . . neighbor.* I sent an image of myself by the wall—at least, of how I thought I might look, having no access to a mirror.

Out of the silence came the voice again, and at the edges, a sprinkling of light. *I remember you.* The image shown to me then was of myself, age six or seven, holding up one of my drawings against a glass room.

I found her, the girl with the fire in her soul. *Tera.*

After that first meeting, we met by the wall every night to talk. Instead of showing Tera paintings on a tablet, I painted stories for her in my mind. Because she spent most of her time in isolation due to her "dangerous powers," she had few memories to share. So I showed her my memories—of my childhood in the institute, but also what thoughts I could pick up on from the scientists, guards, and nurses.

Eventually we were introduced in person, and it was amusing to see Tera act cold to me, as she would to most everyone. Only I knew how warm-hearted she truly was. When Tsuko arrived from Neo Taipei, we became a trio. We went to the lab together, we took our lessons alongside one another, and we trained side by side in the fitness center. We were the successful results of a project started fifty years ago, one worth trillions in investments and that cost countless lives.

We were the hope of the Neo Council. With our superhuman abilities, we were going to change the course of the war, the future. Everything was primed to go exactly as the Tower planned—that is, until 2199, the year I turned sixteen and fell in love.

■ ■ ■

His name was Alex, one of two new recruits from Apgujeong's military academy, brought on board the project to assist with its final stage: implementation. To secure further funding, Dr. Koga needed to prove to the board and sponsors that the project had successfully created "permanently Enhanced individuals" who could be utilized in the various branches of the military "to provide advantageous results to the war." Through injections of the "Tera" serum, Tera 3017, or Tera, developed a dramatic increase in strength, speed, and durability. Through injections of the "Ama" serum, Ama 3016, or me, developed telepathic and mild telekinetic abilities.

Tsuko at this point had already left the Tower the year prior under a veil of secrecy, his association with the project expunged from the records. I never questioned his exclusion. Even from the moment we met, there was a haunted quality about him. Besides Tera and me, he always seemed to walk in shadows.

Into this setup entered Alex Kim, along with his classmates Lee Jaewon, a talented pilot, and Sela, an actress and singer whose mind was a constant blend of loud and colorful music. It made it hard to extract any of her actual thoughts. Jaewon's mind was the opposite, quiet and intuitive, and as open as the sea. As for Alex . . .

His mind was like a storm, at times chaotic and moving fast, at times brewing in the distance. He was the only son of the most powerful man in the city. And because of this, he was somewhat of a celebrity, his name connected with a variety of famous and beautiful people, each with a salacious twist. He was arrogant and rich, ambitious and ruthless, and these were just the thoughts I picked up on before he'd even arrived.

"Is it true what they say about you?" I'd scrounged up the courage to ask him that one evening when we were left alone in the labs.

By then, I already knew how I felt. I just wanted to know which rumors were true and which weren't, so I could defend him the next time I heard one. I'd been practicing new ways I could use my telepathic abilities with Dr. Koga, one of which was creating illusions in the mind. A well-aimed spider would make anyone regret having cruel thoughts.

"In the past two weeks we've been together, when has anyone had the time to say anything about me to you?" Alex was standing while I sat on the examination table. We were waiting for my blood pressure to stabilize before returning to my room. It had spiked after the latest Enhancer. I think that's why I'd had the courage to ask. He'd been more attentive than usual.

I rolled my eyes. "Let me rephrase. Is it true what they *think* about you?"

There was a beep on the blood pressure monitor, and Alex began to unwrap the strap from my arm. "Why won't it go down?" he said to himself.

I pressed my hand over the numbers on the display. "Won't you answer my question?"

He carefully began to wrap the strap around my arm again. "How do you want me to answer?"

"With the truth."

He frowned. "I don't want you to think badly of me."

"No, that's not—" I could have kicked myself. Sometimes I forgot that other people couldn't read minds. "I would never think badly of you. I just wanted to defend you either way. Of course, I could have defended you regardless, I realize now. Silly me. Even if the rumors were true and you kissed a hundred people, it wouldn't matter to me!"

"It wouldn't matter to you . . ." he repeated slowly.

"Yes!" I said, taking his hands in my own. "You could be the most awful person, and it wouldn't matter to me."

He raised a brow at this nonsensical statement. And soon I was laughing, and so was he, a low, rare sound, and my heart filled with how much I adored him.

The monitor beeped. We both looked down.

I sighed. "For a super soldier, my body's weak. It's unfair. The serum was supposed to make me healthy and strong. If anything, it shortened my life span."

"Don't say that." Alex let go of my hand to run it through his dark hair, turning away from me. His mind was a thunderstorm of anger, frustration, and fear. I wanted to slip off the exam table and wrap my arms around him, but I was still tied to the monitor.

"Are you reading my mind?" he asked.

"Not on purpose," I hurried to explain. "Unless I close the door of my mind to block out your thoughts, I can see whatever thoughts you're projecting. Like right now, I know that you're upset. I—"

"Close the door."

I slammed it shut. Turning, he took one step, grabbed my face in both hands, and kissed me. His mouth was soft against mine, his breath warm. He pressed my lips open, deepening the kiss.

I pulled away first.

"I—I love you," I blurted out.

His eyes widened. Then he laughed. "You don't hold back, do you?"

"I think it's unfair to hide the truth, not when I can read people's minds. I always say what I'm thinking."

"Good," he said, carefully sweeping a stray hair back from my face, his cool fingers gentle against my heated skin. "I always want to know what you're thinking."

"And I want to know what you're thinking. Quite literally."

"Then open the door."

When he kissed me that second time, all his thoughts were of me.

Where did it go wrong? Of course, it had been wrong from the beginning. Everyone had warned me. He had everything to lose and nothing to gain by being with me. He was under an immense amount of pressure—from the public, but most of all from his father.

Yet the way he looked at me, the way he listened to me, attentively, with his whole being, as if he didn't want to miss a moment of me, how could I doubt him?

I thought I couldn't be fooled. After all, I knew all his

thoughts; those that made me laugh, and made me blush, and made me love him all the more.

How could I know the truth when Alex didn't know it himself? That he had fooled himself into believing he was in love with me.

The morning before the Battle of Neo Seoul, we stole away together out of the Tower.

"You can have anything you want," he'd said. "Name it, and it's yours."

"I want to see where you are when you're not with me."

Alex took me to his school, Apgujeong Military Academy. The classes were in session, but we managed to sneak up to the rooftop. I waited as he broke open the lock to a large storage container at the back. An errant breeze swept across the open space, and I pulled Alex's coat around me, warm despite the chill. All I wore beneath the coat was a yellow dress. It was a summer dress, but I liked the way it felt against my skin, so soft after the standard gray Tower uniform. More to the point, I liked the way Alex's eyes lingered on me when I wore it. I slipped my hand into the pocket to feel the soft petals of a single yellow rose, a gift from him.

"Ama?"

I turned to find he'd succeeded in breaking the lock. I took the hand he offered, stepping across the threshold as he closed the door behind us.

Though the storage container appeared large on the outside, it was crowded inside with overflow materials from the school, folded-up desks and chairs, cleaning supplies, and gym mats.

While Alex cleared a space for us at the center of the room, I uncovered a small heater in a pile of lowTech gadgets. Huddling on gym mats around it, Alex started to unpack the plastic shopping bag of snacks he'd purchased from a nearby convenience store. He handed me a bottle of hot chocolate and cracked open a beer for himself. I sat with my feet tucked beneath his legs. His hand on my back trailed patterns that I could feel even through the coat. It was less than romantic, but it was real, and it was perfect.

Alex leaned forward to raise the temperature on the heater. "I wish I could have taken you home," he said, "but my father . . ."

I knew that Alex lived outside the city limits in a huge mansion built into the side of a mountain. I'd been there briefly once before. He lived there with his father, the Director of the Neo State of Korea and the main backer of the Amaterasu project. I'd never met him, but I knew from Alex's thoughts that he was a cruel man, and that he would never approve of our relationship.

What did we think we were doing? Even I didn't know. With all the forces working against us, did we even have a chance at a future together?

Alex emptied the rest of the contents of the bag onto the mat. He picked up a container of hard candy and popped one into his mouth.

"I didn't think you liked sweets," I said.

"I don't," he said, the truth of his words evidenced in his exaggerated grimace. "It helps with the craving, though." He meant the craving to smoke. He'd had the habit since he was fifteen years old. "I'm trying to quit. I know how you don't like the smell. And well . . ." His looked up, a teasing glint in his eyes. "I like kissing you."

I kicked him. He shook his head, offering me a candy which I refused. A sudden rush of doubt came over me, a tugging at my heart. Why *did* Alex like me? Was it because he liked to—as he said—kiss me? But as I'd been told repeatedly, he'd kissed a lot of girls. Was it because he thought I was pretty? Was it because he could tell how much I loved him? Or was it because I was forbidden? Alex would do most anything to get his father's attention, and I was the one girl he couldn't have.

"What's wrong?" he asked, noticing the change in me. "Was it something I said? Damn it, I'm sorry. Please don't cry." He wrapped me in his arms. This close, I could feel the wild beating of his heart.

"Why do you want to be with me? You could have anyone you want. I'm not like one of your classmates. I'm an experiment. I'm a m-monster. I could hurt you."

Alex moved back so that he could see my face. "It's not like I haven't been hurt before." He meant by his father. "Do you avoid doing things because you think you'll get hurt?" I started to nod. "I do things *because* they hurt."

I flinched. Was *that* why he was with me?

"All my life, I've acted recklessly, chosen the path that'll hurt the most people. Best if it hurts me most of all. Because if the pain is worse than what my mother did to me by leaving, what my father does to me by staying, then what they do can't be that bad, can it? It's all in perspective. I'm constantly chasing after those pieces of me that they've torn apart."

"Alex." My heart broke at the pain in his voice.

"But not with you. With you, I feel whole. My mind is full of chaos—you said it yourself—but with you, for the first time in a long time, I have peace. Look and tell me what you see."

The storm of his mind was present, but it was subdued. On the horizon was a spark of sunlight, a longing for me.

Most of what came next is a blur. He reached for me, or I reached for him—I can't remember.

Later, we woke to the door slamming open. We'd been discovered, reported by someone who had seen us sneaking up to the roof. Alex's father had arrived at the school.

Alex was taken, first beaten in private, then dragged outside. Wanting to make a spectacle of his son, the Director had assembled the student body in the courtyard. I'd caught a glimpse into his father's thoughts, and what I saw there made my heart grow cold.

Desperate, I'd run to help Alex. I'd have done anything, maybe thrown an illusion over the guards or put pressure on their minds until they dropped their weapons, which would have at least given Alex the chance to escape. But before I could attempt anything, Alex turned to me, his mind as clear the sky on a sunny day. I saw his choices laid bare. Choose me and lose everything—all his privileges, his wealth, his status, his father's approval. Or throw me away and keep it all.

He didn't even hesitate.

I was sent away, shuffled onto a small transport carrier

where, in one of the guards' minds, I saw our destination: Neo Beijing's Tower. The one bright spot was that Jaewon, who'd arrived to help me, was there for a short while before he was dropped off at the Tower for a formal arrest. Apparently he had turned against the state, joining the United Korean League, becoming a rebel like his father. The last image he left me with was one pulled from his own memories, an image of Tera smiling, at him, full of love.

When the transport ship had a critical system failure over the Bohai Sea, preparing for a crash landing, my last thought was that I wanted to see them all again. Tera. Jaewon. Tsuko. Dr. Koga.

And in that last moment, I also didn't hesitate.

I wanted to see Alex again. Even in a world where I was a government experiment, where the boy I loved betrayed me and broke my heart, I still wanted to live in it.

I wanted to survive, I wanted to live, I wanted to love again.

07

CHERRY BLOSSOMS

Cherry blossom season brings new life to the people of Neo Beijing, the streets crowded with families and groups of friends catching up after the long winter months. Small children run down the pathways between trees, trailing holo-balloons resembling stars and moons. By the bridge in Yuyuantan Park, a little girl trips, her pink plastic cherry blossom crown falling into the serene waters of the lake. Soon the surface begins to ripple, accompanied by the whirring noise of machinery at work, and a large mechanical red-and-white carp breaches the surface. Mouth gaping wide, it swallows the crown whole. Later, the girl can retrieve her crown at the park's guest service for items lost and found. Into this rather strange and bucolic scene, Shun and I stroll hand in hand down one of the small walking paths beside the lake.

I glance at him from beneath the brim of my white baseball cap. Most of the bruises from his sojourn in the Tower two months back have healed, his handsome face once more smooth and unmarked. I tug him toward a nearby bench. With a warm smile, he sits and stretches his arm out behind me. Sighing contentedly, I snuggle close into the crook of his shoulder.

"If I didn't know better," a teasing voice drawls into our earpieces, "I'd believe you two were a real couple."

Shun gazes warmly into my eyes. "That's the point, punk. What's the status on the video?"

"Ten minutes until launch," Shiori responds. Then with her usual cheek, she adds, "Try not to enjoy yourself too much, Shun."

I hear the familiar click as Shiori closes the link to check on Helen's status at the broadcasting station. On the bridge, the little girl who'd lost her flower crown is tugging at the sleeve of her father's coat, begging for a sweet from the bridge cart vendor.

"How can she tell I'm enjoying myself?" Shun says with a flirtatious wink. "Don't tell me telepathy is contagious."

"It's not." I roll my eyes. "Though even if it were, Shiori wouldn't be able to read your mind over a communications device. She'd have to be close by you." Right now our talented hacker and the youngest member of our team is several kilometers away in the basement of a repair shop, our hideout for the time being.

"How close? This close?" Shun wraps his arm around my shoulder until I'm practically sitting on his knee. For a moment, a memory rises of Alex drawing me gently across the examination table. Blushing, I scoot away. Shun grins, clearly enjoying himself.

Ever since he learned that I'd come back to help Helen and Shiori save him from the Tower, he's declared his undying devotion to me. The flirting is innocent and fun, neither of us taking ourselves too seriously. At least, I hope not. Sometimes I glimpse a question in Shun's eyes.

"What?" he says. "Are you reading my mind?"

"You know I don't," I chide, "not without your permission." It was one of the rules Helen set in place when I regained consciousness after the events of the Tower. Weakened from my powers, with bots roaming the streets in search of us, I accepted her offer of protection. Not reading their thoughts was a rule to safeguard her people and PHNX as an organization.

"I understand that sometimes you won't be able to help it," Helen had conceded, "especially if I or others express strong emotions while in your vicinity, but I trust you to not actively seek out information moving forward."

It cost me nothing to agree. In fact, I felt honored that Helen would trust me to keep my word. My first impression of her from that night in my apartment was correct. She was a good leader—calm, intelligent, capable, and patient.

Over the park, holo-screens move lazily through the air, showing the latest news updates. I count about five above the lake. In the distance, the screen atop the broadcasting station— the largest in the entire city—plays the same segment, a high-light reel of the battle that took place on Lunar New Year, culminating in a decisive victory for the Alliance.

It was because of this battle that most of the attention was diverted away from the Tower's search for us. Helen began sending the team out on missions, mostly surveillance and information gathering. To repay them for saving my life, I offered to help as long as nothing was asked of me that I couldn't handle, namely with regard to my powers.

I promised myself I'd stay only a few weeks at the most, but I'm still here, two months and counting.

"Four minutes until launch." Shun stands and takes my hand, tucking it against his side. We move slowly through the park toward the bridge. Someone has hung a wind chime in a branch of the nearest cherry tree. It chimes a light, twinkling melody above our heads. "Helen says my problem is that anyone could read my mind. What I'm thinking, how I'm feeling, it's all here, written on my handsome face."

I lift a brow. "You lasted well during the interrogation."

"That's different. They were looking for new information. If they'd asked me to confirm or deny a fact they already knew, that'd be a whole other story. For example, had they asked me if I thought you looked pretty today . . ." Shun backs me against the railing of the bridge, leaning close. Two children accompanying their parents erupt into giggles. An old woman *tsks* at the public display of affection. Shun's light brown eyes look almost golden in the sunlight. "Would it matter if I said no?"

"Your hypothetical interrogators need new jobs," Shiori interrupts. "Helen's set the timer. Two minutes until showtime."

Shun and I stare at each other. "Want some cotton candy?" He points to the vendor at the center of the bridge spinning the sweet cloudy confection for the children in the park. The young girl from earlier has joined the eager crowd. Her father stands behind her, scrolling through images displayed on his tablet.

"I would, actually," I say.

We approach the vendor. The holo-screens flicker above the lake, then black out. Many of the cherry blossom viewers take notice and turn their faces toward the sky.

"The truth is," Shun says, "I've never felt this way about anyone before."

"You're doing this *now*?" I ask incredulously.

Shun continues, his voice rising in volume as his passion grows, "I've never met a girl as brave and beautiful as you. Who's as special and unique. Just give me a chance."

There's an audible gasp from the crowd. I don't have to look to know what they're seeing. The video Helen and Shiori put together with the surveillance footage from the labs begins to play. Children locked in cells, experimented on, brainwashed and abused.

By now the broadcast station is scrambling to shut down the segment, but not without a passcode override from the president of the company, given both verbally and through a handprint signature, in order to effectively shut down every holo-screen in the city. They'll be contacting him now . . .

"I'm just not ready." I take a step a back. "I'm in love with someone else."

I begin to turn, but Shun grabs my wrist, desperate. "That can't be true. Please tell me that's not true!"

"Stop!" I shout. "Let me go!" I rip my hand away, twist around—

And bump hard into the girl's father, standing behind me. His tablet, blinking with an incoming call from Neo Beijing Broadcasting Company, falls over the side of the bridge into the water, disappearing in one bite of a giant mechanical fish.

■ ■ ■

Before we can return to our hideout, Shun has a shopping list of items to pick up for Helen at the old street market, a labyrinth of small shops sitting side-by-side almost atop one another located right outside the Dome. These shops deal in antiquities, prewar Tech, knickknacks, and herbal remedies. And of course black market goods, if you know where to look.

While Shun haggles over a pair of EMP Tech nullifiers, I maneuver down the alley, stepping over crates of wires and old batteries. A weathered-faced woman hands me a small plastic cup of hot broth with a gap-toothed smile. Grateful, I accept the cup with both hands, moving farther into the warren of shops. Hopefully I'll be able to find Shun later; otherwise, I'll be trapped here for all eternity.

Most of the shopkeepers don't pay me much attention, instead focused on their lowTech television sets that replay the news of this morning's incident at the broadcasting station. The official statement from the company is that the one-minute segment had been "fabricated to spread untruths about the government," and that "anyone who condones such false advertising will be branded traitors of the state and lawfully imprisoned." This crowd of hardened men and women see through the noise—in fact, many of the shopkeepers frown at the replayed images meant to prove their fabrication but only illustrate again in stark detail the atrocities sanctioned by the government.

"Children are to be protected and cherished," an old woman says to a group of her fellows squatting around a small, round tea table, who nod and grumble as she speaks. "We've gone too far if we believe even children should be sacrificed for the war. There is no logic in sacrificing the future for the future."

I move past the group and enter a shop filled with curios, finding a secluded corner to revel in the joy and satisfaction sweeping through me. This must be why PHNX and the other rebel groups are doing what they're doing, risking their lives for such a small thing as sixty seconds on the news. So that the people can know the truth and, if not directly join the resistance, at least aid it with hope in their hearts—in little ways, take steps toward a bright and safe future for all.

A grandfather with tortoiseshell glasses peeks his head out from above the precariously stacked shelves. "Can I help you?"

"Yes." I rub my eyes to compose myself. "I'm looking for . . ." I quickly search up "paper crafts" in Mandarin through my interface, then repeat the translation.

"Oh, yes," the man says. "Behind you, on the shelf second to the bottom."

Following his directions, I find a small mahogany box with silver inlays, filled to the brim with stationery. Reverently, I flip through the selection of loose-leaf papers and cards, some of which are already written upon. I find a folded letter the size of my palm, dated 16 May 2151, First Act of the Pacific War: *I regret not having said these words to you in person, but here is my confession now, whether I live or I die: I love you, I love you, I love you.*

I carefully tuck the postcard back between the others, and select a blank one with a simple photograph of a rose.

Shun finds me as I'm finishing up my note, leaving it unsigned. I lift it up for his inspection. "Does this look all right to you?"

He scans the short message. Educated in international schools overseas, Helen and Shun can speak and write in several languages, including Mandarin and Korean. Shun grimaces. "It's legible, if that's what you mean."

"Perfect." I borrow glue from the proprietor, squeezing thick drops onto the small stamp, and secure it with the press of my thumb.

Afterward, I drop off the postcard at the nearest hotel that has a mailing service.

"Who is TingTing?" Shun asks casually as we make our way toward the shipping yards.

"A friend I used to work with at the bakery. She was drafted shortly before I joined PHNX."

"Ah." Shun smiles. "A friend, you say? That's smart of you to send her a postcard. It should be untraceable without a return address."

"Thank you."

"How will she know it's from you?" he asks. "You didn't sign it."

"The rose," I say. "It's my favorite flower."

■ ■ ■

PHNX B Team's hideout is beneath a machine repair shop west of the shipyards, where the clank and groan of great machinery at work can be heard at all hours of the day. Inside the small but well-ventilated space is an open-floor concept with one bathroom and two bedrooms. The single bedroom is occupied by Helen, the double by Shiori and me. Shun sleeps on the couch at the center of the living room, beneath the low glow of thirty surveillance monitors that take up the entire back wall.

As we enter, they're tuned to different news channels covering the "telecommunication blitz," though the sound is muted.

Helen emerges from her room carrying two large suitcases. "Good work in the park. The segment played at least twice before it was shut down. Did you get everything on the list?"

We watch as she throws the suitcases onto Shun's makeshift bed and grabs clothing from the drying rack. "What's going on?" he asks before I can.

She rolls and stuffs the clothing into the bags. "New mission came in about an hour ago. We leave tonight on a train headed for the NIC."

Shun walks over and places his purchases on the small kitchen table. "By the NIC, do you mean 'Neo International City,' the capital of the Neo Alliance, *the* most dangerous place to attempt a rebel operation?"

Helen rolls her eyes. Then she says briskly, "We have our orders. Pack for an extended stay."

I'm sure there are parts of this mission Helen would like to discuss with Shun in private before filling in either Shiori or me. As siblings, they'd been a team long before we joined. I gather up my own laundry and move to the small room I share with Shiori, closing the door behind me. Inside the room, I'm met with the familiar low staccato sounds of gunfire.

At fifteen, Shiori's the youngest on the team. When not breaking encrypted software or hacking into top-secret government data, she's playing first-person-shooter games online. She waves at me over her shoulder as I enter, though I don't know how she can tell I'm here. She wears bright pink headphones the size of her face, presumably blasting music from the band whose holographic image adorns our wall: Shiori's idol and C'est La Vie's lead singer, Sela.

One day I'll tell her that I've met Sela. To tell her now would dredge up memories I'm not ready to share. It's strange, though, to sleep at night with Sela's image glowing across the room from me, a constant reminder of my past.

"I can't take her with me." Shiori says. She's turned off the console and gazes starry-eyed up at the holo. "But she'll be safe here. Don't know what sort of sharks infest the waters around the NIC."

"You've never been there?" I sit down on the bed, sinking into the soft mattress.

"No way! Only the superrich are allowed on that island.

Helen and Shun have, I think. Their father was a diplomat of some sort."

This is news to me. I'm not the only one who doesn't talk about my past.

"I'm excited, though. They say it's the most technologically advanced city in the world, with the best of the best from every state in the Alliance—Japan, Korea, North China, Taiwan. It's located between all the states too, on a great artificial island on the sea that's visible from the mainland, a whole city of lights. I wonder how we'll get in. It's supposed to be impossible without either a sponsorship or a load of cash."

"Maybe the latter."

"Mm . . ." She stands abruptly, her chair swiveling behind her. With a running start, she leaps across the room to land on my bed. "Shun is totally in love with you. *'I've never met a girl as brave and beautiful as you.'*" Her impersonation is terrible. I can't help laughing. "*'Who's as special and unique.'* Don't tell me that actually works for some people."

"I'm sure it does. But we were only following a script that, if I remember correctly, *you* wrote."

"Oh, did I? Then did it work? Did your heart feel all fluttery inside?"

Not for the reason she might expect. *I'm in love with someone else.* "I'm afraid not."

"Good. You can do better. I've seen Shun scratching his butt in his sleep. Don't go into the living room after midnight if you can help it." Suddenly she sits up. "Do you think they have ramen in the NIC? I mean, it's, like, a superrich city. Would they even have convenience stores?"

Before I can answer, she races out of the room, returning a few minutes later with a large cup ramen, chopsticks stacked over the covered top.

After glutting herself, she grows bleary, swaying toward the bed. She falls immediately asleep upon contact. Gently, I tuck the blankets around her, then take a cleansing tissue and sweep the oil from her face. I then check to see if her bag is packed, finding it half full of electronics, a stuffed penguin, and several changes of clothes. I include some undergarments and basic toiletries before zipping up the bag and bringing it out into the kitchen, where Shun sits at the table, fiddling with the EMP Tech nullifiers.

I return to the room and pack my own belongings, a fairly quick process as I haven't accumulated much since leaving my old apartment, just the items I brought with me when I left, including the red dress at the bottom of my bag.

When I finish, I take my bag out to the main room and place it beside Shiori's. Shun's gone, and the shower in the bathroom is running. The door to Helen's room is open, but the lights are turned off. I head out the back door and climb the stairs to the roof, where I find Helen, a thin shawl wrapped around her shoulders, drinking a glass of red wine as she gazes out at the shipyard.

We share the silence, watching as the sun sets over the dry dock, the workers having turned in for the night. This is one of the few places in the city with such a wide and open space. Most of the buildings are factories manufacturing ship parts that are then transported to the huge shipbuilding facilities on the coast. Helen once considered blowing up the factories, as most of the ships built nowadays are bombers and other types of war vessels, but the risk to the city was too great. Most of the communities nearby are low income and residential.

Helen always thinks of the people first, the war second.

She offers me the last of the wine, and when I decline, she finishes it and places the glass on the edge of the balcony. "Though our orders came a bit suddenly, they're not unexpected."

I wait for her to elaborate.

"The fact of the matter is this," Helen says quietly. "The South Chinese rebels took a huge hit during the battle on Lunar New Year. Many believe the Alliance won the war on that day. In a week's time, there's going to be a benefit gala in the NIC, thrown to honor the heroes of the Lunar New Year Battle, but also to drum up money for the next battle on June Solstice. No matter what, we cannot be defeated a second time. I have a feeling our missions, whatever they may be, will involve ensuring our success in this battle. As you can imagine, the risks and danger will be at a much higher level than before."

A rogue wind sweeps over the dry dock, and I rub my hands together to keep them warm.

Helen turns fully to face me. "I was remiss not to mention it earlier, but though you are welcome and we strongly hope you'll join us, know that the choice is yours."

A part of me expected that we would have this conversation.

It was easy after the Tower to stay with Helen, Shun, and Shiori, to help them as repayment for saving me. But leaving with them now means I'll have joined PHNX in truth. I'll be responsible for their lives, and they for mine, working against the Alliance, using my powers as they were meant to be used, in spying, in espionage, possibly in violence.

I'll have chosen to take part in the same story that began with Neo Seoul's Tower, so long ago.

"I cannot read your mind, Ama," Helen says gently. "Tell me what it is you fear, and I will give you my honest opinion."

I nod and attempt to express my thoughts. "What we did today," I begin, "showing the truth about the government to the people, it felt good, like we were doing the right thing." I think of the shopkeepers in the old street market, huddled around the television. "Even if only one person is inspired to fight back because of our actions, it's enough for me."

"Hopefully more than one," Helen says with a self-mocking curve of her mouth, "but I understand what you mean."

"I really admire you, Helen. I respect your wisdom and leadership. I—" I blush. "I've always been drawn to stronger women than me, women with goals and the courage to achieve them." An image comes of Tera as she looked on the roof of the Tower when she escaped that second time, before Alex or Jaewon ever came into our lives. I didn't know we were living in a cage until she broke it. "I think . . . a part of me wants a little bit of that fire for my own."

Helen says softly, "You cast your own shadow, Ama."

Not like Tera's.

But I keep that to myself. "The missions in the NIC won't be like how they've been here, will they? Not in the capital of the Neo Alliance. I don't know if I'm ready. You saw what happened in the Tower. I overexerted my powers. If I collapse again during one of our missions, I'm a liability. I can't depend on you to save me every time, nor do I want you—any of you—to risk your lives for me."

For a long time, Helen doesn't say a word. Then, "I'm glad you think I'm a strong woman, Ama. As a wise and capable leader, trust me when I say I am not a charity worker."

My blush deepens, but she presses her point. "I didn't seek you out because I thought you were weak. I wouldn't have asked you to join me if I thought you were a danger to my team. It's true I don't know the extent of how your powers work, and sometimes that element of the unknown does intimidate me. But more powerful than the fear of the unknown is the hope of it. You came back when you didn't have to. You saved my team. It's true you have a lot to learn when it comes to your powers, but with practice, you'll grow stronger. It will take some time before we're settled at a new base and given our mission. Shun, Shiori, and I will help you."

I smile, grateful for Helen's steadfast logic and confidence in me, but my powers were never in my control, even with practice. If Helen and Tera cast shadows that raise them up, that make them strong, mine was always uncontrollable, apart from me. Dangerous.

I have a sudden longing for Tsuko, who knew exactly what I was experiencing as he experienced it himself. He said he'd help me control my powers. I wonder where he is right now, if he's put into action his plan to stop the war, with whatever means possible.

"We leave in a few hours," Helen says. "Get some rest."

I nod, though I don't move away. The sun is now just a speck on the horizon, a sliver of light in the vast darkness. I should heed Helen's words, but I want to prolong this moment of peace. "Shiori mentioned that you've been to the NIC before."

Helen nods. "When I was eight, I traveled to that city with my father."

That city. The edge in her voice doesn't escape me.

"He was there for business, but he brought me along because my favorite opera was being performed at one of the theaters."

"I didn't know you liked opera."

"Not anymore. After the show, we returned to our hotel room. An assassin was waiting in the room. He murdered my father. Afterward, I was told to lie to the police and say my father had killed himself. Otherwise those who murdered him would kill my mother and brother. Shun was only five years old. My mother always blamed me for making my father out to be a coward."

Helen's voice is soft, but her eyes are hard. "It's strange. They say there are no ghosts in that city, but you'll feel it when we get there: it's the most haunted place in the world."

08

TRAIN, PART 1

The train to Neo International City is a massive luxury conveyance, boasting three restaurants, a casino, hyper sleep chambers, and even a pool and spa on the upper floor decks. After storing our luggage in our own private car located toward the back of the train, Shun and Shiori bound off to explore the facilities, while Helen and I check our surroundings, pinpointing possible threats and locating the nearest exit routes. Businessmen occupy the cabins to the left and right of us. Across the hall, a young couple and their small child settle down for the long journey. It's estimated to take around nine hours—eight hours to Neo Shanghai and one more across the East China Sea road.

Helen and I take seats at the far window. She slides an envelope across the white flip-down table. "Your new identity.

Take the next hour to memorize it, and then I'll toss it down the incinerator."

I carefully read over the documents. Like before, I'm the second daughter of the CEO of a joint Chinese-Korean tech company, this time joining my father in the NIC in order to attend a benefit gala. I wonder if one day I'll ever meet this powerful and rich father of mine, who must exist in order to lend credence to my false identity. Shiori travels as my attendant, hired due to her gift with languages—she's multilingual—but also her training in martial arts, making her a bodyguard of sorts. As for my connection with Helen and Shun . . .

"Engaged?" I look up, surprised. Helen is watching me as if anticipating my reaction.

"It's easy to pair the two of you," she says. "You're the same age. Shiori is too young to be engaged, and I'm the head of my family. You're both second children, far less likely to attract notice. Moreover, your engagement provides a perfectly reasonable explanation as to why the four of us are traveling together."

After a short pause, I nod. "I agree. I think this setup has the least amount of variables. Also, Shun and I have natural chemistry. It's easy to fall into a role with him as my partner." I just worry it might be too easy and that one or both of us will get hurt.

I don't need the full hour to memorize the file. Afterward, Helen leaves the cabin to dispose of it. Shiori returns, bearing a cache of snacks from the food carts that patrol the halls. We stuff ourselves with breads and cakes before falling asleep together on one of the two pullout cots in the room.

I wake a few hours later to find her snoring lightly beside me. Helen occupies the other bed, her back turned toward the room. There's no sign of Shun. I check the time. We left the station at around 21:00, and it's well past midnight. Grabbing my jacket, I slip out the door.

The lights in the hallway are dimmed, the once-translucent windows frosted over to give privacy to passengers. The hall is silent as I make my way down the carpet runner. I pass through two more cars before entering the first of those that contain the public rooms. These are wider and illuminated by bright wall sconces, giving the appearance of antiquity, an ironic choice considering this is the most technologically advanced train there is.

I wander from one car to the next, only finding direction when I come across a sign leading to the sky deck. I take the short elevator to the third level, where the doors open to a spacious room scattered with small, intimate round couches decorated with blankets and throw pillows. The walls and ceiling are entirely made of transparent glass, giving me a one-hundred-eighty-degree view of the outside, mostly darkness with pinpoints of light—towns, perhaps. It's peaceful here and, thankfully, not well populated. I find a small chaise in an alcove separated from the room and stretch out. I'm alone only a few minutes when I feel the presence of another human being draw near.

"Good evening, my love, light of my heart, darling, angel, queen of all that I have and am—"

"You read the file."

Shun grins, pressing his back against the wall beside me. "Who needs a matchmaker when you have a sister?"

I laugh. Why did I think this might be hard? As long as we don't take ourselves seriously, no one will get hurt.

"If you want," Shun says, crooking his arms behind his head in a casual pose, "it could be one of those marriages of convenience where we despise each other but are bound together due to money and the political aspirations of our parents."

"Why can't we just be a normal engaged couple? Who admire and respect each other?"

"Ah." Shun pats my head. "What a quaint and naive concept of *normal* you have."

I bat his hand away.

He laughs, his smile easygoing. "Did you know they have an aquarium here? It takes up an entire train car. How much energy do you think they're using just to transport fish *across an ocean*?"

I glance at him. "You should get some sleep."

"I did. In the hyper sleep chambers. You lie down for twenty minutes, and it's like you've slept for six hours."

"What were you doing with the rest of your time?"

"I swam a few laps in the pool. Ate a sandwich in the dining car. Then I came up here to look at the sky."

I follow his gaze. "It's clear."

"No ships tonight." From now until June, when the next battle is scheduled, the skies will be clear.

"Why did the rebels agree to schedule battles?" I ask, keeping my voice low, though a cursory mental probe of the area shows no people within hearing distance. The closest people are half asleep, their minds hazy and quiet.

"Because we're losing the war." Shun sighs, his expression grim. "We don't have enough manpower or resources to stay our current course of guerilla warfare and small skirmishes. Eventually we'll be routed and destroyed. This way, we can even the playing field, regroup and strategize without the threat of an impending attack."

"But the same can be said of the opposing side. The Alliance has time to plan *their* attack."

"Yes, but their priorities are divided. This war has made some people very rich; what those in power care about right now is keeping it that way. Because of this, most of the concessions were made on the Alliance's side. Besides the temporary ceasefire, they allow us to pick the location of the battles. In return, we allow them to set up cameras in the zoned areas of the battlefield."

"But what about the people who actually do the fighting? The families whose children are drafted into the war? They can't condone this."

"Most, if they thought about it, wouldn't. But what can they do? They exist within the system; they benefit from it. Every item they buy, every product of the media they consume, even the very air they breathe, circulated as it is by the Dome, funds the war machine. The cycle keeps them safe and rewards those who take advantage of it."

"And some even choose to fight on purpose," I say, thinking of the boy I'd met in line outside the recruitment office and the ace pilots featured in the commercials.

"I think every kid in the Neo Sphere wants to be a pilot when they grow up. But then . . ." Shun sighs again. "You grow up. And you realize shooting people means killing people."

Neither of us speaks for a time. Out of the darkness rises a great city, sparkling red and gold.

Neo Shanghai.

We only pass it from a distance, heading straight toward the coast and the sea.

An announcement plays over the intercom, stirring the nesting stargazers.

One hour until arrival at Neo International
City. Please have your passport and
identification papers ready for inspection.

I uncurl myself from the chaise. "I'm going to head back to the room."

"Yeah, okay," Shun says, his head tilted back, still gazing up at the sky. "I'll be there soon."

I leave him to his thoughts.

The public rooms are more crowded as people leave their rooms for a final stretch before arrival. Most gather at the large floor-to-ceiling windows to watch the sun rise over the Pacific. I catch sight of the young couple occupying the room across from ours. They walk hand in hand with their daughter, swinging her up into the air by the arms. On closer inspection, I see the father wears civilian clothes, an elegant light blue hanfu, and the mother the plain green uniform of the Alliance military. *She's a soldier.*

They must be traveling on vacation before her deployment. Perhaps they have family in the NIC, or she received a special dispensation from the government for acts of heroism in the war. I wonder if she fought in the battle that occurred on New Year's, and if she'll fight in June at the Summer Solstice, the battle that the rebels must win at all costs.

I wonder . . .

By wishing for our victory, am I wishing for her death?

She lifts her daughter. Their noses touch. I watch the young father as he watches mother and child. What must it feel like to love a soldier? What must it feel like to love someone whose very life can't be promised—to him or to herself?

"Tera."

Tera, whose enhancements would otherwise make her the perfect soldier if it weren't for her love of a human boy, for her own mind that questions and challenges the world presented to her, that rejects it and asks for better.

I wonder where she is now. The last time I saw her was the night before the Battle of Neo Seoul. She'd been worried because Jaewon had returned injured from a mission. I hadn't been able to say goodbye to her. The following day I was discovered at the school with Alex and taken away. One of the first things I did when I arrived in Neo Beijing was scour the Net for any hints of what might have happened to her after the battle. But all the news articles were censored, even the gossip forums.

"Tera, we need to go."

Someone is talking. A girl, perhaps sixteen, with hair shorn close to the skull. She addresses another girl, her back to the room as she stares out to sea. The second girl is thin with long, dark hair.

My breath catches. It can't be. *Tera*. What is she doing here? Joy, boundless, spills out of me. I stumble forward, reaching out a hand. She turns. Our eyes meet—

It's not her.

I've never seen this girl before. She's of a height with Tera, but she's younger, with sharp, aquiline features. She holds my gaze for a moment, and then her eyes slide past me. "Ama," she says.

I blink in confusion. Then, slowly, I turn to see the first girl staring at me. That's when I feel it. A pulse at my brain, as if someone were knocking on the door in my mind. I've only felt this with one other person—Tsuko, whenever he attempted to breach my thoughts.

"Can I help you?" This in Mandarin from the girl with long hair.

"I'm sorry," I respond in my halting Mandarin, which I hope at least gives me the impression of innocence, and take a step back. The girl, as if on instinct, takes a step forward. "I made a mistake. I thought you were a friend."

She glances at the short-haired girl, and I realize she's *waiting* for her to confirm the truth of my words, *by reading my mind*. The knock grows insistent. The sharp-eyed girl steps closer. It goes against instinct, but I open the door. The mind-reader sweeps through like a sickness, boring into my thoughts. I keep them cluttered with noise. *They looked familiar; that's why*

I stopped them. I thought they were old classmates, but they're much too young. I wonder what school they attend. They're wearing odd uniforms. Gray. Nondescript.

I clench my fist to keep from screaming. "I have to get back to my cabin."

"I hope you find your friend," the dark-haired girl says. Her words are delivered deadpan. For a second, I meet her eyes. They're dull and cold. I bow, and she returns the motion.

Neither girl moves as I walk away. I can feel their gazes on the back of my neck. The first girl's mind drills into mine again, searching and ripping through my thoughts. I focus on nonsense. The sort of shops I want to go to while in the NIC. The latest chapter in the serial novel I've been reading. My head hurts so much I can hardly think straight. I exit the hall, stumbling through a few more train cars to put space between us, finally collapsing against a wall.

What just happened? Who *were* they? They called themselves "Ama" and "Tera."

At Neo Seoul's Tower, the project ended with Tera and me, but there were other Towers running experiments, like in the labs we destroyed in Neo Beijing. It's possible that in another program, there were others who might have survived the serum. Another Tera. Another Ama. Hope kindles within me. Could they be like me, fugitives? I didn't see any guards accompanying them. And yet they were wearing the gray suits issued to Tower subjects. And their eyes . . .

They were empty. Without light.

"Ama."

I turn abruptly, heart racing, but it's only Shun.

I glance at the door to the train car closing behind him. "Did you come through the public rooms?"

He nods. "What's wrong?"

I grab his hand and lead him down the hall at a brisk pace. "Did you see two girls around our age wearing gray clothing?"

"I did. They were exiting the public rooms toward the front passenger cars."

"Did they notice you?" I keep glancing behind us, but the hall of the car is empty. "What were you thinking about when you saw them? About the mission? About me?"

He shakes his head. "I can't remember."

Reaching our cabin, I lock it behind us. Shiori and Helen are on their feet. "What happened?" Helen asks, immediately alert.

"Super soldiers," I say, trying to catch my breath. "Onboard the train. Two of them. They addressed each other as 'Tera' and 'Ama.' I could feel the other Ama reading my mind. I couldn't risk blocking her thoughts in case she'd notice. Instead I filled my own thoughts with noise, but I can't be sure if it worked."

Helen turns to Shun. I don't have to read her mind to know she's making calculations. "Were you there?"

He shakes his head. "I came later, but I did walk through the train car. I don't think they noticed me."

"But *you* noticed them, and if this other Ama was in range, she would have noticed you noticing them."

"It's possible."

For a moment, Helen closes her eyes. Then she opens them.

"Okay. This is what we're going to do. We're going to assume two things as fact. One, that the soldiers are hostile and working under the direction of the Alliance. Two, that they have identified our group as a threat and will take actions accordingly."

She turns to Shiori. "Check the video surveillance for the train. If we can pinpoint their location, we'll be better prepared in case of an attack." Shiori nods, reaching into her bag and pulling out her tablet and portable keyboard. "Shun, check the weapons. My main concern is the telepath. We know what to expect with a physically Enhanced soldier, but we have no defenses against the mind. Our best course of action is to take her out first. Until then, I'm relying on you, Ama, to shield us from her influence."

I nod, though doubt creeps in. If the other Ama is a part of the Alliance, then she'll be better trained than me.

"It's possible they won't attack until after we disembark, in which case—"

There's a knock at the door.

We all turn to Shiori. "I can't see who it is," she says. "I'm loading the hack. It won't go through for another three minutes."

Shun throws Helen a handgun, which she tucks in the back of her skirt. "Who is it?" she calls, keeping her voice steady.

"Customs before arrival." It's a woman's voice, low and clear.

Helen looks to me.

"I don't think it's them," I say. The woman had sounded older.

Gripping the handle of her gun, Helen disengages the lock

to the door, and it slides open. A woman and man enter, wearing the dark green uniforms of the railway employees. Helen releases the gun. Out of the corner of my eye, I see Shiori closing her notebook.

Both the woman and man bow, their faces plastered with accommodating smiles. "Excuse the intrusion, but we'll be arriving shortly at the Neo International City. To ensure a safe and orderly arrival, we ask that all your belongings be accommodated for and stored in advance. Will you be needing a luggage service?"

"No, thank you," Helen says.

"Splendid. Now we'll just need you to fill out this customs form, and you should be all ready for arrival. Are you the head of the family?"

"Yes," Helen says. "I'm traveling with my younger brother, his fiancée, and her attendant."

The woman nods, and I see the man checking our faces with the photos he has saved on the tablet. "Your files are all cleared in the system. After disembarking, you may bypass the security checkpoint and exit through the elite passengers' aisle."

They bow once more, then leave. Helen secures the lock behind them. We let out a collective sigh of relief.

Shiori wipes an arm across her brow. "That was close. I thought for sure it would be those super soldiers."

The cabin door explodes inward.

09

TRAIN, PART 2

Through the smoke and debris from the explosion, Helen calls out, "Is everyone all right?"

"Affirmative," Shun and Shiori respond.

"Affirmative," I repeat.

I see Helen dart toward the control panel. She jams the HELP button and shouts into the receiver, "There are rebels on the train. Hurry and send security. Now!"

"Clever." The other Tera steps over the blasted door into the train car. "Though they won't arrive in time." Like before, she speaks without emotion, yet there's an unmistakable malice to her words and actions. "You can all leave. There's only one person I want." Her eyes are on me. She *knows*.

Who I am. What I am.

"Go," I tell Helen before she can protest. "You'll be more of a help to me from outside the room."

Grimacing, Helen leaves, but not before grabbing her bag off the floor. I notice that Shun and Shiori have also taken their bags, mine included. Other Tera doesn't seem to notice.

Through the window behind her, I can see the front of the train as it curves on the watery track; in the distance shine the bright lights of Neo International City. The conductor must have determined it was better to keep going and reach the city rather than stop and have an emergency evacuation on the water.

Tera closes in on me, stopping when we're a few centimeters apart. She has no visible weapons on her body. Then again, she doesn't need weapons to get what she wants. She *is* the weapon.

This close, I can see the black of her irises, blue-limned with the glow of the Enhancer. "I know who you are," she says, her voice soft, drawing me toward her, "Ama 3016. You were the first to survive the Amaterasu serum, you and my predecessor, Tera 3017. At Neo Seoul's Tower."

I can see her studying my eyes, really looking at them. Can she see the green in mine, the proof that I'm just like her? "I didn't know—" I say. "I didn't think there were others." Again, that feeling of hope. Tsuko, Tera, and me—we're not the only ones. "Were you at Neo Beijing's Tower? Was there only the two of you?"

"Not at first." Her words are accompanied by an influx of memories. The terror of the forced injections. The agony of friends dead and gone. The painful brainwashing simulations that made it all seem *good and right*. Until there was nothing left of her except this emptiness inside, so cold it burns.

I gasp. "I'm so sorry."

Tera lowers her eyes. "Are you?"

"They stole your childhood, they took away your freedom, they killed your friends. The scientists were all adults. They should have protected you. Instead, they betrayed your trust. You should have never been forced to endure such pain." Am I trying to convince her or myself? "What you are right now, what they made you, isn't your fault."

Her eyes remain downcast. I probe her mind, but I see nothing, only blackness.

"Come with me," I say, suddenly, recklessly. "Let me help you."

There's a beat of silence, and then, "The thing is . . ." She speaks so quietly, I have to lean closer to hear. "The scientists weren't the ones who betrayed us." She lifts her gaze, fury written across her features. "The real traitor is you."

She grabs my neck. I gasp and struggle to pry her hand from my throat, but it's like steel. Her nails bite into my neck, sending blood trickling down my skin. "I'm disappointed," she says. "You're not the prototype they made you out to be. You're just another failed experiment."

Her hand cinches tighter. My vision darkens at the edges. I reach for her mind, but she blocks me, a new technique she must have learned in conjunction with the other Ama. If only I had listened to Tsuko back in the alley, when he told me I needed to grow stronger, to train my powers.

He believed in my powers more than anyone else. He said that's why PHNX wanted to recruit me, why the Tower—had they known I survived the crash—would have sent soldiers to get me back.

If it were them, they wouldn't hire an assassin to kill you quietly in an alley. You're worth trillions in investments.

"Wait!" I manage to choke out. "Who ordered you to kill me?"

Doubt creeps into Tera's mind, and I leap into the crack, widening it. "You're acting on your own, aren't you? You never received any orders. You know this isn't what your superiors would want. I *am* the prototype, at least in their eyes. I'm not something that can be thrown away."

"They don't know you exist. They think you're dead! I intend to keep it that way."

But the doubt in her mind is a weakness. I exploit it. Breaking through her defenses, I take control of her mind. Her hands drop, and she stumbles back.

Turning, I rush through the door. Shun's ready. He grabs my arm, pulling me to the side just as Tera barrels after me in pursuit. Holding a charged ion gun, Helen aims it at Tera's back and pulls the trigger. The impact blasts her into the empty cabin opposite the hall, the family having fled. "Shiori, now!"

Shiori presses the key and the door shuts, locking Tera inside. Immediately there's a loud bang. The metal of the door caves outward.

Shun grimaces. "That won't hold her for long."

"Where is security?" Helen asks. Down the hall I see the

other car passengers, cowering—civilians all. The man and woman who had checked our cabin earlier lie unconscious on the floor. "They should have arrived by now."

Shiori flips her tablet, holding it up. "They're not coming." On the bisected screens, uniformed guards idle in the halls, unmoving. Passengers shake and berate them, but none react to the abuse, acting like bodies that have lost their souls.

There's only one explanation. "Where's the other Ama?" I ask.

Helen reaches the same conclusion. "She wasn't in the hall. My guess is she's still in her room, in one of the front passenger cars."

Shun frowns. "You think she can control that many people from that far of a distance? Is that even possible?"

I shake my head, trying to think. "It's not. It shouldn't be."

There's another loud bang from somewhere inside the room.

Shiori gets up to check the rooms on either side. "There's no damage," she shouts. "I think she's breaking through to the roof."

"We're not her target anymore," Helen says. "She's trying to get back to the other Ama."

Shun frowns. "The train should reach the station in under ten minutes. Is it even worth going after her?"

Helen shakes her head. "Why do you think they're on this train? Instead of a transport ship or commercial aircraft? We decided to take this route because it's the easiest way to smuggle weapons into the NIC, as our tickets and luggage are pre-checked and paid for in advance. The train goes straight through the Dome into the station, unlike the airships, which have to pass through checkpoints."

"They're likely doing the same thing," Shun says. "Transporting something important."

Helen nods. "I think so too, but what?"

A weapon that augments the power of the mind.

"When I was at the Tower," I say slowly, "they were developing a new defensive weapon that would amplify the reach of my powers. They called it the Helm. They were developing it alongside its counterpart, armor that Tera wore— or, more accurately—piloted. The Extension was a God Machine, the most advanced in creation."

"Which disappeared during the battle of Neo Seoul," Helen says.

I nod.

"Then the Helm is still in the Alliance's possession."

Shun groans. "This was never part of our mission, Helen."

"We don't win a war without risks. Ama, your new directive is to retrieve that Helm. We have eight minutes and forty-two seconds before arrival. Shiori, go with her. Shun and I will stay behind and prevent Tera from blocking your advance. We also need to blow up some rooms to secure our escape."

Not for the first time, I'm impressed with Helen's leadership—her mind that is always thinking two steps ahead. By blowing up the other rooms, she's essentially making it appear as if the attack was random, not singling out our cabin. Later, the investigators on scene will conclude the rebel attack was focused on the train, not on the affairs of its individual occupants.

Leaving Helen and Shun behind, Shiori and I race down the hall. The public rooms are packed with distressed passengers shouting at the blank-faced security guards who stand like broken automatons. Shiori grabs me as a group of people approach us, having witnessed our exit from the rear train car.

"What's happening back there?" a wide-eyed woman asks.

"Rebels!" Shiori cries. "I think they're trying to blow the train off the tracks!"

This statement rouses a renewed fervor of panic as passengers move to blockade the door we just exited.

I glance at Shiori, who shrugs. "Helen and Shun will be fine."

We push our way through the crowded car until we near the door leading to the front passenger cars. Shiori takes out her tablet. "I can unlock the doors to the rooms, but it's a guess as to which one is theirs." She pulls out a layout of the first of the front train cars. Seven of the ten have open doors, most of the people having fled their rooms to congregate in the common areas. "So of the rooms that are locked—"

"One must be theirs," I say. "And it's likely they're not traveling alone."

"Guards, you mean." Shiori hands me Helen's handgun. "How good are you with this?"

"Not very."

"Still better than me. It's a myth that playing video games prepares you for the real thing." She steps forward, and the door slides open.

The hall is identical to the rear passenger cars, five rooms on either side of a carpeted hallway. Evidence of the panicked flight of the passengers is strewn across the floor—brightly-colored clothing spilling from overturned suitcases, shattered glass, maid-and-butler bots tilted over with their gears still whirring. We approach the first locked door on the right. I raise the gun and nod. Shiori overrides the lock on her panel. I brace for attack.

Empty.

The third door on the left is empty as well.

We check the last door on the right. A man lies inside a portable hyper sleep chamber, oblivious to the chaos.

"How many front passenger train cars are there?" I ask Shiori.

"Same as the rear. Eight."

We find more people in the second and third cars. By the fifth car, I have a hunch of where Ama is located. "We're running out of time. How many doors are locked in the last car?"

"All of them."

"That must be it. Let's go." We sprint the rest of the way, stumbling through the final door into . . .

Sunlight. I pause, momentarily disoriented. The presence of the train beneath me, that subtle forward momentum, has disappeared.

The sunlight streams through open windows on one side of a short hall; on the other side are empty classrooms.

My mind struggles to adjust to this new reality. It was hours before dawn. Now it looks to be midmorning. The train had been catapulting at a great speed toward the city, but now it's as if I'm not on the train at all. Through the window, I can see the tops of several trees, and beyond them, huge skyscrapers with holographic signboards written in Korean.

Something tugs at the edge of my mind—*I've been here before.*

Out of the corner of my eye, I catch a movement at the end of the hall. "Shiori?"

I take a step forward. A high-pitched scream rends the air. It seems to come from right behind me, but when I turn, there's no one there. The hallway extends far past where the door to the train car once stood. Which makes no sense, and yet . . .

Like a dream, my mind blurs all outside thoughts—doubt and reason—distilling them into this single moment. My bare feet slide against the cool tiles. I'm wearing a yellow dress, the hem of which tickles my ankles. Someone screams down the hall, and though the urgency to discover the source remains, I've forgotten who I'm looking for.

I walk slowly in the direction of the sound and soon reach a stairwell. From the brief glance out the window, I surmise I must be on an upper floor of the building, and yet the stairwell has no stairs leading down. The landing drop off into darkness. My instinctual fear wars with the druglike haze of the dream. I push the darkness from my mind and look up. Light streams through an open doorway.

I step outside. Immediately I know where I am. Apgujeong's premier military academy. If I turn my head to the left, I can see the athletic fields where the students run drills. To the right is the front courtyard where assemblies are held. I've only been here once before, led by someone who knew this school well, his hand tugging on mine until we reached the rooftop, breathless. Like then, the open space is sparsely furnished, a few potted plants and square platforms for sitting. The only other feature of the rooftop is a large storage container tucked in the corner. The last time I was here, it was locked to keep out enterprising individuals. Now the door is slightly ajar, through which looms that impenetrable darkness.

Up until this moment, like all good dreamwalkers, I've accepted the scenario rendered for me. Perhaps I accepted it because I can't differentiate between a dream and reality. Or perhaps I accepted it because I wanted to see how far this unreality would take me.

I approach the door. What lies inside the darkness, across the boundaries of the subconscious?

The world shakes around me, edges chipping away. First the sky splinters into fragments of illusory glass. Then the fields and building crumble into dust.

I sprint toward the door.

It opens.

Alex steps out. He appears as he did the last time I saw him, wearing his Tower uniform, young and happy and unbearably handsome. The world is breaking apart around us, but he doesn't seem to notice, his eyes on me. "Why did you leave, Ama? It's cold out here. Come back inside."

A stray piece of debris sweeps toward him at an alarming rate. "Watch out!" I shout, but it goes right through him, as if he were a hologram. Or a ghost. Or a dream.

"You're not real," I say. "You're not here."

"Maybe not, but that doesn't mean you can't talk to me." He raises his hand, an invitation to take it. "Or be with me."

"It's not the same." Though I'm tempted. If I reached out now, would I feel him—the texture of his hand, the warmth of his skin?

"What are you doing here?" he asks. Behind him, the storage container begins to peel away.

"I'm not here. Not really. I'm in a train car en route to the NIC. I was attacked by someone like me, a super soldier, a telepath. I believe she's using the Helm to augment her abilities, reaching into my mind and pulling out my darkest fears. But she doesn't know how to control it. Look around you. The world is falling apart."

"Your darkest fears," Alex repeats, then looks up with a frown. "You fear me?"

Slowly he begins to crumble, pieces of him breaking away to join the swirling darkness.

"I don't."

"Then what do you fear?"

"I fear the me who longs for you, even now. Though I can't have you. Though you're lost to me."

In a few more seconds, he's gone. I reach for the door to the storage container and step through.

I'm in a cabin of a train car, identical to the one I traveled in with Helen, Shun, and Shiori. On the ground are two guards unconscious from blows to the head. The third and final person in the room is also unconscious, her head lolling beneath the weight of a gigantic helm.

Shiori stumbles in behind me. "What the hell was that?"

"An illusion. Whatever it was, it wasn't real."

She shivers. "Thank God. Now what?"

There's a loud bang, and the room buckles inward.

Tera. She must have climbed across the train from the outside. Another loud bang. She'll be inside within moments.

"We can't beat her," Shiori says, and she's right. Tera is too strong. Without firepower, we don't stand a chance of winning. I rack my brain for ideas. What were *my* Tera's weaknesses? She had none. Her only weakness was . . .

"I have an idea." I move toward the other Ama. First I need to secure the Helm. I grab the silver contraption and give it a sharp tug, only to stop when I see a trickle of blood slip from beneath the Helm down the young girl's cheek. I stare in horror.

Another loud bang and the outer wall of the train car caves in. "Ama!" Shiori shouts.

I blink away my shock. "Grab her arm!" Shiori and I lift the other Ama together.

Tera punches a hole through the wall. Before she can come through, we throw Ama off the train.

"No!" Tera screams, her voice caught by the wind. She doesn't hesitate. She jumps into the water, and the train rushes forward, speeding into the night.

10

THE PARTY

We arrive at the station and manage to slip away amidst the chaos; Helen flashes her signed customs forms to the security droids. For three days, we lie low at our new hideout, a penthouse apartment in the middle of the city, stocked with food and shiny new surveillance equipment, paid for by PHNX supporters. Shiori uses the equipment to hack outgoing calls from government facilities, but there's no news on the super soldiers, whom Shun nicknames Tera 2.0 and Ama 2.0. The attack on the train is attributed to insurgents and then quickly covered up, the Alliance discouraging any attention, even negative, to the rebellion. After a few more days of quiet surveillance, Helen concludes that the super soldiers, though a threat, are not the immediate concern. We have a more pressing matter to attend to: our first mission arrives.

A week after the incident on the train, Helen, Shun, and I are on a small boat floating down one of the wide canals of Neo International City, an artificial island comprised of waterways, much like the cities of Suzhou and Venice. Tonight, the mayor of the NIC hosts a charity ball to honor the heroes of the New Year Battle. The venue: the mayor's own residence, a palatial mansion of red and gold, a modernized simulacrum of the grand palaces of long-ago emperors. The boatman, a cheerful uncle with bright beads braided into his weatherworn beard, slides his paddle through the thick black water, circumventing a nest of golden lanterns. On either side of the canal, cherry trees shed their blossoms, pink and white against the dusky water. Already the short season of their blooming is at an end.

A chill sweeps over the Pacific. I raise my shawl to cover my shoulders, bare but for the thin straps of my dress, the same red one I brought all the way from Neo Beijing.

Across the bench, Helen speaks, keeping her voice low so as not to alert the boatman. "Tonight marks our official debut into the NIC's elite circles. There will be some scrutiny. Stick to the script and you should be fine."

By "script," she means my false identity—Wang Jangmi, second daughter of Wang Yunpeng, second-year engineering student at a university in Neo Beijing, engaged to Li Shun in a political match engineered by the ambitious heads of our families.

Speaking of my fiancé, Shun moves to the other end of the boat, presumably to take a call from Shiori. She'll be monitoring the party through the mayor's security cameras, already hacked for that purpose.

I glance at the boatman. A gentle probing of his mind shows he's more interested in the music pumping through his interface than his secretive passengers. "Can we go over the mission objectives again?"

"Of course. Tonight you accompany Shun and me as our honored guest. While we volley the many questions inevitably aimed our way—as new blood with old money—you will stay abreast of the conversation and concentrate on the things that are left unsaid."

"A lot of my ability is up to interpretation," I remind her. "Most thoughts aren't expressed in words." In fact, the majority of thoughts are expressed in images, emotions, and memories. It's why, though I need Tour Guide for words spoken aloud, I don't always need it for the mind.

"That's fine. A lie is felt, after all, whether in guilt or satisfaction." Helen leans forward, her dark eyes glittering. "Tell me who lies and who tells the truth, who is a staunch supporter of the Neo Council, with everything to lose should the Alliance fail, and who can be bought. There's one man in particular, Tanaka Kenichi, a veteran of two acts of the war. He's been retired for ten years. Yet according to the recently released guest list, he's to make an appearance tonight. Gossip speculates he's looking for a political match for his only granddaughter . . ." She trails off, biting her lip.

"You suspect otherwise."

"Recently he was offered a hefty incentive to leave

retirement and lead the Alliance forces during the June Solstice battle. This would be catastrophic. He is the only person in all three acts of the war to have led the entirety of the army at one time, when he commanded the Alliance forces to victory against the west during the Second Act of the war. Afterward, he retired, and for ten years he hasn't claimed a side in the ensuing Third Act of the war, which is essentially a civil war, neither supporting the Alliance nor the rebels. More than that, he's popular, a hero. If he should agree to lead the forces into battle, that will give the Alliance the moral advantage, at least in the eyes of the people."

"What will PHNX do if he does choose to fight?"

"We can't assassinate him. That would be just as bad. I'm not sure. Perhaps he can be persuaded."

Shun rejoins us, plopping down on the bench. "That was Shiori. She intercepted a call not too long ago about the transport of two assets, picked up off the coast of China."

"Ama and Tera," Helen says immediately.

"Shiori thinks so. Though she can't be certain."

"What will happen to them?" I ask.

Helen appears to consider my question. "Their behavior on the train revealed their lack of discipline. If they'd been thinking clearly, they would have waited for our arrival before notifying the appropriate authorities. Instead, they took forceful actions against us, sidelining their superiors. It's likely they've been called to a Tower to undergo more . . . training."

"You mean brainwashing," Shun says with a shudder.

Helen nods, though she doesn't appear happy about it.

Tera and Ama might have attacked us, but there's a sense of wrongness in blaming them.

The boatman whistles for our attention and Shun stands, making his way over to him.

"How are you feeling?" Helen asks quietly when we're alone.

An image flashes through my mind of myself earlier in the week. In Helen's memory, my face is wan, my eyes bloodshot. Shiori had told Helen about the illusions, how we had each faced our greatest fears. Shiori had seen spiders; I told them I'd seen Neo Seoul's Tower.

Just like then, I lie. "I'm fine."

The canal opens up to the sea. The mansion on the islet is resplendent with red-and-gold lanterns hanging from a thousand open windows. Boats alight like stars on the crescent-shaped shore, releasing gorgeously wrapped individuals who laugh and sparkle as they climb wide stone steps that ascend up and up to great bridges that lead like heavenly pathways to the glittering depths of the mansion.

The boatman maneuvers our vessel between elegant luxury yachts, lilting wind gliders, and small personal crafts similar to our own, until we reach a small opening on the sandy shore. Shun confers with the boatman while Helen and I disembark. I adjust my shawl and gaze at the long train of people climbing the steep steps of the cliff face. Should one choose to forgo the stairs, there are glass elevators built into the cliffside as well as a cable car.

"He'll wait for us in the cove," Shun says, joining us a few minutes later. "I said we'd be out at around midnight."

Together, we join the rest of the partygoers, the steep climb broken by small viewing platforms every twenty or so steps, where refreshments and energy boosters are available in iced buckets. At the top of the stairs are great wooden bridges that lead to the heart of the mansion; below, the darkly shifting sea. Music beckons, a beautiful rhythmic melody. A silvery voice sings of memories and moonlight.

Shun and I follow Helen through a gilded archway. Below is a grand courtyard, open to the sky. Couples dance at the center of the floor, a dreamy, shifting mosaic of azure and turquoise meant to mimic an underwater grotto. Moving outward, individuals gather around long tables laden with decadent appetizers—marbled oysters with crème fraîche and caviar, halibut rolls smeared with fermented bean paste, and cocktails of crab bisque.

A server passes by carrying a tray of yuzu and matcha bonbons.

Helen gently takes my arm. "Remember," she says, "our main objective is to discover why Tanaka Kenichi came out of retirement to attend this party. Reconnaissance is second to this objective. If you find yourself exerting too much power, close it off in reserve; should you feel light-headed, Shun will escort you somewhere secluded to recover."

In my mind, I feel a loud knock on a door.

"Did you get that?" Helen asks.

I nod, and we share a smile. We'd been thinking of a signal Helen could use when she wanted me to probe the mind of an individual. It was her idea to focus a thought into an image and sound—a knock on the door. We'd been practicing all week.

"And what am I?" Shun says. "The devastatingly handsome sidekick?"

"Yes." I laugh.

Helen wrinkles her nose. "Handsome? Let's be honest, little brother."

I'm still laughing as Shun and I follow Helen to a liveried footman. Helen produces our invitations from within her coat. Our names are read aloud as we descend the gilded steps. Hardly anyone glances in our direction—we are of no consequence. An attendant approaches, motioning for our coats. I'm reluctant to give up my shawl, but then I notice the heat orbs floating overhead, seeping warmth into the atmosphere.

Helen removes her coat and hands it to a porter, catching the attention of a group of young socialites who stop and stare. I don't blame them. She's stunning in a dark green evening dress, her midnight hair falling waterfall-like down the open back, her skin glowing and pearlescent.

"Ms. Li." A handsome young man approaches, accompanied by two older women, one of whom shares his wide cheekbones and full mouth—presumably his mother—and the other with hair the color of ice and eyes narrow like a cat's. "May I have the pleasure of introducing you to my mother and her close friend, Mrs. Peng?"

A knock on the door. I open my mind, blurring out the many voices around me and focusing on Mrs. Peng. In my concentration, I hardly hear Helen as she introduces Shun and me to the group, who pay us little attention. As an affianced couple, nothing is gained by an association with us—our worth having already been spent in marriage.

"You're so young to be the head of your house," Mrs. Peng says, her mind assessing Helen's monetary value. "How old are you? Eighteen?"

"Twenty-one. And my mother is alive; she remarried when my brother and I were young. My father passed away in this very city."

"Oh, yes. So sorry." Pity flashes through Mrs. Peng's mind, though brief. Her attention wavers as a server walks by with a tray of champagne flutes.

"I would love to meet your husband," Helen continues. "I'm interested in investing in his company, I so admire his work in shield technology. Many claim that the Dome over the NIC is twice as strong as Neo Beijing's Dome."

"Strong enough to withstand a blast from the Ko Cannon?" This from Helen's acquaintance, who has inadvertently helped us with our line of questioning. In the Battle of Neo Seoul, the massive Ko Cannon destroyed the Dome and the Tower in one powerful blast, effectively bringing an end to the battle.

I sense a wall go up in Mrs. Peng's mind, as her thoughts slip into a memory of signing an NDA and the hefty penalty fines attached. Though it doesn't prevent her from snidely remarking, "I wouldn't think your family has that kind of money."

"Our father left us a respectable inheritance," Helen says coolly. She looks over Mrs. Peng's shoulder. "Is your husband with you tonight?"

"Of course."

She's lying.

For a moment, Mrs. Peng's mind slips into a dark pit of disgust and jealousy. A woman's face appears, perhaps not more beautiful than Mrs. Peng, but jolly and bright. It seems Mr. Peng has a mistress.

Helen glances at me, and I give an infinitesimal nod. "It was so nice to meet you," Helen says. A lie.

We move amongst the partygoers. Languages wash over me in waves, Tour Guide quickly translating anything within audible distance. Most, if not all, the individuals in this courtyard have apps like mine. It would be impossible to communicate otherwise. I see delegates from South Asia and the American Neo States. English and French mix with Tagalog, Cantonese, Hindi, and Urdu. Minds blend together in vibrant colors and sounds. My grip on Shun's arm tightens.

Between every set of songs, the mayor calls an individual to the stage and the crowd cheers as they accept a medal for their performance in the New Year Battle. An open link to a donation portal is accessible through every interface. Whenever a hero of the battle receives an award, there's a sharp rise in donations. Right now the total is at fifty million.

"Helen!" A cheery-faced young woman approaches wearing a silk dress suit. Immediately both Helen's and Shun's minds brighten with familiarity.

"A university friend of Helen's," Shun explains with a smile. "Helen and Mei were coeditors for their school's journal."

"It's been so long!" Mei says. "How have you been? Had I known you were in the city, I'd have invited you to all the parties this past week. There are more, of course. You will come, won't you?"

I rub my head where a gentle throbbing has taken up root. It continues to grow the longer Helen talks to Mei.

"Did you hear about Jing?" Mei asks, glancing around the room, but no one is paying them any particular attention. "Can you believe she was arrested?"

Helen's thoughts dim with sadness. "I heard. I sent some money to her family."

"Oh, that's good of you." Mei smiles kindly. "You and Jing were always so close."

The pain in my mind intensifies, building in pressure. It's similar to the pain I felt back in The Alchemy of Dreams, when the girl came in with a secret. I probe Mei's mind but meet resistance—her mind's natural defenses.

I have to get closer. A server passes by, and I reach for a deviled egg, purposefully twisting my foot and losing my balance.

Helen's friend catches me. "Are you all right?" she asks, all concern. In the recesses of her mind I find it. The memory of a young woman, smiling. *Jing.* A dark night. A phone call. An arrest.

Mei is an informant for the Alliance.

"I'm fine," I say, tucking the deviled egg between my teeth.

Turning, I grab Shun's arm and squeeze, practically shouting *DANGER* into his mind.

"Helen," Shun says, catching on quick, "I think Jangmi has had a little too much to drink."

Mei laughs. "Go see to your little brother and his fiancée. We have all the time in the world, now that you're in the city."

When we've walked a far enough distance, Helen brings us to a halt. "Something's wrong. What is—?" She breaks off. Shun and I look to see what's caught her attention. An elderly gentleman sits alone on a bench, his eyes closed—Tanaka Kenichi. The Hero of the Pacific is *napping* in the midst of a party.

"I aspire to such heights," Shun says in awe.

"I hadn't expected to get him alone," Helen muses, her voice low. "But how should we approach him?"

"Let me go," I say. "There's only room for one other person on the bench, and I need to be close to get a good peek into his mind."

I also wouldn't mind sitting down. My head still pounds from the encounter with the informant, though I can feel the pain receding, more quickly than it had in the café or on the train.

Helen nods. "We'll meet you at the entrance to the gardens."

We separate, and I walk over to take a seat beside Tanaka Kenichi, catching the end of his dream. A sea of gold beneath an azure sky. Then the image disperses. I wait as his mind becomes aware of his surroundings. For a while, we sit in companionable silence, watching the partygoers laughing and dancing. In a lull between songs, Tanaka Kenichi asks kindly, "What's wrong, child? Is the party not to your liking?"

His voice is gravelley and quiet. I don't know much about Tanaka Kenichi other than that he's a general and a grandfather. As an orphan, I have little experience with either. Then I remember that Dr. Koga always said I was like a granddaughter to him. I imagine that he were the one beside me.

"I feel overwhelmed," I say honestly. "I'm not used to crowds this size. And I know so very few people."

"Ah," he says in a grandfatherly rumble, "perhaps I can help. Sometimes when I'm feeling overwhelmed, I think of the one place where I feel safe and most at peace. I remind myself that this place is waiting for me. And because I know that I can go home, I can enjoy the time I spend away."

"What is it like, this place of yours?"

And though he describes it in words, it's more beautiful in his memory.

■ ■ ■

Later, I find Helen and Shun to make my report. Shun must have told Helen about Mei, as her thoughts are tinged red with pain.

"Even if the Alliance offered him the position of general," I tell them, "I don't believe he'll take it."

"Why do you say that?" Shun asks.

"His thoughts were of a house in a golden field."

"Gold?" Shun frowns. "What does that have to do with anything?"

"I think it was rice. The heads turn gold in time for harvest. He wasn't thinking of the war. He was thinking of rice in a field."

Shun looks befuddled.

"I see," Helen says, "and I agree with your assessment. If he's dreaming of peace and harvest then it's unlikely he'll accept the Alliance's offer. Good work, Jangmi. I want to follow a few potential leads, but I won't need either of you to help with that. Meet back here at midnight and we'll leave."

Helen disappears amid the crowd, and Shun and I move to the edge of the courtyard. We step out into a garden with night-blooming flowers and low-hanging wisteria trees. Couples stroll down lantern-lit pathways, and children bob for candy fish in small glass pools. At the edge of the garden is a cliff, beyond which lies the East China Sea.

We meander down one of the pathways. It's quieter here, with fewer people. I shut off my interface and let my mind go still, breathing in and out, practicing the meditative exercises Dr. Koga taught me.

Behind us, a great cheer rises out of the inner courtyard. The couples who've been strolling around the garden make their way inside, followed by the children, until only Shun and I remain in the garden.

"A celebrity must have arrived," Shun says, glancing over his shoulder. "Perhaps the guest of honor himself. Some war hero."

I sigh. "We should go back."

"Wait, there's something I want to tell you." He takes my hand.

Instinctively, I know what the right thing to do is. I should refuse his request. I should insist on returning to Helen. But there's a question in Shun's eyes, and a reckless part of me wants to go with him, to hear what he has to say, to feel what it's like to be wanted again.

We move down a pebbled walkway and slip between a copse of trees. The ocean stretches ahead, a few stray lanterns wandering into the moon-drenched sea. Dropping Shun's hand, I step to the edge of the cliff. I can hear the low hum of an unseen barrier. If I were to fall, I'd likely bounce right back into the wet grass. Inhaling sharply, I breathe in the salt-slick air.

Tanaka Kenichi's words flit through my thoughts: *The one place where I feel safe, the place that is waiting for me.*

A stray wind slips across the sea, and I wrap my arms around myself. How did I come to be here? So far away from Neo Beijing. So far away from Neo Seoul. Why, even after traveling such great distances and experiencing such new and wondrous things, do I feel like this? When will I ever be satisfied?

"What are you thinking?" Shun asks from beside me.

"I don't know," I say truthfully. "I have so many thoughts that I can't put into words."

"Try."

"I look at the sea, and I feel sad."

There's a pause. Then he says with a smile in his voice, "What did the sea ever do to you?" I know he means to put me at ease. "I think you'd be happy if I was someone else."

"Forgive me. What is it that you wanted to tell me? I'm listening. I would like to hear what you have to say."

Shun sighs. "You won't read my mind?" I shake my head. "Then I'll have to put it into words."

I try to mimic his light tone. "Unless you want to say how the sea makes you feel."

"Happy," Shun answers immediately. "Because I'm with you."

I swallow hard.

"I like you, Ama. I don't think my confession surprises you. I've liked you since the beginning. Being with you is easy. Natural. I think it's because we're so similar."

"Are we?" I whisper.

"Younger siblings to strong, capable women. Thoughtful. Romantic." He takes a deep breath. "I know you have ghosts that haunt you. Helen wasn't the only one paying attention to how you reacted after the train. But what you saw in that illusion is the past."

"And what are you?" I laugh shakily. "The future?"

He takes a step forward, pulling me into his arms. "I'm the one who wants you now."

His kiss is soft, gentle. His thoughts are filled with wonder and respect and desire for me. It should be everything I've wanted to feel in so long, and it is—for a moment—but then a billowing ache fills my chest and Alex's dark, piercing eyes fill my thoughts, the illusion from the train so fresh in my memories.

I break off the kiss. "I can't do this. I'm sorry."

I race across the garden. Inside the courtyard, the place is packed, and I can't find Helen in the multitudes. I'm attracting curious stares. With my flushed cheeks, anyone can guess what I was just doing. I circumvent the crowd and slip into the nearest restroom, running water in the sink and splashing it against my face.

In the mirror, I stare at my reflection. There are dark circles beneath my eyes. Shun and Helen were right. I haven't been myself since the incident. The illusion rattled me like nothing else has in the past two years.

But it was just an illusion—it wasn't real. What is real is PHNX—Helen, Shun, and Shiori. What is real are Tsuko and Tera, wherever they might be in the world. And me. I'm learning to control my powers; I have barely a headache even with how much I've used them tonight. And on the train, though the other Ama's powers had been augmented by the Helm, I could still tell that I was in an illusion. If she hadn't fainted, I would have broken it myself.

Even in just these two months with PHNX, I can feel that I've changed, becoming braver like Helen, becoming stronger like Tera. If I continue to work alongside PHNX, I can use my powers to help people. And after this is all over, I can go in search of my own place of peace and safety.

I can find my own field of gold.

As I turn to leave, a group of women enters the bathroom. I move to the side to let them pass.

"Did you see him?" One grabs the sleeve of her friend

who's applying lipstick with a deft sweep of her hand. "I thought he was handsome on TV, but in real life he's magnificent."

The friend puckers her lips. "Is it true he's dating that pilot? What's her name—?"

"God, I hope not. But I wouldn't be surprised. With a face like that, he could have anyone he wants. Though I've heard he's quite dedicated to his career. Just imagine, to be appointed commanding officer at the age of twenty!"

One bumps into me, and I bow in apology, but she hardly spares me a glance.

Helen is with Shun when I emerge from the restroom. "Are you all right?" she asks.

"I'm fine. Are we leaving?"

"Yes. It's almost midnight. The boatman should be waiting."

Shun doesn't say anything, and I'm careful not to read his thoughts. I follow him through the crowd toward the steps. The crowd is quiet, only a soft murmuring, everyone turned toward a stage set up at the front of the room. They must be handing out the last medal of the night, presumably to the soldier who outshone the rest. Anticipation sweeps through the crowd—I can feel it in their thoughts, like a rising wind.

The microphone hums as the mayor's sonorous voice breaks over the room. "Thank you all for coming tonight." He continues to make announcements and speak pleasantries as I receive my shawl from the porter, and Helen her coat. We reach the stairs and begin to climb.

"Now for the moment you've all been waiting for."

The crowd already begins to cheer. "I'd like to welcome onto the stage—"

I reach the top of the stairs, my hand poised on the banister.

"—the hero of the New Year Battle—"

Helen and Shun step out onto the bridge.

"Alexander Julian Kim!"

The roar of sound is deafening. Slowly, I turn. Alex walks from behind a red-gold curtain, dressed in a lieutenant's uniform. What the girl had said was true. He's magnificent. His dark hair is swept back from his face, displaying his handsome, arrogant features. He walks with confidence to the podium in a few long strides, bowing to the mayor and receiving with both hands the Medal of Honor. He turns toward the crowd, his face exultant. The crowd is wild.

This is all he's ever wanted. This is all he's ever dreamed of. His gaze sweeps over the crowd and toward the stairs.

I turn my back on the room and flee, applause like thunder at my heels.

ACT 2

11

THE WAR HERO

I catch a fever in the night, for once a result of a bad bug in the air rather than an overuse of my powers. I wake to Shiori pressing a cool cloth to my neck. Beside the bed, Helen adjusts an IV drip attached by a catheter to my arm.

Noticing I've regained consciousness, Helen helps me to a sitting position. She hands me pills and a glass of water. Afterward, I'm tucked into bed. "Sleep," Helen says.

I sleep.

I wonder if this is my body's way of protecting me—in a strange, self-injurious way—from the agony of my mind.

Alex. In this city. A hero! The hero of the NIC, just as he was the darling of the NSK. No, that's not true. It's different now. There, he was lusted after, envied, adored. Last night, he was admired. As he walked out onto that stage, he appeared confident, triumphant. Last night, he'd appeared . . . happy.

What did I expect? That he'd be broken, pining after me, filled with regret for his betrayal? Of course I didn't expect that, nor would that have pleased me. And yet . . .

His middle name is Julian. I never knew. I never knew *him*.

If I had been in good health, my curiosity would have driven me to look up everything about him, where he has been the past two years, what he has been up to. How did he get to this position of honor and prestige? Through his father's connections, most likely.

True love is happiness for the other person, regardless if the love is requited.

I am not happy.

In order to speed up my recovery, I'm given low-level medical Enhancers and ordered to sleep the rest of the day, yet not before debriefing Helen on the thoughts I had picked up on at the gala. I watch her carefully as she jots down notes that she'll compile later into a report for her superiors. Her face is expressionless, even as she names Mei as an informant, which may not be as treacherous as a spy, but is just as much of a betrayal.

"You'd think I would have gotten sick too," Shun jokes later, alluding to the kiss, when he brings a bowl of rice porridge for my lunch. I must turn bright red, because he quickly flops onto the bed, proceeding to eat half my porridge, and as a result, getting howled at by Shiori, who catches him through the doorway with the spoon halfway to his mouth. I'm laughing as they wrestle on the bed, reaching my arm out to catch the bowl before I lose the rest of my lunch to the floor. And just like that,

Shun's and my relationship returns to how it was before the kiss, an easy, effortless camaraderie. With so many people surrounding me with complicated thoughts and emotions, it's a relief to be around a mind like Shun's that lets things go.

Honestly, I need to be more like him.

I sleep a few hours, only to wake in the night from more dreams of Alex. Of him in the Tower and at the school, telling me that he loved me, of him that last time, showing me it was all a lie, and lastly of him on the stage, triumphant, beautiful—everything he's ever wanted his for the taking.

Through the door, I hear the murmur of voices. A blue light glows from the sliver between the door and floor. We must have received another mission. Slipping out of bed, I release my arm from the IV.

In the living room, the lights are dimmed. The blue glow comes from a projection cast on the wall. Alex gazes back at me from a photograph, his name and stats displayed on the right side of the screen. Born: 2181, Neo Seoul. Age 20. 180 centimeters.

"Our target is the newly appointed commander of the Neo Alliance's troops in the Pacific." Helen stands by the wall, a clicker in hand. Shiori and Shun are sprawled on the leather couch facing her. "The last commander having died in the New Year Battle. Alex, only a second lieutenant at the time, took control of their unit and finished the battle without major casualties. More than that, he finished it in style."

On the monitor, the screen switches to a recording from the battle. A God Machine—standard issue, tall, and slate colored, armed with an assault rifle—flies through the air at a dizzying speed, dodging enemy gunfire and returning it with stunning accuracy. Alex leads a troop of similarly outfitted GMs that tear through the enemy ranks with aplomb. It's an impressive display of skill, rendered, as Helen pointed out, with finesse.

The screen switches to a recording of Alex emerging from his GM after the battle, a host of reporters and floating cameras converging upon him, capturing every detail—his sweat-streaked brow, his eyes alight with triumph, his smile to capture the hearts of the people—as well as the war sponsors eager to have him wear their products into battle.

"Damn," Shiori says. "Is he a soldier or a drama star?"

"Is there a difference?" Shun quips, though without humor.

"Regardless," Helen says, switching the screen back to Alex's photograph, "he was chosen as the next commander for the NIC's main base. According to the mission report, our objective is to work our way into his inner circle, become someone he trusts."

"Why isn't the objective to . . . uh, dispose of him?" Shiori asks.

My heart constricts at the suggestion.

"We're not assassins," Helen chides. "He's just a weapon wielded by a greater opponent. If he dies in combat or by the work of an assassin, the Neo Council will simply replace him. Right now he's our best chance to gain access to much-needed knowledge. Battle plans. The locations of supply depots. Weaknesses among their ranks. If he has secrets, we're to exploit them. We'll take anything we can get from him, bleed him dry."

Her words are mercenary, and yet they give me a grim satisfaction.

"This plan is all fine and good," Shiori says, "but how do we even get him to notice one of us, let alone infiltrate his inner circle?" The whole time Helen has been talking, Shiori's been scrolling through articles on her tablet. "Just glancing at the reports—the official ones, but also checking out netizen gossip—it looks like he's the most sought-after person in the NIC." Hijacking the monitor, Shiori pulls up a live feed of reporters outside what looks like a luxury apartment building in the inner quarter of the NIC. "He'll be overly cautious of anything that even smells like sycophantic behavior. Who's acting point on this? I'll say this without shame: I have zero confidence I can get him to look at me twice."

"It'll have to be you, Helen," Shun says. "You have more practice playing the femme fatale than I have playing the homme fatal." He strikes a seductive pose, and Shiori erupts into giggles.

Helen frowns. "You both see him and think of one thing, which is how the media portrays him. Treat him in this way and you'll be sure to earn his scorn."

This shuts them up.

"Maybe he wants a lover," Helen says. "Maybe he wants a friend. We won't know until we're at the base, living in his world. Whoever acts as point needs to know he's not someone who got to his position through just good looks and charm. He's dangerous. He's our enemy. And he deserves your respect. For now, we'll hold off on choosing who will play point until—"

"I'll go," I say.

Shiori and Shun whip their heads around. Helen must have already noticed me because she doesn't move.

I stare at Alex's photograph. A part of me knew the moment I saw him on the screen—or even before that, the moment I saw him on the stage—that this outcome was inevitable. Neo Beijing's Tower was only the beginning. If I want to move on with my future, I need to face my past. With this mission, I can finally close that chapter of my life.

Crush it, if I must.

"You're unwell," Helen says after a short pause. She hasn't outright denied my offer.

"I'm feeling much better now." I take a deep breath, plunging forward. "It makes the most sense for me to go. You're our leader. You can't afford to be out of contact with us for the length of time you'd need to be undercover as the point operative. Shiori is too young. Shun is of an age, but . . ."

I hold Helen's gaze. "I was engineered for the sole purpose of being a spy," I say quietly. "I was trained in infiltration tactics. Let me do this. I won't let you down."

There's another pause. Then Helen nods. "All right."

Shun opens his mouth as if to argue, but then quickly thinks better of it. We're a team, but Helen is the indisputable leader.

"Join us," she says. I take a seat at the table behind the couch. "It seems you're already aware of who our target is."

"Yes."

"Good. These are the people closest to him." She pulls up two photographs on the monitor. One is of a young woman around my own age, with striking good looks, high cheekbones, and narrow, intelligent eyes.

"Who is she?" Shiori asks. "A lover?"

"His first lieutenant. Na Gayoung, an ace pilot who made an impression as a show pilot before enlisting into the corps. In rumors, they have been linked romantically. However, I wouldn't regard rumor as fact. They've both been paired with numerous others, she more often with women than men."

The other photograph is of an older man. I recognize him immediately.

"Tanaka Kenichi," Helen says. "Also known as General Tanaka. Turns out the reason he was at the gala was to support Alex, his godson, a fact that was unknown to the public until last night. He was a friend of Alex's maternal grandfather."

Alex's maternal grandfather, his mother's father. Little is known about Alex's mother, who abandoned him when he was a young boy and moved to the American Neo States. Later he lived several years overseas studying in an international school in the Neo States, though it's unclear whether he met with his mother then. Whenever I asked him about her in the past, a wall would go up in his mind.

"They're recruiting new candidates in three weeks' time at the naval base right outside the NIC," Helen says. "Your 'father' will purchase you a place in their regiment.

I nod. It's not uncommon for wealthier citizens to purchase their children placements in higher-ranking military positions.

"But . . ." Shun begins, scratching his arm, then pointing at me. "What if he recognizes her?"

I go still. I knew Helen and the others had researched my past, but my personal history wasn't in any private files, let alone public ones. No one knew about my relationship with Alex, apart from Jaewon, Tera, Tsuko, and Alex's father. Even that day at the school, when Alex was dragged to the courtyard to be beaten in front of the students, they didn't know the reason why or who I was. They only knew that Alex had disobeyed the Director. Even Alex's position at the Tower alongside Jaewon, as retainers for Tera and me, was sealed information. All PHNX would know is that Alex secured a high-level internship in his senior year at the military academy.

"Well, maybe not Alex," Shun continues nonchalantly, oblivious to the tailspin he's thrown my thoughts into, "but his father is bound to visit him on base. Wasn't he on the board for the Amaterasu Project? He'll recognize Ama for sure."

"Oh, yeah, that's true," Shiori says.

I panic as my position on this mission slips from my grasp.

"Ama can change the way people see her," Helen says, turning to address me. "You did it at the Tower. You changed the soldiers' perception so they thought they were looking at a scientist they recognized rather than at you. If the illusion is close to your actual appearance, do you think you can sustain it for long periods of time?"

"I believe so." I nod slowly. "Yes," I say with more confidence. "I can."

"Oh, my god," Shiori says, "you're so cool."

"You can tweak a photo of her, can't you?" Shun asks her. "We'll have to submit a photo of Ama for processing, and you said when you saw her through the security camera at the Tower, the illusion didn't hold."

"That's right," I confirm. "I need to be in physical proximity of a person in order to influence their mind."

"So I'll just tweak your official photo to an altered version of yourself," Shiori says. "And you can make it so that anyone you might have known at the Tower sees that version of you. For others, you won't have to cast the illusion. They'll see the real you. And if they do happen to look at your official photograph, they'll just think you got plastic surgery or something."

Once more I stare at the photograph of Alex, emotions warring inside me—anticipation, worry, and fear. In three weeks' time, I'll stand before him, and the person he'll see won't be me but a stranger.

Helen shuts down the monitor. "I think that's enough for tonight. Tomorrow we start your training."

Shun turns around on the couch to face me. "First things first. Do you know how to pilot a God Machine?"

■ ■ ■

Over the next three weeks, I get a crash course in GM piloting. And I memorize everything I can about Alex, including his schedule: two-hour morning workouts, followed by GM drills and meetings with his officers. Twice a week he takes a cruiser into the city to meet with sponsors as well as Alliance senior officers. These meetings take place at elaborate venues, like the party at the mayor's home, but also at restaurants, clubs, galas, and benefits. Though from most of the reports, it seems as if he shows up to these meetings, takes the business, and leaves the pleasure. He always returns to base before full night, much to the disappointment of the paparazzi clamoring outside.

I'm surprised to discover that his fame is fairly recent, attributed to an exposé that ran directly after the battle at New Year's. His good looks first captured the attention of the public, singling him out of the many junior officers who would take part in the battle. However, his daring exploits, captured live on camera on the field, earned him their fervent devotion. After receiving the Medal of Honor and his promotion from lieutenant to commander, his status as a war hero—and media darling—was sealed.

His skyrocketing fame also dredged up old articles of his life from two years ago when he was a student in Neo Seoul. The fact that he'd dated a lot of high-profile models and actresses teased that he might do so again, and reporters attached his name to many celebrities in the city, including his own first lieutenant, Na Gayoung.

Strangely, there are little to no news articles from the years prior to the exposé. What Alex had been up to in that two-year interim is a mystery even to the observant public. The last he'd been mentioned was a great scandal in his home city of Neo Seoul, the details of which were covered up by the NSK, of which his father was the Director at the time. Afterward, Director Kim was forced to retire when past corruptions come to light, namely his connection with Red Moon, a powerful crime syndicate that was bribing the Director to overlook its illegal activities. Still, after two years of lying low, Director Kim has been appointed as the head of a new security division for the NIC. A brilliant comeback.

Like father, like son.

"What's that?" Shun leans on the back of my chair, reading over my shoulder.

"Nothing." I close my notebook. "Is it time?"

Every afternoon Shun and I run simulations to sharpen my GM piloting skills, which were never strong to begin with, even when I was in training at the Tower.

"You don't have to be an ace pilot," Shun says. "Just know the basics enough to get by in training."

God Machines. The weapons of modern warfare. Giant humanoid machines the size of small buildings controlled by human pilots. The extra armor, height, and arsenal of weapons makes them lethal killing machines—like tanks, but with legs and arms, capable of advanced mobility. Not every soldier is a GM pilot, but every soldier needs to know how to manage one.

After hours in the simulation, I run five kilometers on the treadmill, then meet up with Helen for the other half of my training.

"The illusion is starting to waver. I can see your true face," Helen shouts from across the parking garage beneath our apartment complex, the closest place we could find in this crowded city where we could test my mental range.

"I think it's safe to say that thirty meters is your limit," she continues as we take the elevator back up to the penthouse. "Any farther and you'll risk the illusion. How are you feeling?"

"Really good," I say, and I do, both physically—I don't have any headaches—and mentally. It feels *good* to use my powers in a way that I can control. "Maybe it's because the illusion is so close to my actual appearance or maybe it's because of the practice, but I hardly have to concentrate to hold the illusion once it's set. I don't think I'll have a problem with that part. It's the other stuff I'll have to be careful with."

Helen and I have thought up some active ways I can use my powers on the mission—namely, pulling information out of an individual's mind like I did with Dr. Yu, manipulating the minds around me to avoid suspicion, and if need be, using telekinetic energy, though as a last resort, as that particular end of my powers expends most of my strength. I can't risk fainting, which would break all my mental ties, including any ongoing illusions, though Shiori wonders if, after repeated conditioning, the illusion will remain even without conscious effort on my part.

■ ■ ■

Three weeks after the party, I'm ready.

Helen is the one to see me off at the port. "We won't have contact with you during training," she says, as we pull up to the wharf where new recruits are already forming a line to board the ferry. It'll take us a few kilometers outside the NIC to a small island where the base is located. "Afterward, you should have supervised access to contact family and friends through phone or video. At this point, use the code to report any initial findings or impressions to Shiori." We'd come up with a coded language for basic communication. "If there's something that can't be shared electronically, we'll have to plan for an in-person meeting. Shiori's been looking out for the whereabouts of the other super soldiers, but so far hasn't discovered anything. Until it becomes an issue, I don't want you to worry. Concentrate on the task at hand."

I nod, trusting the others to keep me informed and safe. I check my knapsack one last time. I have my personal items, undergarments and such—uniforms will be provided on base— my identification papers for Wang Jangmi, and my reading glasses.

"Ama."

I look up. For the past two weeks, Helen and the others had been calling me Jangmi so I could get used to responding to that name. That she calls me "Ama" now is significant.

"Yes?"

Helen places her own rough palms over mine. "I—" she begins, then stops. It's the first time I've ever seen her hesitant.

"What's wrong?"

Like always, I respect the privacy of her thoughts, keeping the walls raised around my mind.

"Would you tell me if I asked too much of you?"

"You don't ask for more than I would ask from myself." I slowly wrap my arms around her. "Thank you for believing in me."

"I do believe in you. More than you know."

Now it's my turn to hesitate. For the past three weeks, I've had more than enough opportunity to tell Helen the truth, that I *know* Alex, that this mission isn't like the others, that it's personal to me. But there's a chance that telling her would mean being pulled from the mission, and I won't risk it. I need this. I *want* this.

And though it might be difficult for others to lie to me, it's not so hard for me to lie to her, or myself, when I say, "I prepared for this, Helen. I am ready. There is nothing and no one who can stop me now."

12

INFILTRATION

As the ferry approaches the base, thick clouds gather overhead, and a sharp wind buffets the boat against the docking platform. No sign of thunderclouds, and yet there's a loud crackle and boom nearby as well as colors in the sky too scattered to be lightning.

"A fine day for new recruits!" a burly man shouts over the lashing rain. I stumble off the shifting boat onto solid, if not dry, land, alongside the thirty other recruits. "Hurry before the wind sweeps you out to sea."

We follow him from the docks up a steep path, which levels out to an area with many large buildings, indiscernible in the darkness. We're then ushered into a gymnasium, our feet tracking water on the hardwood floor.

"Line up!"

I take position beside a girl around my own age with a braid down her back. A glimpse into her thoughts reveals she's nervous. She's not sure she's capable of holding a gun, let alone going to war. Like my false identity, Wang Jangmi, her position here was secured through connections and bribes.

A cursory sweep down the line discloses that, other than a few others, most of the recruits are students from the various Neo states' top military academies. From PHNX's research, we knew this would be the case. Still, I feel an inkling of unease. I'll have to compete with the best for a position close to Alex.

A loud rumble shakes the gymnasium. Our guide displays no reaction, undaunted. "Leave your belongings here," he informs us. "They'll be delivered to your dorms. Any and all electronic devices will be confiscated. If you have a translator app, set it now before we take your phones." Recruits scramble to shut down all apps on their interfaces but their translators, which we're allowed to keep for communication purposes. I only have a few apps to shut down before placing my phone in a basket carried by a service droid.

Our guide points across the gym. "Through those doors you'll find the showers. Wash up and change into your uniforms inside the lockers assigned to you. Orientation is after lunch in the auditorium located behind this building. Lunch is in the cafeteria between the dorms and the gym. My name is Instructor Yang. Move out!"

I take the prescribed five-minute shower, then change into the green-and-brown uniform, jogging with the rest of the recruits into the canteen where a lunch of seaweed soup is served with stewed vegetables and minced meat. Afterward, we hurry back through the rain into the auditorium. Here, Instructor Yang is joined by our other instructors—a tactician, a weapons specialist, and a GM piloting instructor.

So far there's no evidence that either Alex or his first lieutenant, Na Gayoung are on base. In order for our plan to work, I need to see Alex before he sees me. I'm tempted to pry his whereabouts from the recruit instructor's mind, except that I can't spare the energy it would take. I need all my mental faculties in order to deceive Alex.

Fortunately, most of the recruits are as anxious to see him as I am.

"Sir." A girl raises her hand mid-orientation. "When will we meet the commander? My mother won my position here at an auction, and I want what I paid for."

I stare at the girl, both horrified and impressed at her audacity. Half of the minds in the audience express a similar shock, and the other half nods in agreement.

Instructor Yang bursts into laughter, only to sober up quickly. "If you joined the army to get closer to the commander, you're in for a rude awakening. He has no patience for sycophants and even less for the sick in love."

The girl scowls, clearly displeased.

Another sound like thunder pounds the air, but it's too metallic and high-pitched to be natural. This time Instructor Yang can't ignore it. "To answer your question, you'll meet the commander after orientation. He and his lieutenants are running GM drills with the rest of the battalion as we speak. The weather forecast predicts it'll be a storm the day of the Solstice battle. Therefore Commander Kim has ordered GM drills to be conducted in every storm from now until June. Something for you all to look forward to."

Another blast and boom shakes the auditorium.

Alex is out there now. *After the orientation.* I press my hands into my lap, my anxiety keyed up now that I'll see him soon.

"Because of the short time frame between now and June Solstice, the senior officers have decided on pushing forward a new program."

I drag my attention away from the booming outside to concentrate on Instructor Yang's words.

"One-on-one mentorship. One recruit will train directly under either the commander or the first or second lieutenants."

I sit forward. I'm not the only one. Recruits are calculating what this opportunity could mean for them—favoritism, the probability of advancement, and the promise of increased social status and popularity. Their heads ring with visions of the future.

Instructor Yang continues, "Though the senior officers will make the final decision on who they choose, only the recruits who we, your instructors, deem most worthy will be recommended as candidates."

The significance of his words is clear. To win this opportunity, we must strive to impress him and the others.

The rest of the orientation is a blur of rules and regulations. Afterward, we're herded outdoors. Though the storm has mostly abated—a fall of rain, rather than a downpour—night has set in. The darkness makes it difficult to see far ahead as we make our way across a grassy field. Ahead, floodlights illuminate a vast stretch of concrete, squared off in GM landing pads for vertical landing and takeoff. Each pad is equipped with a height-adjustable lifting platform for the pilots to safely disembark, as most GMs stand eighteen meters off the ground.

We wait at the edge as lights approach over the sea. I shiver. The waterproof military jacket does little to keep out the chill of the Pacific, as unforgiving as ever.

There's a murmur of awe as the lead GM comes into view, sunlight breaking through the clouds to backlight the massive machine like a wrathful angel come to Earth. It's an apt metaphor. According to the reports, Alex's white-and-gold GM Light Bearer is often called "Lucifer" by the rebel factions. Weighing in at around ten tons and over twenty meters tall, it's an impressive exemplar of modern weaponry. Though GMs are first and foremost advanced weapons purposed to kill and destroy, a key component to their effectiveness is their appearance. A unique and towering GM like Light Bearer has a substantial intimidation factor.

A little behind Alex, on either side, are his two lieutenants. I immediately recognize the sleek red GM on the left: Yeongdeung, Na Gayoung's GM, which she named after the Korean goddess of the wind. Smaller than Light Bearer but highly mobile, its main weapon is a massive red glaive. On the right, however, is a GM I've never seen before, a blue so dark it almost blends with the night sky. This must belong to Alex's second lieutenant, an appointment so recent that Shiori wasn't able to get information on their identity.

Soon we're in sighting distance of the GMs. I take the military cap consigned to us as part of our uniforms, placing it over my head and pulling down the bill.

The other GMs in formation are the standard models assigned to petty officers, each equipped with a machine gun, explosives, and a short wrist blade. All around the field they begin to descend, landing in great gusts that sweep out like mini dust storms. Instructor Yang motions us forward. We follow him through the particle rain toward the center of the landing area where the senior officers are anchoring their GMs to the docking platforms.

Gazing up, I see the chest of Light Bearer slowly open and the figure of a helmeted pilot emerge. He triggers the mechanism for the lifting platform, and it begins to descend. My pulse peals like a chime within me. He reaches the ground and proceeds to approach us, his strides long and steady. I reach out with my mind, but it's like grasping smoke or rain or wind. I panic. This was a mistake. I should have known.

I will never be ready for this.

Reaching up, he removes his helmet. I take in the details of him as if I were starving. This close, I can see the little changes two years have wrought upon his features. The remnants of boyhood are gone. His body is leanly muscled, his jaw more defined, and his eyes—his eyes seem to burn with an inner light even in the darkness. If I had thought him handsome before, he's devastating now. It's unbearable to be so close.

His head turns slowly, as if sensing the intensity of my regard. The memories rise unbidden. His hands on my skin, his lips on my neck. The feeling of sinking into him, the all-consuming emotions—of longing, of desire, of love.

"Sir!" Instructor Yang rushes between us, reaching up to hover his hand over Alex's neck. "You're hurt!"

I take an involuntary step forward.

"It's nothing," Alex says. "Banged my head when Nayoung hit me in the back. Bastard." He laughs.

The laugh is echoed back by a husky, feminine voice. A woman approaches, as tall as Alex, her long hair swept back in a high ponytail. She wraps one arm around his shoulder, and he doesn't push her away, his grin growing even wider. I'm reminded of the way he looked on the stage the night of the party. Happy. Free.

I feel a tug at my shirt. It's the nervous recruit from earlier. She glances at the line, indicating for me to get back in position. I nod, grateful, and take my place beside her.

Looking up, I meet the eyes of the second lieutenant—sharp, intelligent eyes that watch me with an indefinable expression. The newly appointed lieutenant wears a half mask that covers the bottom half of his face. The only indicator of his identity is a small badge worn on his blue-black piloting suit, signifying his rank. I break our gaze, cursing my carelessness. How much had he seen? Did he see how I reacted to Alex? When I risk a glance up, the lieutenant is looking down at his gloved hands, twisting a ring he must be wearing underneath.

"These are the new recruits," Instructor Yang says, leading

Alex over to where we stand. The distraction of the lieutenants' arrival has given me time to gain control of myself. This time when I probe Alex's mind, I manage to grasp his thoughts; his concentration is on meeting the new recruits.

I only have the one chance. It's as if I'm a sniper and Alex the target, as if I sight him through the scope. He shakes the hand of the boy to the left of me. Then he's turning toward me. I need to time it perfectly. *There.* That moment when recognition should register—I switch it out so that he sees not me, the girl he once claimed to have loved, but a stranger. *Wang Jangmi.*

I release the trigger.

I look into his eyes, and there's . . . no recognition. No dawning realization of who I am. No surprise or hurt or guilt or sorrow. There's nothing at all.

Our hands touch. My heart breaks. He moves down the line.

"Yuuki." He addresses the nervous recruit to my right. "Your grandfather said you would be here. I apologize for not being present for your arrival."

My surprise is matched by those around me. Even Instructor Yang raises a thick brow.

"Alex," Yuuki says, blushing furiously. "I—I mean, Commander . . ."

"Alex is fine."

"My grandfather said to expect impartial treatment from you and to—to try not to speak to you as if we—we know each other."

I suspect, suddenly, who she might be. Tanaka Yuuki. The

granddaughter of Tanaka Kenichi, Alex's godfather.

Alex tilts his head, clearly amused by Yuuki's discomfort. "I think," he says slowly, "if your grandfather expected you to be treated with impartiality, you shouldn't have been sent to my base."

I didn't think Yuuki's face could get any redder.

"Regardless, I'm glad you're here. Come to me if you're having any difficulties." He glances down the line at the rest of the recruits and instructors, the message clear. Tanaka Yuuki is under his protection.

"We're on a tight schedule," Alex says. "June Solstice is in three weeks' time. Every one of you will be deployed. There will be no exceptions. Your instructors will prepare you in time. This is war, but I will suffer no casualties."

It's a bold statement, but I sense the excitement in the other recruits. They believe him. They believe *in* him.

When I knew Alex at the Tower, he was smart and driven, but there was a restlessness inside him, a lack of faith in himself, as if he didn't know his place in the world.

He knows it now. He's a natural leader, inspiring confidence in and respect from his soldiers. If I wasn't so resentful, I might have been proud.

"Instructor Yang will have informed you of the accelerated program," Alex continues. "At the end of the week, my officers and I will each choose one of you to train personally and accompany us into battle as junior officers. I look forward to witnessing the reach of your ambition." With that, he turns and strides away, flanked on either side by his lieutenants.

I watch him go, every step he takes putting distance between us. Ten meters. Twenty meters. Thirty meters. My grasp upon his mind loosens and breaks. If he should turn around now, he would see me as I am. I search my heart for guilt at what I'll have to do in the coming weeks—manipulate his mind into believing I'm a stranger, work my way into his inner circle so that I can discover the Alliance's plans, then sabotage those same plans if I can—yet all I feel is bitterness.

My enemy, my beloved.

In order to win, I must get close to you.

In order to win, I must destroy you.

Is it a betrayal if he was the one who betrayed me first?

13

WANG JANGMI

Had I thought this would be easy, that I could walk onto this base, manipulate a mind or two, and obtain the information key to winning the war? No, I wasn't so naïve, and yet I hadn't believed I would *fail.*

Of the thirty recruits, half have earned their place here through skill and grit. The other half might have used bribes, but they along with the rest graduated from prestigious military academies. And though I can manipulate the minds of the instructors, it's only a temporary solution. Once those instructors are out of my proximity, their memories will return—of my subpar piloting skills, of my complete lack of physical combat training. Even Tanaka Yuuki, arguably the weakest candidate after me, looks on me with pity. My only hope is that by my reinforcing a positive impression, the instructors will choose me as a candidate for the program.

Luckily, Alex and the other senior officers aren't present on base. Otherwise I'd have to juggle an illusion as well. The morning after that first introduction, they were called to a joint session between the Neo Alliance and the coalition of rebel factions concerning the June Solstice battle. I want to discuss with Helen and Shun what this might mean for the war, but I have no way of contacting them.

Our instructors have us running drills morning, noon, and night, in simulations and in the Real, in GMs, and on foot, in sunshine and in the storms we were promised. At the end of the day, I'm so exhausted in mind and body that I collapse into bed, a blessing in that it allows the constant whirling of my thoughts to cease—thoughts about whether I'll be chosen and whether I'll be caught, about the way Alex had smiled at Gayoung as if she were a friend and about the way he'd singled out Yuuki as if she were more.

A week after my arrival on base, I wake restless and hot, a heat wave over the sea bringing an unbearable humidity to the barracks. I climb out of my cot, careful not to rouse Yuuki. We were assigned the same room, along with two others, and though I resent her closeness with Alex, I can't help liking her. She's open, thoughtful, and sweet. She reminds me of . . . *me*, at times. Or at least how I used to be.

Pulling on my running shoes, I slip out into the night. The base is around twenty-five square kilometers. I run the eastern length of it, the side that faces the Neo States of Japan and Korea. If I were on the western side, I might see the lights of the

NIC in the distance. As it is, here on the east, all I see is the sea. Tonight, the moon is like a lamp in the sky, casting a low glow over the path.

Tomorrow morning the candidates for the program will be chosen. Alex and the other lieutenants are due back to base to make their final selection. Even if my mind manipulation worked, and I'm put forth as a candidate, I still have to be chosen by one of them. If I can get within reach of their minds before the choices are made, I can force one of them to choose me. But what if they've already discussed which of the recruits they'll pick? What if there are internal politics at play I'm not aware of? Perhaps this competition was never one of merit or skill.

My mind reels with all the possibilities of failure, all the things that could go wrong.

Ama. I stumble as the name—*my name*—is spoken aloud in my head. I turn toward the mess hall, where a figure stands in the shadow of the building. My heart catches. I reach out with my mind, startled when I discover the identity of the person.

"Shun?" I whisper, joining him in the shadows. "What are you doing here? How did you get on the base?"

He winks. "Happy to see me?"

I roll my eyes.

"A GM equipment supplier in the city is hiring temporary workers," he explains. "I snatched a job as a deliveryman, managed to drop off the parts here, and snagged a couple of drinks with some engineers. They let me sleep overnight in the barracks." He grins, his eyes clear and sober. Sometimes I forget that, for years before I joined them, Helen and Shun had switched off playing point operative on missions. He's capable and thinks up solutions to problems quickly. Perhaps he would have been a better choice for this mission.

"And Helen and Shiori?" I ask. "How are they?"

"Helen is Helen. I've hardly seen her in the past week, she's been so busy. She leaves the apartment every night dressed for battle, except instead of wearing fatigues, she's in high heels and lipstick. Remember that woman we met at the gala, whose husband owns a company that specializes in shield technology?"

"Yes, Mrs. Peng. Her husband had a mistress."

"Well, let's just say that mistress didn't last long beneath the undivided attention of Helen at peak glam. She practically spilled information on Helen's designer shoes. The husband's company doesn't just specialize in shield technology for the Neo cities, but also for GMs and other armored vehicles, tanks, and planes. That's why I'm here. In three days' time, he's flying to a meeting in Busan to discuss the weapons that will be used in the battle. The only people present will be other military weapon manufacturers and high-ranking officials of the Alliance. You heard about the joint session between the Alliance and the rebel factions?"

"Yes." The session is why Alex and the others officers aren't on base. I wince at the anger and frustration seeping from Shun's mind. "What happened?"

"The Alliance screwed us over, that's what happened. They demanded a naval battle in international waters—"

I frown. "But I thought the agreement was that the rebels would choose the terrain of the battle."

"It was, but the Alliance flipped on us. They argued a battle on water would 'limit civilian casualties,' which was the exact wording for why the rebels wanted to choose the location of the battle. However, this puts us at a huge disadvantage because most of our artillery is operated from the ground—tanks and hand-operated weapons."

"I don't understand. Why did the rebels agree, then?"

"Because of the concession the Alliance made to bring onto the battlefield the exact number of units that we do."

I blink, absorbing the implications of this news. The Alliance, with all its military might, will meet the rebels with an equal number of units. "But isn't this to our advantage? What is the cap number on the units?"

"Ten thousand units altogether, five thousand on their side, five thousand on our side. And it would be—if not advantageous—at least fair, if it wasn't for the fact that the Alliance owns the greatest military on the planet. Their God Machines are superior; their pilots are *celebrities*. In order to have a chance, we need to know what sort of firepower they're bringing to the battle, makes and models of GMs." He pauses. "That's where you come in."

The plan falls into place. "The meeting Mr. Peng is going to Busan for," I say. "You need me to discover this information."

"All the senior-level officers who are taking part in the battle will be present, including your commander."

"He's not my commander."

Shun grins. "Glad to see you're not in love with him like half the female population of the NIC."

I bite my tongue.

"Ah, before I forget." Shun reaches into the pocket of his jacket, pulling out a small electronic device and handing it over. "Shiori's been working on this all week. It's a location device. All satellite receivers are being monitored, so use it sparingly. Just press down on the device once to release a brief signal. It's undetectable to body scans, so you should be able to keep it on you. This way we can find you, should you move location or need to contact us. We'll come to you."

A clatter from inside the mess hall alerts us to individuals nearby.

"I should go," Shun says. He's only been here a few short minutes, but even they have been a risk. "Take care, Ama."

I surprise myself by stepping forward to wrap my arms around him. I don't want to burden him with my worries—I'll find a way to get the information PHNX needs, with whatever it takes—but it's a relief to take some comfort in his solid embrace. He holds me a moment longer before letting go. I don't take my eyes off him until he's disappeared between the buildings that lead to the engineers' barracks. With a sigh, I turn, slip around the corner, and almost run into the person standing there.

A bank of clouds sweep overhead, shielding my face for the vital few seconds it takes to cast the illusion.

"A friend of yours?" Alex drawls.

The clouds pass, and I'm in the moonlight. Recognition

doesn't register in his mind, nor does suspicion. He must not have overheard our conversation. He's wearing his piloting uniform, a dark blue-black suit that should be sweltering on a night like this, yet he shows no sign of discomfort or fatigue. His expression is carefully blank. "Intimate relationships between army personnel are discouraged."

I could die.

Alex glances in Shun's direction. "I've never seen him before."

The fear in my heart switches direction. "You didn't see anyone," I blurt out. His eyes meet mine. I grab onto his thoughts, his memory. "You only see me." Pain blossoms at the base of my skull. I haven't used this particular power since the Tower, when I'd made Dr. Yu forget she'd spoken to me in the bathroom of the train car after I'd extracted information from her mind. Like then, adrenaline helps focus my powers, but at that time, I hadn't been also expending energy on an illusion.

For a moment, neither of us speaks. I don't think I even breathe.

"It's late for a run," Alex says. I must look startled because he glances down at my running shoes.

"I couldn't sleep," I say. "I thought running might help."

He nods absently. A probe into his thoughts shows that he's losing *interest*. I scowl. "I didn't think you would be back until later."

Alex glances at me. I realize how I must sound, taking note of his whereabouts, another lovesick fool. "I flew in ahead of the others. Not a few hours ago."

"Why?" I realize as I speak how impertinent I must seem, questioning a senior officer. Like with Dr. Yu, I could probe his mind and force him to answer me, but that wouldn't last long, and I'd have to wipe his memories or risk that he'd sense something off about our conversation. And I *want* him to remember this conversation; I want him to remember *me*.

"Remind me of your name . . ."

"Wang Jangmi. I'm one of the recent recruits."

"Jangmi," he repeats.

"My mother was Korean," I say, as a way to explain why my name is "Rose" in Korean, rather than in Chinese to match my surname.

"I see." Sighing, he sweeps one hand through the thick, dark strands of his hair. "The reason I flew back early is because, like you, I couldn't sleep."

"Is something bothering you?" I'm not sure if I ask because I'm looking for weaknesses to report to Helen or because I'm concerned for his well-being. Perhaps both.

"A lot of things, in fact," Alex answers. "But I won't burden you with my troubles."

To prod further would only lead to suspicion, so I say nothing.

Alex glances away from me, toward the sea. "I'll see you later today. I'm going to stay out for a little while longer."

It's a dismissal.

I bow in respect and farewell, though his thoughts have already left me behind.

The next morning when the recruits gather in the

auditorium, the results of our weeks' performances are in, and although I half expected it, it's still a dagger through the heart when Alex chooses Yuuki.

Na Gayoung chooses the top recruit, Wu Fei Hong. Grinning, the handsome pilot from Neo Shanghai climbs the stage as his instructors and peers clap him on the back.

I have very few options left. I could attempt a mind blitz, erasing the memories of a few minutes before and replacing them with a present more aligned to my advantage—with me as Alex's chosen candidate. But there are too many variables that could go wrong. I could miss a few in the auditorium. There could already be written records of those selected. Alex could recognize the symptoms of mind manipulation.

Alex steps forward, addressing the recruits. "Second Lieutenant Go Giwoo is on his way back to base. As for his choice . . ." Instructor Yang hands Alex a tablet, and he glances at it, his brow furrowing slightly. He looks up, and his gaze pins me in the audience. "Wang Jangmi."

My fellow recruits cheer and clap as I make my way to the stage. My mind tries to piece together what just happened. Had I been successful in convincing the instructors I was the strongest candidate?

Alex lifts his hand. I take it. His grip is strong. His eyes, usually guarded, stare at me intensely. I glimpse his thoughts. He—like me—is curious why Go Giwoo would choose me above the more qualified candidates. "Congratulations, Jangmi-ssi."

"Thank you, Commander."

He releases my hand. I bow and walk away, giving off at least the appearance of confidence, though I'm reeling inside. Why would Go Giwoo choose me? There must be a reason. I remember the way I'd caught his gaze after seeing Alex for the first time, how I'd worried Giwoo had seen the expression on my face before I concealed my feelings. In the past week, I've only picked up a little information about him from the other candidates and instructors—that he was a foot soldier who was plucked from obscurity by Alex, that his GM Brotherhood had the most confirmed kills in the battle at New Year's, that he's from Busan, but has no record of friends or relations.

The officers' quarters are located at the center of the base. Passing by security, I wait in a small inner chamber where the only decorations are a coffee table, a couch, and a potted plant. An hour passes as I pace back and forth, worrying the floor with my shoes.

The door slides open behind me. I turn. A tall soldier with unruly hair walks in, slinging a heavy bag off his shoulder.

I've seen him before. Outside the Tower in Neo Beijing months ago, when I accompanied TingTing to the draft office.

He grins at my look of surprise. "Hey, boring girl. It's been a long time."

14

GO GIWOO

"I looked for your friend. TingTing, was it?"

"You have a good memory." Right now, I'm struggling to remember our conversation. He'd spoken to me while holding TingTing's place in line outside the recruiting office. I'd noticed him because he'd been mumbling to himself in Korean. He'd said he was a member of Red Moon.

"Sometimes." He shrugs, then drops his bag to the floor.

Like that first night, I notice the emblem on his chest. "A lieutenant. You've come far in life."

"It's a matter of perspective. I was second only to the under-boss when I took the fall for him."

"Then you should be careful not to repeat past mistakes."

"Are you saying I shouldn't 'fall' for Alex?" His words are teasing, but there's a questioning glint in his eyes.

I don't know what to make of him. You don't rise from nothing to one of the most powerful positions in a group *twice* without a little artfulness. "You should protect him with your life."

His eyes never leave my face. "I can't argue against such conviction." He holds a tablet with a photograph of Wang Jangmi staring back at him, a face like mine but with thinner eyes, nose, and lips. "What an intriguing profile you have, Jangmi-ssi. It almost seems like you're a completely different person."

"I am," I say with confidence, as if I really am the privileged girl in my profile, unashamed of my wealth or status. If I want him to trust me, I need to connect my present with my past. "When we met, I was working in a bakery in Neo Beijing's Starlight District, in an attempt to be independent. My father is . . . protective. After TingTing was drafted, he ordered me back home to apply for a position at this base."

"Fascinating," Giwoo says, though his tone of voice implies it's anything but.

I change the subject. "Why did you choose me?"

He places the tablet on a side table. "I chose you for the same reason Alex chose me."

"And why was that?"

"Because I reminded him of someone he once knew." Giwoo takes a seat on the couch, spreading out his long legs. "Alex lives in the past. To him, sometimes it's more real than the present."

"That's not true," I say.

Giwoo looks up sharply.

I scramble to cover my blunder. "When he lived in Neo Seoul, he was only ever gossiped about and judged harshly for every little indiscretion. As the son of the Director, he was held up to impossible standards, none of which he could ever meet. Now he's gained the respect of his soldiers. He's praised in the media for his merits rather than who his father is. Moreover, he has confidence in himself. If this isn't the present he's always wanted, then what is?"

I've said too much. I knew I was saying too much halfway through, but I couldn't stop. I hold Giwoo's gaze. Hopefully he interprets the flush in my cheeks as part of an impassioned defense of our general, as opposed to something more personal.

"You speak of him as if you know him."

"I've done my research."

I probe his mind, but I'm met only with yellow-tinted curiosity. Suspicion hasn't yet crept into his thoughts. "So," I say casually, "I must remind you of someone you once knew."

"No."

I frown.

"You remind me of you. Literally. I remembered you from Neo Beijing. It seemed reasonable enough for me to pick someone I'd already met. I figured we'd at least have one memory in common. There are so many people in the world, it's nice to see a familiar face—especially someone who hasn't tried to kill me before. At least," he adds, "not that I know of."

"We only spoke for a few minutes."

"The memory stuck. Can't you accept your good fortune?"

My frown deepens. I'm not sure if I would call this meeting fortuitous.

"Sir." A man in the uniform of an engineer appears in the doorway. "Brotherhood has almost finished undergoing maintenance. Would you like to oversee the final inspection?"

"Ah!" Giwoo rises to his feet, an expression of boyish glee flitting across his face. He gestures for me to follow him out behind the engineer.

"I've been speaking to you without due respect," I say. The shock of seeing him again momentarily scrambled my wits. "I apologize."

"What year were you born?" he asks abruptly.

"2183."

"Then we're the same age. It'll be easier to converse if we speak without honorifics."

The GM hangar is located on the northeast side of the base. While most of the standard GMs are stored in the west bay, the senior officers have private stations for repairing and refueling in the east bay. Machinists and off-duty soldiers bow or nod in acknowledgment as Giwoo and I pass.

"Why is your GM called Brotherhood?" I ask as we enter the holding chamber designated for the second lieutenant. The massive metallic-blue GM is laid out on its back on the flatbed of a truck.

"It's named after a sword from a video game."

"Really?"

A machinist approaches, lifting his welding mask. "Repairs

are finished. We replaced the metal sheets on the armored shell and the main rotor. The rifle is still in maintenance, but—"

"I won't need it until the battle," Giwoo interrupts.

"I figured. Still, I attached a handgun just in case."

Giwoo clasps the machinist on the shoulder. "Thanks, Syd."

The man grins back, then moves to the other end of the chamber to fiddle with a rotor.

"God, I love that guy." Like a boy receiving his first toy robot on Christmas, Giwoo begins to inspect the GM from steel-coated chest to iron foot, even going so far as to shine the leg with the sleeve of his jacket. "Brotherhood to me means working with machinists like Syd, fighting alongside friends-in-arms like Alex and Gayoung. It's depending on other people and having them depend on you. Trust. Familiarity. Communion. I had that in the gang, though my brothers ultimately betrayed me. Here I have it again."

"You could be betrayed again." I don't know what makes me say it. I don't know why I keep on speaking my thoughts aloud.

He stops fiddling with his GM. "I could, but I choose not to live my life thinking about the past. Resentment. Regret." He shrugs. "They'll just stick in your soul like needles in an open wound. I don't dwell on my past mistakes. I'm not like Alex."

I bite my lip to keep from arguing *again*. The movement doesn't escape Giwoo's notice. "You disagree, but every soldier beneath his command would say the same. He'd give his life for even the lowliest one of us. Sometimes he fights as if he's trying to do just that, taking increasingly dangerous risks. Half in a bid to save one life, half as an atonement for lives he couldn't save in the past."

Giwoo's description reminds me of another person. *Tsuko.* The whole reason he wanted Tera and me to join the war was so that he could prevent further death of the soldiers beneath his command. I'm not surprised at Alex's and Tsuko's similarities. They were always haunted by the same ghosts.

"He's relentless in battle," Giwoo says, his words almost prophetic in their fervor. "Some say that because he's unafraid of death, it can't touch him. Then there are others who think this way of behaving is reckless. It intrigues Death, and she watches over Alex. Soon she will take him."

■ ■ ■

Three days later, I'm hurrying with Giwoo down a windy airstrip where a transport carrier awaits to take us northeast to Busan.

"Didn't you serve out your sentence at a penitentiary in Busan?" I ask as we finish climbing the ramp into the transport carrier. The doors close behind us, shutting out the wind.

"Oh yes, I told you that the day we met, didn't I? Strange how I shared so much about myself, while you shared nothing at all."

I ignore his mocking tone. After three days of being constantly in his presence, training with his squadron, I've gotten used to his odd personality, a mixture of wry humor and unnerving perceptiveness.

"Will you be all right? You said you fled the state." I know very little about Red Moon, the largest crime syndicate in East Asia, but from what I'd gleaned from Tera's thoughts, they don't forgive and forget easily. Jaewon had been a member of Red Moon.

"Is that concern I hear in your voice, Jangmi-ssi?" Giwoo places a hand on the top of my head, as if I were a kitten.

The doors to the inner chamber slide open. Four pairs of eyes turn upon us— Gayoung, Fei Hong, Yuuki, and Alex. Since the night Alex came upon me unexpectedly, I've been careful to keep track of his whereabouts. If I close my eyes and concentrate, I can pinpoint the light of his mind in the darkness. The illusion slips over him easily.

"So glad you could joins us," Gayoung drawls.

Releasing me, Giwoo strolls inside. The room is small, furnished with a metal table and several chairs bolted to the floor. Each officer is sitting across from their recruit of choice.

"I wouldn't miss this for the world," Giwoo says, plopping down next to Gayoung. I take my seat, nodding at Wu Fei Hong, who acknowledges me with a nod of his own. Yuuki waves from over his shoulder. "There's no place like home. Isn't that right, Gayoung-ah?"

She rolls her eyes. "I'm from Neo Seoul."

Up until a few hours ago, I'd worried they wouldn't include the recruits on this trip, but with a week and half until Solstice, it was decided we would continue the accelerated program overseas, even if our efforts are more secretarial than combat oriented. Though the recruits won't be able to sit in on the meeting for the battle, I have confidence I can extract the information from Giwoo afterward.

In little over an hour, the transport carrier enters the Busan airspace. I glance at Alex, catching the flicker of awareness in his mind before he speaks. "Giwoo."

"Sir." Giwoo sits up. For all his irreverent attitude, he never treats Alex with anything less than respect.

"I don't want you to leave the meeting place at any time while we're in Busan."

Giwoo's gaze lands on me, and in his thoughts, he recalls how I expressed concern for him as well. He nods. "Understood, sir."

In the pocket I've sewn inside my jacket, I press Shiori's location device, notifying Helen and the others that I've arrived in Busan in the Neo State of Korea.

■ ■ ■

At the Alliance's docking port, a limo awaits our arrival. It's accompanied by a smartly dressed driver, since Busan, a non-Neo city, has a normal traffic system. Alex gets in last after me, shutting the door behind him. I've only been inside a limo once before, on my first and only date, ironically with the boy sitting next to me. Though perhaps *boy* is not the right word for the man he's become. Military training has changed his body in small yet significant ways. Ways I'm becoming even more infinitely aware of as the limo moves onto the uneven cement-paved roads. My shoulder taps his arm, my knee his thigh, every point of contact a bloom of heat against my skin. He places the cap from his uniform upon his leg only for a bump in the road to tip it into my lap. I hold my breath as he slowly reaches out to remove it.

Suddenly there's not enough room or air in the limo. The limo picks up speed as we move onto an expressway. Alex pulls a packet of cigarettes out of his coat.

Shocked, I blurt out, "I thought you gave up smoking."

He glances at me sideways. "Did I say that?"

I could kick myself. I was *just* thinking how he wasn't the same boy as he was two years ago. "It's not good for you."

He rolls the cigarette as if contemplating a thought. "Does the smell bother you?"

Across from us, Gayoung laughs. "A soldier who doesn't like the smell of tobacco?"

It's only a passing comment. Afterward, she resumes her conversation with Yuuki, seated beside her. With Fei Hong asleep to my left and Giwoo on his phone across from him, no one but Alex is paying attention to my next words.

"You shouldn't give it up for me," I say quietly. "You should give it up for you."

The limo exits the expressway onto a bustling beachfront street lined with tall, glittering buildings—hotels and multistory shopping malls. Usually I'd be drawn to the spectacle of a new city, but right now, all my attention is on Alex. Slowly he lifts the cigarette to his lips, his eyes never leaving mine. With his other hand, he reaches into his pocket for a lighter, bringing it to my ear. I hear the sharp snap of the spark wheel and the sudden heat of a flame. Out of pride, I don't blink, though my heart flutters wildly. He's the first to break our gazes, his eyes downcast as he brings the flame to the end of his cigarette, lighting it.

With horror, I realize I'm about to cry.

I expected indifference from him, contempt, even, but never unkindness.

"Alex, can you switch with me?" Giwoo leans forward from his seat in the corner. "I want to talk to Jangmi."

Alex frowns. "Are you serious?"

Gayoung leans back, crossing one long leg over the other. "Alex can't believe he's being subjected to the inconvenience of changing seats in a moving vehicle."

"Come on, boss," Giwoo says, giving Alex no choice as he stands, making his way over. Scowling, Alex snuffs out his cigarette in a tray and sidles past Giwoo to take his corner seat. Yuuki, at least, looks pleased with the change in positions. In the commotion, I take the opportunity to sweep my sleeve across my eyes.

"I have something important to tell you," Giwoo says, plopping down beside me. "Your shoes are unlaced."

"Our shoes don't have laces," Fei Hong says, having apparently woken up to make this comment.

"Thank you, Fei Hong, my good friend!"

I'm glad for Giwoo's timely interruption, but I also worry at how much he'd noticed, if he thought to save me—his subordinate—from a tense encounter with our commander, or if he saw through to the latent emotions simmering beneath, at least on my end. "Giwoo—"

He cuts me off. "This is the best seat in the limo." Reaching over, he presses a button on a wall panel. It opens to a small refrigerator full of liquor bottles. "Jackpot."

"You know we're about to attend a meeting with all the major NIC leaders," Gayoung says.

"Ah, an occasion to drink if there ever was one." When Giwoo offers a glass to the others in the car, they all decline.

"Jangmi-ssi?" He holds up a glass of amber liquid.

I know I shouldn't accept it. I've never been able to hold my liquor well the few times I've attempted to drink, and I need all my mental faculties today. And yet I find myself reaching for the glass.

"Geonbae," Giwoo says, clinking his against mine. I swallow the liquid. It burns like fire down my throat.

The rest of the trip is more pleasant. Though I forego a second glass, Giwoo downs two more. He manages to wrangle Gayoung into an illuminating debate about whether GMs will have space mobility in the future. I laugh as their arguments become more heated, Yuuki and Fei Hong occasionally adding in counterpoints of their own. Alex ignores our revelry, shutting his eyes and leaning back in his seat.

Traffic halts around the hotel where the meeting is being held. The reason becomes apparent when we get closer. Hordes of paparazzi stand outside, cameras angled for a shot of the passengers concealed within the limos pulling up to the curb. As our own vehicle approaches, the noise and commotion climb to a frenzy. Hover cameras press against the blue- and black-tinted windows, illuminating the dark interior in flashes of brightness.

Gayoung pulls out a gold tube, twisting the cylinder to release a burgundy lipstick. She proceeds to apply two coats to her wide lips with steady hands, using the reflective cylinder as a mirror. When she catches me watching her, she holds it out to me. I shake my head. She offers it to Giwoo and Yuuki, who also both decline. "Suit yourselves," she says. "Don't come to me tomorrow when you see your faces plastered to all the Netizen boards with bare, chapped lips."

I blanch, but not because of vanity. Photos taken of me will show my real face. It was a controlled risk on base, where hover cameras weren't allowed and where Shiori could potentially sabotage CCTV footage if I was compromised. But a photo taken here today would be spread widely. Those who worked at Neo Seoul's Tower would see it—the scientists and machinists. Alex.

"Jangmi-ssi?" Giwoo says. "You don't look so good."

There must be a way out of this. "I'm camera shy."

"Really?" He blinks. "But you're, like, gorgeous. Not that ugly people can't also take photos."

On any other day, I might be flattered. And a part of me wonders what Alex thinks of this compliment, if he finds Wang Jangmi as attractive as he found me. But his eyes are on the window. "I'll stay behind," I say, trying to keep my voice level, "and come in later through a back door."

"That'll draw even more attention," Giwoo says. "Anyway, we're already here." I whip my head around to see that he's right. Our car has reached the apex of the curb. A gauntlet of reporters and paparazzi line a blue carpet leading into an elegant silver-and-slate building—Busan's Paradise Hotel. "Just stay behind me. They won't look at you because they'll be too busy looking at me." For once, his jests lend me no comfort.

I press my hands together to keep them from trembling. Perhaps I can grasp each individual mind in the car and convince them it's the right choice to let me stay behind. But I can hardly concentrate with the alcohol still thick in my system. What should I do? My heart beats rapidly in my chest. The hover cameras *click-click-click* outside the door. Giwoo reaches for the handle.

"Wait," Alex says. Everyone turns to him. "Gayoung-ah," he says casually, "you go first."

The first lieutenant raises a brow but doesn't protest. Scooting over, she opens the door. Her emergence from the limo is met with a raucous clamor of shouts and earsplitting screams. It's not surprising. Of the six of us, she's the most famous after Alex, a show pilot before she was a soldier.

I'd been momentarily shocked by Alex's interruption, but now I regain my wits—and my fear.

"Wu Fei Hong." Alex nods to the tall, soft-spoken pilot. His exit is not as loud, but the flashing lights maintain their steady rhythm.

"Giwoo, you're next," he says. "Don't draw attention to yourself."

"Easier said than done, boss." Giwoo opens the door and slips out. I feel like such a fool. Why did I not prepare for an occurrence such as this?

"Wang Jangmi." I turn, startled to find Alex so close. I realize belatedly that this is the second time he's called Jangmi's name. I feel a soft weight on my head, pulled low to cover my eyes. It's the cap from his uniform. "Keep your head down." He opens the door and presses me forward.

I'm met with an onslaught of flashing lights and shouts.

"Look over here!"

"Show us your face!"

"This way, soldier!"

Then a hand grabs mine. "Hurry," Giwoo says. He pulls me along behind him.

We're a quarter of the way down the carpet when the attention of the crowd shifts. Like Gayoung's entrance earlier, there's a thunderous explosion of shouts and cheers. Behind the reporters and paparazzi is a roped-off area where young people have gathered, some holding holographic signboards flashing with the names of their favorite pilots. None of the cameras are trained on us anymore, instead focusing on the spectacle behind me.

I risk a glance over my shoulder. Alex stands by the limo, not quite posing, but not moving either. He's drawing their attention away from me. My heart skips with joy. A wide smile plasters itself on my face. Then he turns, reaching back to help the last person alight from the limo—Yuuki, whom I'd forgotten about in my panic.

Alex wraps an arm around her, pulling her close. The crowd goes wild. The smile slips from my face.

There's a tug on my hand. I turn from the scene to find

Giwoo watching me. I catch a whiff of his emotions—empathy.

"I think you've seen enough."

I let him lead me through the glass doors into the hotel.

15

BUSAN

It's blessedly quiet inside the lobby. Miniature koi swim through artificial streams around the edges of the room, while their holographic brethren float like specters through the air. Unlike the chaos outside, the lobby is mostly empty but for a few uniformed soldiers and a smattering of hotel employees.

The only sound is the click of heels against marble floors as Gayoung approaches. "I already checked us in. The passcode should have been forwarded to your interface."

Giwoo's eyes take on the faraway look that occurs when someone interacts with an interface. It makes me wonder if that's how *I* appear when reading someone's mind. "Got it. Are we on the same floor?"

"You and I are. Alex is a floor above us with the other high-ranking officers. He hasn't come in yet?" Gayoung glances behind us. "Ha! He's showing off, isn't he? Though I can't blame him. I'd do the same if I had Tanaka Yuuki on my arm."

"I have to use the restroom," Giwoo says.

Gayoung scowls, disgusted. "Do you really have to announce it to the world?"

"So you know, then," he deadpans, "that you are my world." She moves to kick him. Gleefully he saunters away.

Behind us the doors open to a rush of noise, and Alex enters with Yuuki. His hand rests protectively against her back. Joy, sweet and unfettered, gushes from her mind, striking me like a wave. It's a joy not meant for me, relived in a memory that isn't mine, Alex shielding her body with his own, his hand sliding up her back to grasp her shoulder. I close my eyes to escape the images, but of course that does nothing. In the confines of my mind, they're only heightened more.

"Jangmi? Are you all right?"

I open my eyes to find Yuuki, Gayoung, and Alex staring at me. It was Yuuki who had spoken. "I'm fine," I say.

"You should rest," Yuuki says. "Only the officers are to sit on the meeting. We won't be needed for a while yet. Isn't that right, Alex?"

I risk a glance at Alex, whose expression is difficult to read. Yuuki tugs on his sleeve, and he looks down at her. "That's right," he answers.

I turn away from the scene. I need to get ahold of myself. I can't keep drawing undue attention to Wang Jangmi, who at best harbors an unrequited love for her commanding officer, and who at worst is incompetent, calling for an investigation into why she was even allowed on base. I can't be so wildly affected that I make mistakes, that I lose focus. I can't let my feelings jeopardize this mission.

"Where are Giwoo and Fei Hong?" Alex asks from behind me.

Gayoung answers. "I sent Fei Hong up to the room already, and Giwoo is off who knows where—"

"I told him to stay in the hotel."

"Relax. He's in the bathroom."

"I'll go get him," I say, then hurry off before anyone can stop me. I round the corner toward the bathrooms. The sound of voices travels down the hall. Recognizing one as belonging to Giwoo, I duck into an alcove on instinct.

"It's good to see you, hyeong," Giwoo is saying. "Have you been working here for long?"

"Since last June." The answering voice is gruff and deep. I glance around the corner.

Giwoo's back is to me as he speaks to a man slightly taller than him, dressed in the light blue and green uniform of a restroom attendant. "Almost a year then," Giwoo says.

The man nods. I don't see a family resemblance, but if Giwoo is calling him "hyeong," they must be close enough to be like brothers.

"Is it full-time?" Giwoo asks.

His friend nods again. "Every day except for Friday and Saturday nights. I still—" He swallows, looks away. "The boss has errands for me on those days."

"Right."

"You shouldn't have come back. A lot of people were angry when you disappeared. If they know that you're in town—"

"They don't. They won't. You were always a worrywart, Junhee-hyeong. You don't have to watch out for me anymore."

Junhee shakes his head, as if the thought is inconceivable. "You might have left the gang, but I'm still your brother."

Junhee takes his leave. I wait a few beats before approaching Giwoo. "The others are waiting," I begin. "Is there something you—"

"No." His serious demeanor has vanished, replaced by an easy smile. "Just ran into an old friend. For people like us, there aren't many of those left."

■ ■ ■

Three hours later, I'm sitting on the couch of our two-room suite, watching the sun set over the East Sea. Haeundae Beach is alight with bonfires, couples strolling hand in hand along the white sand for which Haeundae is famous. Before Giwoo left, he said the meeting would last for a few hours and that I shouldn't wait up for him.

But if I'm to extract information from his mind, it's best to do that while it's still fresh. I grimace at the mercenary turn of my thoughts. Regardless of whether I like Giwoo, and I can admit to myself that I do, we're on opposite sides of a war. I'm not really betraying him, but working against the Alliance, to which he belongs.

Or so I tell myself.

There's a knock on the door of my hotel room. I look through the peephole, then open it wide. Yuuki stands on the other side. The skin around her eyes is bright red, as is her nose. She's been crying, her mind limned pink with embarrassment.

"Yuuki!" I exclaim. "What happened?"

"Does this hotel have a bar?" She sniffles. "I don't think I can speak about it without a drink in me."

I walk with her to the elevator, where a directory shows that the bar is located on the top floor. We find seats in the far corner. Yuuki orders the first drink on the menu, and I ask for a glass of water.

"I confessed to Alex," she blurts out once the waitress places our glasses on the table. She picks up one of the silk napkins and blows her nose, then takes a generous sip of her jewel-colored drink.

I blink at her, unable to form a sentence.

"It didn't go well. He said he's always seen me as the grand-daughter of his godfather. Like a sister, though he didn't use that word. He said he cares about me as a friend, but nothing more."

I'm unsure what to say. Expressing my sympathy seems disingenuous. I pick up my glass and take a long gulp of the water.

"Have you confessed your feelings yet?" she demands.

I choke.

"Don't worry!" she says, reaching over and patting my back until I've regained my breath. "It's not obvious to everyone. I've just worn that look for so long I can recognize it on another person."

I briefly consider lying, but Yuuki's honesty must be contagious, because I admit, "I haven't told him how I feel. It's . . . complicated." An understatement.

Yuuki takes my hands. "You have to be brave, Jangmi. If you never tell him how you feel, you'll come to regret it."

Regret. Do I regret having told Alex I loved him that first time?

"I might feel as if I'm suffering in this moment," she says, "but now that I know that he doesn't feel the same way about me, I can focus my affections elsewhere. You have to tell him how you feel. Otherwise you'll never be able to move on."

■ ■ ■

It's 21:00 by the time I return to my room, having sat in the lounge with Yuuki as she spoke about her childhood growing up in Fukuoka.

I check both rooms of our suite, but Giwoo isn't in either of them, though there are signs of his return—his uniform strewn across one of the beds and a towel on the ground from where he dropped it after a shower. I knock on the door across the hall, and Fei Hong answers, saying that Gayoung had returned a half hour ago and is currently passed out on her bed. I check the bar, outdoor pools, and the fitness center. When Giwoo is neither in the sauna nor the simulation rooms, I start to worry.

In the lobby, I approach Junhee coming out of a service door, wrangling a cart of cleaning supplies in front of him. "Excuse me. Can you help me? I'm looking for my senior officer."

Junhee bows, smiling pleasantly. "Of course, Miss. Is he a guest of this hotel?"

"His name is Go Giwoo."

Immediately I feel a wall slam down over Junhee's thoughts, his expression shuttering. "I'm sorry, I can't help you. I don't know anyone by that name."

I glance around, but we're exposed in the lobby. "I have a picture of him." I move into a separated area, blocked from view by a few potted plants.

"I really can't help you. Maybe—"

I grab on to his mind. "Did you do something to Giwoo?"

"No."

"Do you know where he is?"

"I can guess."

"Tell me."

He reaches into his pocket for a pen, rips off a piece of paper from a notebook in his cart, and writes down an address. He hands me the paper.

"You won't remember this conversation." I stuff the paper in my pocket. "You won't remember having spoken to Giwoo until after he's gone from this city." I have no doubt Junhee is a good friend to Giwoo, but I can't take any chances.

Hurrying toward the lobby doors, I release Junhee's mind.

"Wang Jangmi!" Alex calls.

I take a deep breath, then turn toward the familiar voice. Alex jogs across the lobby. "Have you seen Giwoo?"

"He wasn't in the room when I returned." I bite my lip, unsure whether to voice my suspicions.

Alex must notice. "Tell me."

"I fear he might have disobeyed your orders."

He curses. "I suspected as much." He glances at me, then at the door. "You're going after him."

I nod.

There's a spark in his mind, and he says something that surprises us both. "I'm coming with you."

16

RED MOON

After hailing a cab outside the hotel, Alex slides into the seat beside me and shuts the door. The cab driver, an ajeossi with wire-rimmed glasses and silver hair, stares at us through the rearview mirror.

"I have an address," I tell Alex. Leaning over the console, I hand the piece of paper to the cab driver.

His eyes widen as he reads what Junhee had written down. Apparently Red Moon's haunts are well known. "Are you sure you want to go here, agassi?" he asks. "It's not a place for young ladies."

I place a hand on Alex's leg and smile at the driver. "I'll be fine."

As the the cab moves into the street, I remove my hand and

glance at Alex, who's studying me as if he's never seen me before. "Where did you get that?"

"From someone I saw Giwoo speaking with earlier. I think he might have been a friend from his past."

Alex leans back in his seat, watching me with hooded eyes. "Wang Jangmi, you're full of surprises."

You have no idea.

As a non-Neo-ratified city, Busan doesn't have a curfew. At this late hour, the streets are bustling with motorbikes, honking city buses, and a bevy of other vehicles—dingy cabs next to sleek black automobiles—as well as pedestrians, tourists, and city dwellers, all of whom seem to take the crosswalks more as guidelines rather than the law. The city is awash with colors, from the flashing lights of neon signs in Korean and English denoting hotels, restaurants, cafés, and shopping malls, to the constantly shifting mosaic of holograms advertising the latest brands in fashion and beauty products. Speakers pump loud techno-pop music into the air, and every tall building in the vicinity has screen billboards playing music videos, advertisements, or newsreels.

The cab pulls up to a flashy building along the same beach-front street as the hotel, but a few blocks down. As I step out of the cab, I'm met with the rich, salty scents of fried fish and squid wafting from a row of nearby food carts. Alex pays the cab driver and joins me on the sidewalk. Together we stare at the red-and-black building that gives no indication of what sort of establishment it is except for the golden letters spelling out "casino" vertically down the left side. Whoever owns this building must have the local authorities deep in their pocket, as gambling is prohibited in all states of the Neo Sphere.

I notice we're drawing the stares of people on the street. Our military uniforms must be making the locals nervous, like two sharks among a school of mackerel. "We won't blend in well," I say, "not dressed like this."

Alex grimaces, having also noticed the attention we're attracting. He turns from the building, sweeping his gaze along the stores. "Follow me."

Crossing the street is a game of chance as we avoid collisions with cars and people. Shimmying between two illegally parked vans, we enter a brightly lit shopping mall packed with small, stall-like stores overflowing with goods, from toys to electronics to homeware. Shop owners call out to us as we pass by, promising discounts and free gifts upon purchase. Ignoring them, Alex moves farther into the warren of shops, where some of the light bulbs flicker overhead and the shop owners are less aggressive, huddled around low tables inside their stalls with pots of ramen, engrossed in the latest weekend drama.

Muted music plays overhead, a ballad singer crooning about the great love he lost one day on the shores of Haeundae. A display of fashion jewelry catches my attention, little pieces of dove-shaped gems and heart-glass earrings nestled on faux-silk cushions.

"Jangmi-ssi," Alex says, and I quickly turn, joining him where he stands by a small clothing stall that specializes in cocktail attire.

Casually, he flips through the clothing on an outside rack, while the shop owner, a sour-faced ajumma, lingers at his shoulder, adjusting every dress or shirt as he touches it. A glimpse into her mind reveals that she suspects we might shoplift. As Alex reaches to move another shirt, she prematurely whips out her hand, knocking against him. I feel the snap of energy as his mind registers the contact, his anger like a knife.

Slowly, he turns to the woman, sliding her one of his dark-eyed stares. "My colleague and I are looking to purchase some items for an event," he says coolly. "Would you please be so kind as to give us some privacy? I'll pay you double what the clothing is worth."

The ajumma's eyes widen, shocked by such polite words given through gritted teeth. She nods and scurries over to the stall opposite, most likely to gossip about us to that shop's owner.

"Pick out a dress," Alex says, as if he hasn't just scared a shop owner out of her own stall. None of the dresses on the rack outside appeal to me, so I follow him into the small space, about three steps in each direction. A TV is set on a stool at the back. The floor is lined with cardboard boxes and plastic bags of clothing. There are more racks of clothing inside the store as well as dresses and suits displayed against the walls. The affordable prices are boldly marked on colorful cards by each item.

Alex pulls a black dress shirt from a rack as well as a pair of folded-over slacks. Usually I enjoy lingering over clothing when I shop, selecting the one item that feels as if I can't live without it. But as we deliberate here on fashion choices, Giwoo could be in trouble. I pluck two dresses on hangers off the wall.

Both are featured "Deals of the Day." One is a light yellow boat-neck dress with butterfly sleeves, the other a black structured dress with a fit-and-flare silhouette. Both have hems that hit above the knees.

Alex's eyes linger on the yellow dress. My hand tightens, bunching the fabric. Is he remembering that last day at the school? I wore a yellow dress then too.

"Not that one," he says. "You'll blend in more in the black."

I swallow my disappointment and place the yellow dress back on the wall. Alex takes in the small area of the stall. "There's no changing room," he says, stating the obvious.

I bite my tongue from teasing him. I'm sure in the places where he's used to shopping, the changing rooms are the size of this entire store. He might be holding the dress shirt and pants casually, but I wonder at the novelty of this experience for him. I doubt that Alex, in his privileged life, has ever worn clothing not perfectly tailored to his body.

Grabbing one of the racks, he rolls it away from the wall so that it cuts diagonally across the stall, forming a makeshift changing room. "I'll go first."

"Should I—?" I begin, edging out of the stall, but he's already slipping out of his uniform shirt. I catch a glimpse of pale skin and taut muscles before I turn away.

"Finished," Alex says, emerging from behind the rack. Even in a cheap black shirt and pants, he looks elegant.

I take the black dress and move into the corner of the stall. Alex rolls the rack to block me from view, though with his height he can see right over it. He must realize this himself because he steps out of the stall. I watch him walk over to the dagger-eyed ajumma across the way, presumably to pay. Facing the wall, I quickly undress. Shivering beneath the dull ceiling lights, I slip the dress from the rack and step into the skirt, shimmying it up my legs and waist. I reach around me to the zipper, pulling it up halfway before it catches in the fabric. I try to reverse the motion, but it won't budge.

"In need of some assistance?" Alex drawls from outside the stall.

I glare at him over my shoulder. "Maybe the shop owner can help me."

"Knowing her, she'd break the zipper and have us pay for two." He approaches, motioning for me to turn around.

"You can afford it," I say, pulling back my hair to make it easier for him.

"My pride can't." Gently, he tugs at the zipper, releasing the fabric, and pulls the tab upward, closing the gap.

"You're good at this," I note. "Had a lot of practice, I gather?"

"Maybe you should stay here, join the old ladies in front of their television sets. You seem to be fond of drama clichés."

I can't help it—I smile as I turn to face him. "Touché."

He returns the smile, and a thrill races through my body. Alex used to flirt with me, but never like this, with an edge.

He pays the ajumma to watch our uniforms, with a promise to return for them later. Then he offers his arm. "Shall we?"

This time, when we cross the street, the only stares we attract are ones of admiration. The tinted glass doors slide open with our approach. We enter a low-ceilinged lobby, dimly lit, with soothing piano music playing softly overhead. The walls are backlit with shadows that mimic ink spreading across a canvas, depicting traditional brushstroke paintings of the Korean countryside. It's classy, beautiful, and nothing like what I expected from a gangster's den.

A woman approaches at our entrance. "May I be of assistance?"

I can feel Alex's mind working. Perhaps he'd thought we could sneak in with a crowd, but we're alone in the lobby but for the woman. Her smile of welcome slowly deteriorates as she peers closer at our clothing, which, though no longer conspicuous, is still too cheap for such an establishment.

The woman's mind grows suspicious. I see her gaze flick across the lobby to where two burly men stand at attention.

"I know the passcode," I say, and both the woman and Alex stare at me. I clear my throat and pluck the words from the woman's mind. "Even the moon wanes when it is full." A proverb for a passcode, and a humbling one at that. Whatever high-ranking Red Moon boss chose it must have wanted to remind himself that power is fleeting.

The woman nods, and out of the corner of my eye, I see the two guards step back. "This way."

I can feel Alex's gaze on the back of my neck, though he doesn't say a word. If he asks later, I'll tell him Giwoo's friend had been eager to help.

We follow the woman to a far wall with a single elevator. She presses the call button, and the doors open immediately.

Inside is a panel with eight floor selection buttons, including the lobby. A key on the wall delegates floors one through three as meeting rooms, four isn't included out of superstition, five is a pool and gym, six is a sauna, seven is a simulation room, and eight is a restaurant.

"Please select a floor." The smirk on the woman's face tips me off.

I reach into her mind and pull the information from her head. "Five. Eight. Three. Two," I say aloud.

She doesn't mask her surprise well, blinking rapidly; Alex, on the other hand, appears unperturbed, looking down at his nails.

The woman presses the numbers in the correct sequence, and the elevator, instead of rising, begins to descend. Only a few more seconds pass before it comes to a smooth stop.

"Welcome," the woman says, all politeness now that we've passed her tests. "Please enjoy your visit."

I can feel the heavy beat of the bass before the doors open. Alex and I step out into what appears to be an underground club—part casino, part nightclub. It's industrial in design, with gray brick walls and sectioned-off sitting areas with low black tables and plush leather couches.

"It'll be difficult to find Giwoo in this chaos," Alex says, moving aside for a trio of women in matching sparkly red dresses to pass. "Not without leads."

"Should we split up?" I ask.

Alex hesitates. If I was Ama, the girl he knew two years ago, he'd refuse. He'd want to keep me close in order to protect me. But tonight, I'm Wang Jangmi, a soldier, who not only discovered where Giwoo had been taken, but successfully breached a gangster's hideout undetected.

"All right," he agrees. "But be discreet. We want to discover if Giwoo is here, but we also don't want to alert Red Moon if he's not." He lowers his voice. "Also, should they find out we're from the Alliance, they won't take kindly to us being here."

Alex doesn't explain further, but I remember reading an article about what occurred after the battle of Neo Seoul, when the Alliance blamed Red Moon for the destruction of the Tower, though for years the Alliance and Red Moon had been allies, the latter funding the Tower's more amoral projects, like the very one I was a part of.

"I'll be careful," I say.

"We'll meet at the bar in a half hour." He nods at the back wall where a full bar displays an impressive array of wines and spirits in glittering bottles. "Good luck."

We separate, Alex moving in the direction of the table games while I circle the dance floor.

I try to pick up thoughts, but I'm feeling the aftereffects of the recent use of my powers on the woman. My head throbs, and I feel light-headed. The strobe lights above the dance floor don't help; neither does the loud music. But I need to concentrate. Giwoo's in danger. I can still attempt to discover his whereabouts without the use of my powers.

I head toward a crowd gathered around a well-dressed gentleman flanked by two bots. Ever since the Alliance and the rebels agreed to schedule battles, apparently war betting became popular. Individuals shout out numbers, which appear as bets on the droids' screens and are then double-checked by the bookie. Behind the bookie, large monitors show a rolling roster of pilots who will take part in the Solstice battle, the Alliance looking like the favorite to win. Most of the competitive odds are whether certain events will take place. If Alex is killed in combat, several people in the crowd will earn a hefty payout.

An idea strikes me. I maneuver my way to the front of the crowd. "I'd like to place a bet," I say, putting the last of my cash on the counter.

"Oh, yeah?" the bookie says, hardly sparing me a glance. "On who?"

"Go Giwoo."

Several of the people in the crowd stop shuffling to stare at me. The bookie looks up. "That he should die?"

"That he should live."

"The odds are against you."

A man to my right lets out a low chuckle. "If anyone finishes him off, it'll be Red Moon."

"I heard he's back in the city," someone else interrupts, "here for some Alliance meeting. Doesn't look like he'll make it to the battle itself."

The bookie shrugs. "Sorry, agassi." He takes my banknotes and feeds it into a slot in one of the bots. My bet appears on the bot's screen alongside my terrible odds. "No take-backs."

I make a show of being upset and extricate myself from the crowd, but inside, I'm smiling. Giwoo isn't here, or at least these individuals aren't aware he's gone missing.

I find Alex at one of the blackjack tables. He seems to be in deep conversation with the man beside him, so I head over to the bar.

A few minutes later, he joins me, ordering a drink. He doesn't speak again until the bartender moves out of earshot. "Get any leads?"

I fill him in. "You were one of the hottest tickets," I quip.

He raises a brow. "I should place a bet on myself."

I glance around the club. "I'm surprised no one has recognized you."

"It's dark. And people don't expect to see me here." He pulls his stool closer, leaning forward. I almost choke on my water as he brushes a finger against the crook of my arm. His hand traces the sensitive skin, where scars have formed over old Enhancer injection sites. "What happened?"

"I—" I grasp for a believable story. "I was sick."

He leans back, watching me carefully. "With Wang Yunpeng's money, you could have those scars removed."

"I earned these," I say defensively. "They remind me of what I've overcome." *What I've left behind.*

For a moment, he just stares at me. "I'll admit, when I first read your report, I thought you were a spoiled heiress." I scowl. "But everyone deserves a chance to make a name for themselves on their own terms."

I scoff. "Are you speaking of me or yourself?"

He laughs softly. "What was that word you used earlier? Ah, that's right. 'Touché.'"

"Hey, kid." We turn to find the man from the blackjack

table standing close by. "If you're finished flirting, I can take you now."

"This is the delightful Mr. Hong," Alex says, standing up from the stool. "He'll be assisting us in speaking with the local gang leader." He eyes me meaningfully.

I take Alex's offered hand. "Thank you very much, Mr. Hong."

Mr. Hong leads us to a roped-off area, where he nods to the guards standing on either side. We enter a long hall lined with wood-paneled sliding doors and bamboo light sconces. Murmured voices can be heard through the thick walls, punctured by bursts of laughter.

"I got the first installment already, kid," Mr. Hong says. Alex must have promised him a monetary incentive to help us.

Alex glances back the way we came as we slip farther and farther into the recesses of the building. He grits his teeth. "You'll get the rest of it when we get out of here safely."

If Giwoo is inside one of these rooms, it'll be difficult to extract him without bloodshed. Alex slips a hand beneath his jacket, and I wonder if he's brought a weapon. My mind is my weapon, but I can't rely on that, not if I want to maintain my cover.

"Here we are," Mr. Hong says, having reached the end of the hall. Shoes are lined in a neat row outside the door.

"I want to observe for a moment before approaching the leader," Alex stalls.

"If there's something you need to ask a gangster, there's really no point in waiting."

As if to underscore his words, the door slides open, and we meet the eyes of a startled server. Behind her, thirteen pairs of eyes turn toward the entrance, each belonging to a man or woman sitting cross-legged on silk cushions at a low wooden table. They've been drinking. Porcelain cups are arranged in front of each individual, a few stained with the milky essence of makgeolli.

For a beat, no one speaks. Then, "I know you," the man sitting at the head of the table growls. "You're Kim Tae Woo's son."

I realize in this moment that I'd never heard the Director's name spoken aloud.

"You look just like him," the man continues. "Same fair skin, same arrogant pride. And yet here you are in my fine establishment. Did your father send you, think you could make a deal with us, like he did with that fool Park Taesung? Need more pretty little girls for his project?"

"I—" Alex begins, but it's as if he's frozen in shock. No words come out. I wonder how much he knew of his father's role in the Tower, the project.

"Well, I'm not like Park Taesung, who ran away to escape his problems; Neo Seoul's branch was always weak. In Busan, we do things differently."

The gangsters move, reaching beneath the table for their weapons.

"We have to go *now*!" I grab Alex's hand and tug him back down the hall, bypassing a startled Mr. Hong.

We slow down right before exiting into the main room of

the club. I throw a fog over the two guards, buying us a few seconds. Then a gunshot goes off, and the club erupts into chaos.

"Alex, I think I see the exit—" I turn to find him staring at the guards, who aren't moving but looking straight ahead as if transfixed by the strobe lights. Another shot comes from behind the bar. Alex breaks his trance, hurrying behind me into the rush of people. We bypass the elevator and head toward the emergency stairwell.

It's pandemoneum inside as people fight their way up the narrow stairs. Packed into the space, I can hardly breathe. My head throbs from trying to keep the crowd's panic and terror from becoming my own. On the landing, people scream and shout, banging against a locked door. The boss must have notified the guards in the lobby of our escape, hoping to trap us in the stairwell. Someone pushes me against the smooth, mirror-like walls, and I gasp, the wind knocked right out of me.

"Jangmi!" Alex grabs my arm.

Behind us, another shot rings out, and everyone ducks. I have a sudden view of the door above, and an idea strikes me. Leaping forward, I climb the stairs, pushing people aside. I hear Alex shout for me to slow down, cursing when the crowd swells and he loses sight of me.

I'm a few steps from the top of the landing. The door to the stairwell is made of steel, sealed by a deadbolt. Pushing against it with telekinetic energy would be just as effective as the people doing the same with their fists. Instead, I focus on the internal lock and *will* it to move. I'm met with resistance as the locking mechanism catches. I put more pressure on the lock, the force of my mind equal to the force of the deadbolt. The pain intensifies, growing almost unbearable until—

The bolt snaps back into place. Someone manages to get their hand through the small gap of the sliding door, and then the crowd surges forward.

As people rush by, I slowly fall backward, catching a glimpse of myself in the walls of the stairwell. My eyes burn green, like stars of jade.

I faint.

17

HAEUNDAE

I wake in a panic, grappling for awareness. I must have only been under for a few seconds because I'm still in the stairwell, slumped against the wall where I must have been pushed after fainting.

"Jangmi!"

Alex grabs my shoulder from behind. I have a split second to catch hold of his mind before he turns me toward him. "Are you all right?" His eyes search my face. The green must have already faded, because he doesn't react. "Can you walk?" He crouches on the stairwell, turning so that his back is to me. "Here, get on."

I blink in surprise.

Alex glances over his shoulder. "Hurry, Jangmi-ssi."

A shout below jolts me to action. I wrap my arms around

his neck and hook my knees on either side of his hips. He hoists me up, his hands wrapping securely around my thighs. Then he's climbing the stairs fast, grunting lightly from the effort. He follows the tide of people through the door and out into a side alley, where he gently places me on the ground. The cool sea breeze is like a balm against the heat of the stairwell. I take in a long, shuddering breath.

"The streets are congested," he says, peering from the shadows. Vehicles are backed up bumper to bumper as people flood the roads, trying to flag down passing cabs and fighting over who gets the coveted seats. I watch as one man opens the door of a cab, only to pull out another man, taking his place and slamming the door shut. "We'll have to walk."

Together we move down the alley, emerging on the opposite side. A few more blocks take us to the beach.

Haeundae Beach, immortalized in love songs and popular dramas, is beautiful at night. The waters glow neon blue, green, and red, reflecting the colors of the great luxury hotels that line the beachfront. As we walk, we leave footsteps in the soft, crystalline sand. It must be past midnight. Robots roam the beaches, picking it clean of trash and debris from the day.

We're mostly alone, though a few couples pass by, holding hands.

"I don't think Giwoo was there," I say after we've walked a good length of the beach.

Alex answers readily. "It appears not."

I don't doubt that Junhee really believed that Giwoo would be at the club. He couldn't have lied to me when I'd had ahold of his mind. And yet Giwoo hadn't been there. "I apologize for leading us down a wrong path."

"It was a good lead," Alex says quietly. "We did the right thing."

I nod, reassured. Then I wonder at this need of reassurance from him, as if he were truly my commander.

I shiver as a breeze sweeps across the East Sea. "You care about your soldiers. You could have reported Giwoo as missing on duty instead of looking for him yourself. But that would have gotten him into trouble. You could have waited until morning to see if he showed up back at the hotel, but you were worried."

Alex doesn't contradict my words. We've reached a low rock wall that starts at the edge of the beach and stretches far into the sea. A lighthouse is built at the very end, warning off ships in the night.

"Are you cold?" he asks. He removes his jacket and hands it to me. I slip it over my shoulders. "Two years ago, I made a choice that led to the death of a friend."

I remember. In order to place into a high-level internship, he'd taken a simulation test alongside Lee Jaewon and a few others. What made the test so much more difficult than the rest was that if you died in the simulation, you died in real life.

"I didn't have to take that test," he says quietly, speaking more to himself than to me. "Why did I do it? Did I think I was invincible? Did I think their lives were worth the risk?"

"Did you?" I ask.

"I don't know. I wouldn't die for someone on the street. I'm not that selfless. And I won't die now, even if I have nothing to live for."

A memory blooms in his mind, and it's one I recognize. I was *there*. I am there, sitting next to Alex at a table in a restaurant, alongside Tera and Jaewon. Seungri, the twin whose brother died in the test, holds a gun to my head. He wanted to exact revenge on Alex for his brother's death. He was threatening me because Alex might not have cared about his own life, but he cared—desperately—about mine.

Ama. My name.

Alex is calling me. I blink away the memory.

"Jangmi-ssi, are you all right?" Alex's hand is on my wrist, having caught me as I swayed.

"Do you truly believe you have nothing to live for?"

"I'm not like my soldiers, who have homes, who have families."

You do, I want to tell him. But that's not my secret to share.

"My father hardly counts," he continues. "And I haven't seen my mother in years."

"What about Gayoung and Giwoo? They believe in you with everything they have."

"Just them?" Alex's grip tightens. "What about you? Do you believe in in me, Wang Jangmi?"

Maybe it's the night or the look in his eyes, but I say what I feel, what I fear. "I'm starting to."

Far out at sea, a ship blares its horn, the sound muted with distance. Alex releases me, and I back up a step, sand slipping beneath my feet.

"You were right," Alex says after a beat of silence. "I *was* worried about Giwoo."

I take a deep breath, recovering my wits. "Where do you think he might have gone?"

Alex sighs. "I think I know."

■ ■ ■

Alex hails a cab, and we take it to another part of the city, where the buildings are smaller and built side by side.

"He once mentioned his grandparents own a seafood restaurant." Alex fills me in as we move down a well-lit road off the beaten path. Even at this late hour, grandmothers gather outside the local corner market, seated atop low platforms, gossiping as they pluck the tails off bean sprouts. Children run down the street, some playing VR games, others with portable handhelds, and a few even toss around a ball. I dodge a little girl chasing a tortoiseshell kitten.

"And you waited until now to mention this because . . . ?"

"Giwoo hasn't seen his grandparents in years, not since joining Red Moon."

We reach our destination—a small building with placards on the side spelling out seafood dishes in Hangeul. Water-stained fish tanks sit outside the shop filled with clams puffing bubbles, fish swimming in lazy circles, and other presumably edible sea creatures.

From inside the shop comes the clink of dishes and cutlery and the jovial laughter of individuals sharing a late-night meal.

For a moment, I have déjà vu, of standing outside a shop very much like this one in an alley in Neo Beijing. I guess the sound of laughter is the same in every city, when you're on the outside looking in.

Alex ducks beneath the plastic tarp, slides back the wooden door, and enters the shop. I only hesitate a few seconds before following him inside.

We walk into what appears to be a celebration, about twenty or so individuals crammed into the tiny space. Giwoo sits at a back table flanked on either side by one half of an elderly couple and across from a cherub-faced girl who looks to be around ten years old. Catching sight of us, Giwoo jumps to his feet, breaking out into a wide grin.

I would be angry at him for his disappearance if I wasn't so relieved to find him safe, and if he wasn't so obviously happy. He maneuvers around the tables to throw his arms around Alex, then me, his breath sweet with rice wine. Before Alex can decide whether to scold him, Giwoo's grandmother sweeps in, grabbing both of Alex's hands. His eyes widen a bit, but he doesn't pull away.

"You must be Giwoo's commander. Why didn't you tell me he was so handsome?" This she directs at her grandson.

"Didn't I?" Giwoo laughs.

I feel a tugging at the skirt of my dress. I look down to see the girl who'd been sitting with Giwoo earlier. There's a family resemblance in the mischievous tilt of their eyes. This must be his sister. "Sit with me?" she asks shyly. I glance over at Alex. From the way Giwoo's halmeoni is leading him to the same table, it doesn't look like we're leaving anytime soon.

Alex is seated in Giwoo's chair, much to Giwoo's mock-protests. Reconciled to his fate, he pulls up a plastic stool next to me. Already his sister is pointing out the many dishes set upon the table. My mouth waters at the sight. In small plates are a variety of side dishes—baechu kimchi and steamed shishito peppers, rolled omelets, spicy squid, and crumbled tofu. Stew packed with clams and mussels boils in hot stone pots.

I glance across the table at Alex. Giwoo and I watch as Giwoo's halmeoni scoops rice into a spoon, then with her chopsticks places a rolled omelet and slice of kimchi atop the rice. She brings the spoon to Alex's mouth, and he cups his hand beneath hers, eating obediently. Giwoo and I make eye contact, then look away in a poor attempt to conceal our laughter.

The celebration continues into the night, filled with talk and good food. After several drinks, Giwoo's stoic grandfather begins to tell stories of when Giwoo was a boy, the scrapes he used to get in, and how he once caught a fish that weighed more than himself from the wharf. Giwoo's sister, Jiwoo, whose name I manage to coax out after an exchange of shy smiles, hangs on every word of their grandfather's stories, her eyes darting to Giwoo as if soaking in his presence.

Yet even though Giwoo had been gone, it seems that none of them resent him his absence. He'd sent home money in an unmarked envelope on the same day every month, which they'd used for Jiwoo's upbringing. But even then, it wouldn't have mattered. They're just happy to have him home again.

At the end of the night, it's decided that Giwoo will stay to spend more time with his family while Alex and I return to the hotel.

Giwoo's grandmother grabs Alex as he turns to leave, shoving an envelope with banknotes into his hands. "For all you've done for our Giwoo," she says.

A few of the party guests pause to watch, amused and curious. Alex's father is one of the richest men in Neo Seoul. As a commander, Alex's salary for a week is likely twice what they'd make in a year, or more. Not counting the advertisements and sponsorships.

Bowing deeply, Alex accepts the money with both hands, as if it were a precious gift. And I realize, to Alex—who's perhaps never felt like he's earned money, or gratitude—it is. "Thank you, Halmeoni," he says quietly.

The first rays of sunlight can be seen on the horizon as we leave Giwoo's grandparents' home. There aren't any cabs at this hour, so we decide to walk to the hotel, neither of us speaking from sheer exhaustion.

What a strange night, a strange day. It began with the transport ship from the NIC base, then the limo ride, then Giwoo's disappearance and the gangster's den, then finding him safe among his family, and now this, walking with Alex on a deserted street. I can almost believe for a moment that I'm not a spy.

"Alex," I say, and he turns to me. I take his hand and pull him into an alley; I take his mind and pull out his thoughts. I make him tell what information was given at the meeting. I can't make him show me exact images, as he doesn't have an eidetic memory, but I can make him tell me his understanding of what happened, which is enough. I repeat the important information back to him to confirm the details, then release him, wiping his memories of the last couple of minutes.

Alex blinks slowly. "I must have fallen asleep on my feet," he says, making excuses to ease the burden of his befuddled mind. He gives me a sheepish smile, and I feel a deep ache in my chest.

In a few hours, we're on a transport ship returning back to base. And each time Alex glances over at me, I feel my heart break just a little more.

18

PRESS CONFERENCE

Back at base, the final preparations for the June Solstice Battle have begun. In the mornings, Alex meets with his senior officers to discuss strategy—flight formations and offensive and defensive maneuvers, which are later practiced in punishing drills late into the afternoon. At night, I collect my observations from the day as well as siphon further information from Giwoo and store it as a recording in a chip where I've also compiled the data I took from Alex in Busan. However, with the days counting down to the battle, and no way to safely get the information to Helen, I start to worry.

Three nights before the battle, I'm lingering outside the cafeteria, hoping for Shun to appear, though he hasn't since before Busan. I kick the brick wall of the cafeteria building. Should I risk an electronic transfer? Shun had said satellite receivers are being monitored. If the file were intercepted, that would be worse than if it was never sent at all.

The pounding of footsteps alerts me to someone fast approaching. I swing around to see Giwoo sprint past the cafeteria. He halts when he catches sight of me. "Where have you been?" he shouts. "I've been looking all over for you!"

"Why?" I ask quickly, jogging to meet him. "What's happened?" With how on edge I've been with the upcoming battle and PHNX's silence, any surprise is likely to give me a heart attack.

"We're heading into the city," Giwoo says. "Last-minute press conference."

I nod, calmly, though my heart pounds in relief. If I'm off base, there's a chance I can get the file to Helen and the others. I hurriedly follow Giwoo out to the aircraft docking port and board a helicopter, its rotor blades already spinning for takeoff.

Gayoung salutes us as we enter, and Fei Hong gives a cool nod of acknowledgement.

"Alex and Yuuki are already at the hotel," Gayoung shouts above the rotor, "alongside the other commanders. The rest of the senior officers will be joining them for a larger session, which will be open to the public."

I blanch, thinking back to that moment in Busan, with all the flashing cameras.

"The recruits won't be part of the conference." Giwoo buckles himself into the seat beside me. "Your assignment is to observe and debrief with your commanding officer afterward. Simple," he says, and I know he's trying to ease my mind.

I nod. Though as my hand reaches instinctively for my inner pocket where I've stored the chip with the file, I wonder how simple it will be.

■ ■ ■

The NIC has changed drastically since the last time I was here with Helen, Shun, and Shiori. "Battle spirit" has taken over the city. Screen billboards stream constant advertisements promoting the products and brands used by ace pilots like Lee Byul and Fuji Hiyori as well as the clubs hosting the best and most opulent viewing parties. Every band has a theme song for the battle, the most popular playing in a constant loop through all the major shopping districts. Instead of holopets, the newest fad seems to be holomachines, pins that project holographs of God Machines appearing to follow their individual wearer around like colossal specters.

In the limo over to the venue for the conference, Giwoo and Gayoung play a game where they spot how many individuals are sporting their GMs as holos.

"Ha, you owe me a drink later," Gayoung says, counting off the fiftieth sighting of Yeongdeung. Of course, none are as numerous as the sightings of the distinctive white and gold of Alex's GM, Light Bearer, which seem to populate the city like a thousand angels fallen to earth.

The press conference is being held in the Grand Ballroom of the NIC's Asia Pacific Hotel. We pull up to a back door and manage to slip into a service corridor that leads to a side entrance into the ballroom, already packed with reporters and camera crews. Alex sits at a long table behind a phalanx of mics with a moderator and eight other men and women—together, the nine commanders of the Alliance. Most of the commanders are in their thirties and forties. Alex, at twenty, is by far the youngest. And arguably, the most attractive, which is likely why most of the questions are directed at him.

"This question is for Commander Kim," a reporter says, standing up from the crowd.

"Why am I not surprised?" the moderator quips.

"Is it true that your squadron will lead the attack on Friday's battle?"

Alex brings a bottle of water to his lips. His eyes scan the room as he swallows. I haven't spoken to him since that night in Busan, our paths having no reason to cross. Although a part of me wondered if he'd seek me out, perhaps stumble upon me by coincidence on the path I took every night as I ran around the base. In Busan, we'd shared *something*—

"Commander Saito and Commander Tsai will lead the attack," Alex says into the microphone, his voice calm and collected, "alongside me."

Speaking softly into a recording device, the reporter sits down. I'm reminded of my own file, burning a hole in my pocket. The moment the helicopter landed, I'd activated the location tracker, but I press it again now for good measure and glance around for an escape from the room.

"One last question," the moderator says, "before we switch to the next session. Yes, you in the front."

A reporter stands up from where she'd been seated directly in front of Alex. "This question is for Commander Kim."

The moderator chuckles good-naturedly. "It's a veritable fan club in here! Should I ask the other commanders to leave?"

Fei Hong leans over to speak to Giwoo, providing me the perfect moment to slip away.

"Is the rumor of what happened two years ago true?" the woman asks, her voice clear and sharp like glass.

"You'll have to be more specific than that," Alex says, his expression cold but otherwise calm.

"That you were expelled from your military academy in Apgujeong," she says. "That you never graduated."

"All true."

"What were the circumstances for your expulsion?" she prods.

"I think that's it for our hour," the moderator intervenes. He claps his hands. "Now we'll take a fifteen-minute break and reconvene for the next session in the East Ballroom."

"Was it because your father, Kim Tae Woo, the senior member on the advisory board of your school, caught you with a girl undergoing a lucrative experimental project at the Tower, with whom you were forbidden to associate . . . on a personal level?" No one could miss the significance of the reporter's pause.

"Well, isn't that a mouthful?" The moderator chuckles nervously.

Commander Saito bangs his fist on the table, "Is this a

circus you're running?" He places a hand on Alex's shoulder. "You don't have to answer that, son."

"Yes."

The room is silent as everyone stares.

"Yes," the reporter presses, "you were expelled because of your relationship—"

"I was expelled because of the circumstances that you just spelled out." Standing, Alex bows down the table. "I'd like to apologize to the other commanders for the inconvenience that is my personal life. If you'll excuse me—"

"What happened to her?" someone else shouts out from the crowd. "The girl."

For the first time, an expression flits across Alex's face, gone in a moment—but a moment captured on every TV screen in the Neo Sphere. "She died."

There's a collective gasp—of surprise, of titillation, of empathy.

"Did you love her?" It's the same woman. How she knows about the Tower, about Alex, about *me*, is anyone's guess.

Alex turns to look at her, unflinching, his black eyes seething with an unnamable emotion. "Desperately."

As the reporters rush up to the table, security guards scrambling to keep them back, I have only one thought: *he's lying.*

"This isn't good," Giwoo says. "He hates any mention of his past."

"But it's not true," I say flatly. "He wasn't in love."

Giwoo frowns. "How do you know?"

Again, the memory of that day in the courtyard comes back to haunt me, when I looked into Alex's mind and saw the truth there—that though I loved him with all my heart, he never loved me in return.

"He might say whatever he wants, but the mind doesn't lie."

"The mind?" Giwoo asks softly.

I realize my mistake. "If he truly loved her," I amend, "he never would have left her."

"Perhaps . . ." Giwoo says, though he sounds uncertain.

"Wow, talk about a rout." Gayoung appears, her makeup fresh and dazzling. "Whoever coordinated that publicity stunt deserves a bonus. The public loves a tragic hero." She grabs Giwoo's arm. "We're up next. If anyone can steal Alex's spotlight, it'll be me."

"Please do," Giwoo says, with one last look at me. "At this point, I think he'd be grateful."

■ ■ ■

The session open to the public goes more smoothly than the one that came before. Alongside the nine commanders, there are eighteen senior officers, including many ace pilots, who spend most of the conference plugging their sponsors. Giwoo and Gayoung deflect most questions aimed at Alex.

Afterward, we head back to the limo, and I make one last desperate sweep of the room, searching for Helen.

"Alex." A man approaches. He's middle-aged, with broad shoulders and streaks of gray in his otherwise dark-black hair.

Alex bows. "Father."

The former Director of the Neo State of Korea. Kim Tae Woo.

Immediately, I reach into his mind. When he glances in my direction, I blur his perception of me.

His gaze slides to Giwoo, then back to Alex. "I've only been here a few hours, and yet all I hear is talk of you." The pride in his voice is evident.

Alex says dully, "I didn't know you were traveling to the Neo International City, Father."

"My new appointment isn't one I can speak of," Kim Tae Woo says. "But there's no need to stand on ceremony. You've done well for yourself, son."

Alex's expression gives nothing of his feelings away, though his thoughts have a chilly edge to them, like the calm before a storm. "Giwoo, call the driver. I'm going to take my father back to his hotel."

After a brief shuffling, I find myself in a car with Alex, his father, Giwoo, and Gayoung, with Yuuki and Fei Hong in a separate car.

During the ride, Alex and his father exchange pleasantries. Giwoo is apparently beneath the Director's notice, for he speaks to Giwoo not once. At one point, the Director asks me my name. When I give it, he acknowledges that he's heard of Wang Yunpeng, though he's never met my "father."

When we pull up to a sleek black-and-white hotel, it's almost full night. As Alex attempts to see his father off with a bow, the Director places a hand on Alex's shoulder. "No need for such formality." He waits until Alex lifts his head, their eyes meeting as equals. "I am proud of you, son."

The car is quiet after the departure of the Director.

Giwoo clears his throat. "We should head back to base."

"I agree," Gayoung seconds. "It's been a long day, and the June Solstice battle is in three days."

"No," Alex says, shocking all of us. Danger glitters in his dark eyes. "I have a better idea."

19

KARAOKE

I am having one of the worst nights of my entire life. Somehow I'm sandwiched between Giwoo and a wall, watching as Alex consumes enough alcohol to fuel a tank. We're in a private upstairs room of a club, reserved for VIPs. Upon arriving on the packed main floor, we'd been swarmed by people recognizing Alex and Gayoung. The paparazzi go berserk when Alex invites two beautiful women, models by the looks of them, to join us upstairs. Now they sit on either side of him, taking turns to hook their arms with his for love shots.

Upon arrival, Gayoung makes a quick call and is soon joined by a striking young woman in a business suit to whom she gives a most enthusiastic welcome, eliciting hoots and hollers from Alex's companions.

I refrain from drinking. I need to keep my wits about me.

I still have the file, and Helen and the others should know my location, though I worry at their lack of response. I might be deep undercover, but so are they.

The bottle service continues. The large square table that takes up the whole of the room fills with more liquor bottles, glasses, and food. For entertainment, a sleek karaoke machine is set up against the far wall that doubles as a screen flashing a constant display of vibrant and sensuous images. Gayoung's and Alex's companions select songs to serenade us—out of tune but enthusiastic. The models invite a few of their friends into the room, crowding the space as they salute Alex, buying him even more drinks and taking turns in front of the screen to sing him a song. I'm pushed farther and farther into the corner.

"He's going to regret this in the morning," Giwoo says, my only ally in this onslaught of noise and debauchery.

"Why don't you stop him?" I shout to be heard over the music.

Giwoo sighs, grabbing his glass off the table and swilling the last of it. "He's my commanding officer. It's not my place."

"As his friend—"

"As his friend," he cuts me off, "I'm much more likely to encourage him than not. If you haven't noticed, he keeps all his emotions bottled up. Maybe it's better he get this out of his system now, before the battle."

"What are you two talking about?" Alex stands up from his seat. There's a lull between songs, though the beat from the club below can be felt through the floor. Alex's slightly slurred voice carries, and everyone in the room turns to stare. "You've been whispering to each other all night. Care to tell us what could be so interesting?"

Though his words include the two of us, his eyes flicker to me. There's an edge to his voice that keeps anyone else from speaking or moving.

When I remain silent, Giwoo says with a shrug, "We were talking about you." I stare at him, shocked he'd tell the truth. "June Solstice is only a few nights away. With this much drinking"—Giwoo's eyes slide to the girls—"and activity, you're going to be pretty much nonfunctional tomorrow. A whole day wasted. I think we should head back."

Giwoo's suggestion is met with cries of protest from his companions. Alex's arms give out, and he slumps back onto his seat, promptly swarmed. He doesn't push either of the girls away. One is practically in his lap; the other wraps her lithe arms around his shoulders.

Gayoung clicks her tongue. "Giwoo-yah, don't be such a killjoy. Alex deserves to let off some steam after living like a monk for two years." She pours a shot glass and raises it to the girls. "The Alliance thanks you for your service."

As one girl giggles and raises a glass of her own, the other looks at Alex with a sad smile. "Two years? Is it because of the girl you spoke of at the press conference?"

I don't wait to hear his answer. "I have to use the restroom," I tell Giwoo, rising to my feet. I make my way around the table.

"Jangmi-ssi," Alex says as I almost reach the door, "before you go, why don't you sing us a song?"

I turn slowly. Alex is leaning back from the table, his eyes intent and calculating. When I don't respond, he shifts his gaze. "Gayoung-ah," he says, "put on a song for Jangmi."

"No," I say, intercepting her as she reaches for the machine to control the song selection. "I'll choose."

Now that I've agreed to sing, most everyone in the room resumes what they were doing before Alex's interruption—pouring drinks, gorging on the many bright snack foods. I'm not sure what song to pick. One of the girls sweeps a hand through Alex's thick hair, turning his face toward her. His lips graze the edge of her neck.

Not a love song.

I make my selection. The lights automatically dim to accommodate the music. A few of the girls' friends glance in my direction, then roll their eyes, annoyed that I've chosen a ballad. The instrumentals begin, a simple, rhythmic guitar. I bring the microphone to my lips. Gayoung knocks over a pitcher, and the room roars with laughter. Their inattention doesn't bother me. Sometimes at the bar lounge, people would grow rowdy and disruptive. At first, their disregard felt cruel and dismissive, but Jimmy, the piano man, told me not to take it personally. Everyone has a world inside them.

I sing to share with them a little bit of my own. I might not be loud or commanding or witty or glittering, but when I sing, I sing with my whole heart.

In my mind, I shed the karaoke room, the loud and laughing people, the air that smells of alcohol and smoke. I imagine I'm in the lounge, looking out into the room. All the faces are in shadow except one. Alex sits at a table directly in front of the stage, his eyes on me.

I sing a song to let him go. The lyrics begin melancholic, and my naturally quiet voice subdued, but the microphone accentuates the softness of my voice until it cuts through the revelry. Giwoo sits up in his chair. Gayoung places her glass on the table. The song moves to the chorus, and I sing of loneliness, the feeling of moving through the world without direction, unseen and unheard.

In the second verse, the tone of the song subtly shifts direction. Though the melody remains the same, there's a change in the spirit of the lyrics. In the final refrain, I sing of moving on, of letting go of the past, of finding happiness and peace within myself. I don't need anyone else to make me feel whole. In this moment—in this song—the world is inside me.

When I finish the song, there's a brief moment of stunned silence. Then everyone—the girls and their friends, Giwoo, Gayoung and the businesswoman—claps enthusiastically. Only Alex refrains, an unreadable expression on his face.

With a short bow, I place the microphone on the table and leave the room.

■ ■ ■

Outside is a long corridor dimly lit by strobe lights, doors on either side leading to private rooms. Moving to an alcove outside the restrooms, I press down on the location tracker and wait. I lean my head back against the cushioned walls and close my eyes. There are so many things I should be worrying about— getting the file to Helen and the others, the battle in three days, the Director's presence in the NIC, Tsuko's whereabouts, the super soldiers, the war. And yet here in the dark, all I can think about is Alex, the triumphant way he had looked at the mayor's gala, the guilt-ridden way he had looked on the beach in Busan, and the haunted way he had looked tonight at the press conference.

Footsteps approach. I move away from the wall.

Alex steps into the alcove.

From this close, I can see the strain these past weeks have brought on him. His beautiful, slender eyes are rimmed with red; his usually immaculate hair falls in sweeps across his fore-head, a few errant strands clinging to his eyelashes.

"Commander," I say, glad for the steadiness in my voice, "is there something I can help you with?"

"That song. Why did you choose it?" His tone is harsh, accusatory.

Instantly I'm on guard. "No special reason."

"Don't lie to me."

The door to the restroom opens and a girl and boy exit. They glance over at us, their minds filled with thoughts that make me look away from Alex.

When they leave, Alex continues, his voice dropping even lower. "Did you choose it because of what I said at the press conference? Were you mocking me?"

"How arrogant of you to think the song was about you."

"Who was it about, then?"

I meet his gaze. "Me."

Alex scoffs, pushing his hand through his dark hair. "A past you need to move on from, to forget? You? The daughter of Wang Yunpeng, one of the richest men in the city?"

"Not forget," I say softly. "Forgive." *Though you make it so hard.*

"I won't be looked down upon by my subordinate officers!"

"No one is looking down on you. And if they were, perhaps it might be a humbling experience."

Alex steps forward, close enough that I can feel the heat from his breath, but I don't step back. "You don't think I've been humbled enough? I started with nothing. I spent *two years* building up to what I have now."

"I think you've finally gotten what you've always wanted, damn the consequences!"

Both of us are breathing heavily, shouting to be heard over the loud thump of the club music below.

"Consequences? As if you have any idea of what I've lost—"

"Yes, I remember." I grit my teeth. "The girl."

Alex's eyes flash. "You doubt my love?"

"It's not so difficult. Given tonight."

For a moment he looks embarrassed, his cheeks flushed, but then he shakes his head. "Am I to live chaste for the rest of my life? A life that might not extend past the battle in three days?"

"Is that what this is?" I laugh harshly. "One last hurrah? One last kiss goodbye?"

His eyes immediately flit to my lips. A shiver races down

233

my back. "That's all this is. It's enough for other soldiers; why isn't it enough for me? Because I loved a girl once, in another life? Well, she's gone now. You can't kiss a ghost."

He reaches out, his strong arm circling my waist, his hands at the curve of my back, pressing me gently, inexorably closer. My arms curve around his neck, as if by memory. Because I remember this. I remember him. My body trills with anticipation.

"You can't hold them," he whispers, his mouth against my neck, trailing searing kisses from my throat to my jaw. "You can't feel their warmth, their breath. All you can do is find someone to distract you from the pain until there is no past, no future, just a present that swallows you whole."

And then his mouth is on mine, and I catch a glimmer of what it must feel like for him, because in this moment all I want is to give in to this desire, to forget the mission, the battle, the project, the war; to forget the hurt he's caused me and the hurt I'll cause him in the end.

He smells like smoke and the night air. He tastes like liquor, tobacco, and mint. I return each of his kisses with as much fervor, lust, and need, my hands sliding through his thick hair, his hands pulling up my uniform shirt to graze the bare skin of my stomach.

I gasp at the contact. And strange, but my eyes are wet. All day I haven't cried, and yet I can't stop the tears that slide down my heated cheeks. Because I remember this. I remember him— the way he used to kiss me with care and wonder, as if each moment with me was not the last, but one of many in the long chain of our future. He had hope in us, in me. He had dreams of tomorrow.

He kisses me as if it's the last kiss he'll ever have, and I can't bear it.

I stumble back, and he lets me go, though he watches me with a pained expression, his eyes red, his lips raw.

"Go," he says.

He doesn't have to say it twice.

Down on the club level, the party is in full swing. I press between people, trying to reach the exit. Bodies bump into me, the noise of the music as loud as the thoughts of the people. I press my hands to my ears, but that doesn't help. The noise is in my mind.

"Jangmi!" A hand grabs my wrist. I almost sob in relief. *Helen.*

She pulls me to the edge of the crowd. "We couldn't approach you again on base," she says. "The Alliance has appointed a new security division. But that's just a fancy way of hiding what it really is: a secret police force. Kim Tae Woo is leading it. You have to be careful. He's searching for spies."

I nod, taking a shaky breath. "I'll be careful." I reach into my pocket. "I have something for you. It's a file of the battle plans and the weapons."

"My God, thank you. You've saved us." She slips the file into the inner pocket of her jacket. She then takes my hands. "Jangmi, you must remember. In the battle, our forces won't know that you're on our side. They'll attack you, same as the rest. When the time comes, don't hesitate to defend yourself."

"Will you fight in the battle?"

"No," she says, "I'll be watching it live from the mayor's house. He's hosting a viewing party."

"And Shun and Shiori?"

She shakes her head. "Because of the treaty, every soldier is registered. We couldn't risk our covers."

I sigh in relief. I don't think I could bear to know they were on the battlefield, let alone across from me, an enemy I might have to kill.

She squeezes my hands tight. "Know that I trust you, that you shouldn't have to carry the decisions you make on that battlefield alone. Do what you must, but come back to us whole."

20

SOLSTICE BATTLE, PART 1

Three days later, the base receives the green light to mobilize for war. Camera crews are sent out ahead to set up along the field of battle. Thousands of computer-operated mobile droids will populate the airspace in order to relay the most varied optimal live streaming to viewers. According to the ratings report, about 82 percent of Neo citizens are tuning into the prebattle coverage, with an estimated jump to 99.3 percent by the official start. From beginning to end, the whole of the battle will be recorded and broadcast through live feeds in every single village, town, and city of the Neo Sphere.

I meet Giwoo in the GM hangar, where Syd the machinist is putting the last touches on my GM, a standard model outfitted for midrange combat and quick maneuvering. It was recently painted silver and blue to match Giwoo's Brotherhood.

A silver flag flies from the GM's shoulder to indicate my status as a junior officer, a recent promotion due to the accelerated officer program.

Giwoo clasps my shoulder. "Don't die."

"You either." I step onto the lifting platform and it ascends—past the great legs of the machine, the pelvis and stomach—to the chest, already open for boarding. I climb through to the deep cavity where the piloting seat is situated, surrounded by dashboard monitors. Settling into the seat, I flip a switch to close the hatch. The screens automatically light up.

I have five screens. The largest is front and center, offering a wide view of everything directly in front of me. The left and right top screens are for my blind spots. The bottom right screen allows me to talk face-to-face with anyone in my unit or vicinity. Right now it shows Giwoo as he settles into Brotherhood, making adjustments to his cameras. The bottom left screen serves a variety of purposes, but for now I switch it to the live broadcast of the battle.

"The countdown has begun!" a cheerful announcer shouts from within the NIC's City Hall, now packed with people sitting on picnic blankets and foldout chairs. A huge monitor situated against the back wall displays the announcer's jubilant face. Behind her, several children, excited to be on television, wave the black-and-white flags of the Neo Sphere. "In only one hour, our great forces of the Alliance will meet the combined rebel forces over the East Pacific in the first sea battle of the war!" The crowd cheers alongside the raucous beating of noisemakers.

"Now to my associate, Grey Reed, who will be covering the battle from the Alliance's main battleship, the Neo Sphere Alliance aircraft carrier, Genesis 8! Grey, are you there?"

The screen switches to a handsome man of mixed Asian and European descent. He stands beside a tiny dark-skinned woman wearing a gigantic poncho and huge goggles that cover her head. "I'm here, Ling," Grey shouts over the wind. "I'm joined this morning by the esteemed Admiral Chen, who will be commanding the Alliance forces during today's sea battle. Admiral"—Grey turns to the goggle-eyed woman—"do you have any thoughts on what today might bring?"

"Victory."

With that, the admiral races through a door with Grey struggling to keep up. I watch as Grey follows her across the rain-drenched deck of a ship, his suit soaked within minutes while the water slips easily off the admiral's poncho. As she goes, she shouts orders to different soldiers, though her exact words are caught only by the wind. When she finally returns to the bridge, out of the rain, the beleaguered Grey manages to get another question in. "Will you be leading the charge yourself or—?"

"Didn't you watch the press conference? What do you think my commanders are for?" With one strong hand, she swipes the camera out of the air, ending the transmission.

"I just received the order," Giwoo says. "We're moving out."

"Affirmative," I respond.

I move my left hand to the control stick and press forward. My GM reacts to the direction, taking a step. The great hangar doors open, blasting wind and water inside. I quickly follow Brotherhood out to the broad stretch of concrete. Soon the three squadrons of our battalion have gathered on the field.

In total, our battalion consists of nine hundred units, three hundred in each of the wing squadrons. Giwoo and I take our places in front of Blue Wing Squadron, comprised solely of long-range shooters. Down the line, I see the bright red of Gayoung's Yeongdeung standing opposite Red Wing Squadron. Beside her, Fei Hong's GM is painted crimson to match. Lastly, Yuuki is situated in front of Light Wing Squadron, though her GM isn't painted white and gold like Alex's Light Bearer. I wonder if that was on purpose. She won't stand out as a target.

Light Bearer is positioned at the helm of the battalion. On the bottom right screen, Alex's face appears, replacing Giwoo's. I haven't seen him since that night in the NIC. Dark circles mar the pale skin beneath his eyes. Still, he wears the expression of a commander, confident and determined.

"I'm not one for speeches," Alex begins. "All I ask of you today is observance of your orders, and survival by whatever means necessary. Our number of units might be matched by the rebels, but our weapons are superior, as are our soldiers. Lieutenant Na Gayoung"—Alex's gaze moves downward. His bottom right and left screens must be showing Gayoung and Giwoo, respectively—"Red Wing Squadron will follow Light Wing Squadron's formation. We'll be part of the initial assault."

"Affirmative, Commander." Gayoung's response echoes through Alex's feed.

He addresses Giwoo next. "Lieutenant Go Giwoo, due to

the storm, visibility will be poor. Your snipers must shoot only if the enemy is confirmed as the target."

"Roger that."

"We're moving out." Alex ends the transmission, and Giwoo reappears on my screen. I flip a switch on the control stick, transitioning the GM to air mobility, and press down on a pedal to ignite the thrusters. The GM ascends slowly into the sky.

According to a countdown clock that appears on the left side of my central screen, we'll arrive at the battlefield in twenty-eight minutes. I place the GM on autopilot, sit back, and unmute the news.

A voiceover is narrating details about the battlefield to viewers. "Not all the terrain for the battlefield is sea and air, however. There are also small islands out in the far Pacific. Our battle tacticians believe that some enemy units might be hiding in the forests and caves of these islands."

The screen flashes with a red news bulletin. "The enemy has been sighted on the battlefield!" A hazy video shows a blue-black skyline, though storm clouds make it impossible to catch any details. Lights appear in the distance.

Thirteen minutes until arrival.

Already the battalions from the eight other bases across the Neo Sphere have made it to the arrival point, including those from the Neo States of Japan, Taiwan, and Korea. The biggest battalion is from North China. Our battalion from the NIC is the smallest.

As our GMs come into view of the battlefield, my heart picks up speed. On the turbulent sea, I count a dozen aircraft carriers, each carrying hundreds of GMs. Even more have already taken to the sky, hovering in droves of colors representing the many Neo States of the Alliance. Blinking mobile cameras can be seen congregating around the more famous ace pilots—Fuji Hiyori in her bright neon GM and Lee Byul in their dark-blue-and-gold one, meant to mimic the night sky.

We arrive exactly as scheduled. Alex flies off in Light Bearer to confer with the other commanders. After a few minutes, he returns, and our units break off into two groups, Alex's and Gayoung's units moving to join the frontal assault, Giwoo's unit taking our place among the support line at the back.

And now we wait.

It's nerve-wracking. I switch the news channel to one that shows the aerial view of the battlefield, complete with heat signatures, though they're unreliable in this weather.

Giwoo taps a melody on his dashboard. "Stand by," he says to our units, which have positioned themselves on the warships and in the sky, the barrels of their giant sniper rifles pointed north.

Through my front screen, I watch as the rebel forces appear in the distance, hundreds, thousands of blinking lights that seem to swallow up the horizon.

A flash of lighting breaks over the sea, followed by a boom of thunder.

Admiral Chen releases a flare into the sky, as bright as a shooting star.

The battle has begun.

21

SOLSTICE BATTLE, PART 2

In a thunderous roar, the frontal assault units press forward, three thousand, five hundred units flying in a V formation with Alex's Light Bearer at the vanguard, a golden beacon heralding the battle. Below, massive waves rock the great assault carriers like they're little toy boats. The snipers positioned on deck keep their footing, shooting ceaselessly into the void of storm clouds. Their beams rip through the darkness in bright arrows of blue, red, and silver light. I have no way of knowing whether they reach their intended target; the storm swallows up the light.

I'm tempted to unmute the news. Ironically, the watchers at home have a better view of the battle than I do at the moment, as the video cuts from view to view, offering the best angles from the many mobile cameras darting around the field. I watch for Light Bearer amid the chaos, wincing at every explosion, but catch no hints of white and gold. My trembling hands tighten around my control stick. On the screen, Alliance soldiers and rebel fighters tear one another apart. There is no blood, just sparks and ripping metal, yet in this moment, soldiers are dying, and others are killing, and all of us are watching.

"Incoming missile!"

I barely manage to dodge out of the way as the missile plummets, smashing through a turret of one of the carriers.

"They've broken past the assault line!" Giwoo shouts. "All units surround the carriers." He sends me a direct transmission. "This isn't good. Our support units aren't equipped for close combat." Another missile hits the same carrier. On the deck, machinists scramble for cover as the great ship begins to sink. Giwoo swings the barrel of his sniper wildly, aiming toward the sky. "Where are they?"

Lightning splits the firmament, branching across the darkness, and I see them. Hidden behind the cloud cover are the massive shadows of great machines. The rebels are flying *over* the battle, using the storm as camouflage. It's a smart plan, especially given the offensive-heavy battle plans I'd shared with Helen. I should be relieved that my spy work has given the rebels a much-needed advantage, but the cost weighs heavy on my soul.

Another missile plummets through the air, this time finding a different target. Shocked, I watch as a GM in our battalion explodes, instantly killing the pilot inside. That was someone I trained with, someone I *knew*.

"Wang Jangmi!" Giwoo shouts. "What the hell are you doing? Take the squadron and get above the clouds!"

I jolt back to the present, joining the squadron as we make our way into the storm. It's like entering another world, a world of massive gray and black thunderheads, rolling in slow, rhythmic motion, the rain present but less violent. In the darkness, it's difficult to see your allied neighbor, let alone an enemy waiting in ambush.

To my left, there's a scattering of gunshots, staccato and muted by the wind. I veer to the right as the cloud beside me explodes and a rebel GM drops broken to the sea. All around me are blasts of noise and bright explosions as Blue Wing Squad engages with the rebel forces. I should be fighting alongside them, but fear pins me in place.

Helen's words repeat in my head. *They'll attack you, same as the rest. When the time comes, don't hesitate to defend yourself.* My monitor beeps a loud warning signal. A rebel GM fast approaches, northeast, from above. I barely have enough time to lift my shield, blocking the barrage of bullets aimed at my GM's core, aimed at *me*. I brace for impact. My GM is rocked violently to the side; my head bangs against the leftmost monitor.

"Jangmi!" Giwoo shouts.

I don't have time to respond. I see a flash of silver, lit by lightning. A dagger. The rebel GM rams it into my side. My damage count drops to 70 percent. All the screens on my dashboard flash red in warning.

I raise my rifle and release two blasts into the rebel GM's legs. It doesn't seem to hinder the pilot. They reach for another dagger. I aim my rifle at their arm—and miss. The dagger jams into my other side. 48 percent.

"What are you doing?" Giwoo screams, panic making his voice crack. "Aim for the core!"

I know what he expects me to do. A GM is only defeated when either the damage taken is too great that it can no longer function, or the pilot is killed. It's why the rebel pilot has been repeatedly jamming daggers into my side, aiming for where I sit inside, at the core of the GM.

Yet, though I have a clear shot at their chest, I hesitate. *Do what you must, but come back to us whole.* Helen's words. I'll do the former, but I'm not sure if I can hold on to the latter.

All I ask of you is survival.

Alex.

The rebel pilot releases their dagger and reaches for their gun. I reach for mine at the same time.

A sharp, buzzing sound cuts the air. A powerful beam pierces through the chest of the rebel GM. It shudders, sparking, then drops from the sky.

The shot came from below. Giwoo. He must have sniped the GM from the deck of the carrier. I glance at my bottom right screen to find him glaring at me. "We'll talk about this back at base. Retreat. Now."

He shot the soldier to save me. I nod, feeling worn and shell-shocked. I might not have pulled the trigger, but I still have blood on my hands.

I plunge below the cloud line. Most of my squad returns with me, having eliminated the rebel threat to our defense line.

On the left screen, I see the jubilant face of the news anchor from City Hall. I unmute the feed. "It's only thirty minutes in, and our victory is all but secured! Glory to the Neo Alliance!" Behind her, the crowds camped out in the large space are on their feet, clapping and cheering.

Was it a complete rout? If only there were a way I could contact Helen and the others. How great are our losses? What has this battle cost the rebellion?

"Wait." Giwoo leans forward, squinting at something on his screen. "What's that?"

I raise the volume on the news. The video feed has switched to the main battlefield. The Neo Alliance forces now outnumber the rebels by thousands. They're closing in on the last remainder, a scant hundred left in pockets, fighting for their lives. I see Light Bearer among the multitude, somehow unscathed.

Relief and dread sweep through me as Alex bears down on a rebel soldier. They're already defeated, their GM heavily damaged. *Let them live!* I want to scream. *Have mercy, please.*

This isn't war. This is a massacre.

"There!" Giwoo shouts.

On the screen, a figure has appeared. A rogue GM, painted entirely black. It floats like a wraith above the battlefield, unmoving even against the rain and wind.

A voice, loud and clear, issues through my speakers: "Cease all fighting. Disarm your weapons immediately. This is a warning. If you do not comply, you will be destroyed."

On the news, gray Reed badgers a frowning Admiral Chen. She stares hard at her own screen showing the lone figure. "It's not one of ours," she says finally.

"Then it must be one of the enemy's," Reed shouts. "Shoot it down!"

Admiral Chen nods absently, but her jaw is set. "I have a bad feeling about this."

"I repeat," the voice announces again, slightly electronic in sound, as if to mask the identity of the speaker. "Cease all fighting. Disarm your weapons immediately. If you do not comply, you will be destroyed."

"He's missing a line," Giwoo says.

The warning. He's missing the line about the warning.

Admiral Chen hesitates a second too long.

At first the wraithlike GM seems to fall, as if pushed by the wind. As it draws level with the closest line of soldiers, it surges forward, lightning quick. In either hand it holds two silver blades. GMs explode and drop from the sky, their chests gaping open.

The battlefield erupts into chaos. Every GM in the vicinity attempts to shoot the rogue GM down, but it's too quick, dodging blows, dodging *bullets*, slicing through GMs as if it were a reaper and they wheat in a field. Ten fall beneath its double blades, then fifty, then hundreds.

On the screen, the newscasters are frantic, not sure what to make of this third player on the field of battle. It moves with inhuman speed, its reaction times too fast, its ability to track possible threats and suss out weaknesses too uncanny.

I have a sudden thought. The pilot must be Enhanced.

Yet if they're killing Alliance soldiers, then they can't be the other Tera I'd run into on the train. And I don't recognize the black GM as the one *my* Tera fled with after the Battle of Neo Seoul. I don't recognize this GM at all.

The rebels, reinvigorated by the newcomer, begin to fight back, believing they have a chance. One rebel darts near the wraithlike GM, as if to provide backup. But the rogue GM raises its weapon, piercing the rebel through the chest.

"What the hell?" Giwoo frowns. "Was that a mistake?"

I watch as the rogue GM destroys another rebel soldier, then another.

If it's not Tera, then it can only be one other person.

"I can't stand by and let this futile war go on."

Tsuko.

All the pieces fall into place. When he was a general in the Alliance, he piloted an all-black GM called the Shi, after the Chinese symbol for death. He must have had it rebuilt, though its appearance is almost unrecognizable without the Alliance flag plastered across its upper shoulder or the stars on its chest signifying Tsuko's rank as General of the Army. I'm surprised no one recognizes it, or its pilot's superior fighting skills.

Then again, Tsuko is supposed to be dead.

A streak of red flies through the sky. Na Gayoung inside Yeongdeung. She manages to clip Tsuko in the shoulder with one of her silver blades. She's fast. The fastest pilot in the fleet. But she's not a super soldier. Tsuko dodges her second attack and, with one swift motion, slices off the entirety of Yeongdeung's arm. He grabs her GM by the neck.

"Gayoung-ah!" Giwoo shouts. I see him reach for his sniper rifle, aim, and shoot. Tsuko moves to the left, and the beam

249

misses. Giwoo blinks, shocked. I don't think he's ever missed a target, not with this clear a shot. He shoots again and again, but it's as if Tsuko can tell the direction of the beam, shifting side to side, dragging Yeongdeung along as if it were a doll. With the last beam, Tsuko casually places Gayoung in the line of fire.

"No!" Giwoo sits forward in his seat, banging his fist against the dashboard.

The beam heads straight for her. Right before contact, there's a flash of color as a GM zooms through the sky. *Fei Hong.* He wraps his GM's arms around Yeongdeung, wresting her from the Shi's grip. The beam blasts a hole in Fei Hong's shoulder, but he's already retreating. They make their escape. For a brief moment, Tsuko looks to follow, but then stops.

He turns to face a new opponent.

Alex.

Tsuko must know who pilots Light Bearer. He must know . . . but will the knowledge stay his hand or impel him forward? He's always hated Alex, thought him spoiled and privileged, hated him even more when he became involved with me.

But that's not the reason he hates Alex the most, the reason that fuels his hatred like an ever-burning coal in his heart.

Tsuko fires the first shot. Alex dodges it, taking out his machine gun to riddle Tsuko's shield with bullets. Then the fight really begins, and there's no doubt in my mind: they intend to kill each other.

Through some unspoken code of honor, the soldiers on the field give the combatants a wide berth. The fighting between the Alliance and the rebels resumes, though on a more equal footing now that Tsuko has cut a swath through the Alliance's forces. At the center of it all, Light Bearer and the Shi break away, only to clash swords. They both seem to have given up firearms entirely, making this a duel in all but name.

Alex is a skilled pilot, but he's not an ace like Gayoung, nor is he an Enhanced human like Tsuko. He bears down with his sword. Sparks fly as Tsuko raises his blade to meet it, then, spinning, gouges a deep slash across Light Bearer's chest. Alex thrusts forward, misses. The Shi stabs downward into Light Bearer's shoulder, close enough to pierce the pilot compartment within.

On the screen, the crowd inside city hall goes quiet. The ending is inevitable now.

"I have to save him."

I don't realize I've spoken aloud until Giwoo warns, "Jangmi-yah, don't even think about it. Your GM is at a critical level. You can't pull a stunt like Fei Hong did to save Gayoung. You won't make it!"

I jam my thrusters to full throttle. My GM jets forward. Giwoo is still shouting through my monitor, so I cut off communications.

It's not Alex I want to save. In this moment, all I can think about is Tsuko. I must stop him from going down a path he can't return from. If he were to kill Alex now, I would never forgive him. Worse, he would never forgive himself.

There's a thorn in your heart, Tsuko, but this isn't how you remove it. Removing it like this, it'll tear you apart.

My GM smashes into the Shi, and we go careening out of the sky.

22

JUNE SOLSTICE, PART 3

We crash-land on one of the small islands.

"Tsuko!" I raise my arm to cover my mouth, coughing from the heavy smoke billowing up from small electrical fires all around my GM cockpit. I'm at 18 percent functionality. It's a wonder my GM hasn't exploded yet.

"Su!" I press down on the comm device. "Pick up!"

Call not received flashes across the screen. He's blocking my calls. Or they're not going through. I've already lost signals in two of my monitors, both on the left, crushed when my GM slammed into the ground. I try reaching out with my mind, but he's too far away.

I pound on the comm. "Please, Tsuko. Please pick up! It's me. It's Ama."

Through my front-view camera, I watch the Shi rise to its feet, towering over my broken GM. I try to mimic its movements, but my controls have lost all operational capability.

Raising his arm, Tsuko points his gun directly at my chest.

I punch the button to open my hatch. The rain lashes downward, soaking me in seconds. "Su!"

The Shi doesn't lower the gun, but it doesn't shoot either. Over its shoulder, an Alliance GM approaches fast, carrying a rocket launcher aimed directly at Tsuko's back.

I won't survive the blast, not outside my GM. The Alliance GM releases the missile.

The Shi lunges forward. It grabs my GM, bringing it to its chest. I tumble back into my cockpit. The missile explodes upon contact, and I press my hands over my ears. The roaring seems to go on and on and on. My whole GM is shaking, my body too. But I'm alive. Tsuko's GM is blocking my GM from the blast, blocking me. He's *protecting* me.

Then it's over. Smoke and a dull, aching silence.

Tsuko twists around and shoots the Alliance GM out of the sky. My bottom right screen flickers on—call received.

"Ama? What the hell are you doing here? In an Alliance GM, no less! I almost killed you!"

I'm so relieved to hear his voice, even raised in anger. To see his face, though he appears pale and tired. "Su, have you been sleeping?"

"That's not the question you should be asking right now. You— You—" He sputters, blinking rapidly. "You're bleeding."

"Am I?" I raise my hand to the crown of my head. "I am."

Tsuko grimaces. "Why are you in an Alliance GM? They can't know your real identity. Otherwise you'd be at the Tower. What have you gotten yourself into, Ama? Why are you in the middle of a battlefield, the most dangerous place you could possibly be, when you should be far away from here—where I thought you were *safe*?" His voice cracks.

"Su, you don't understand—" How much time do we have before they send down more GMs?

Tsuko leans forward in his seat. Even through the flickering screen I can see the disbelief in his eyes. "Don't tell me. You're here for *him*, aren't you? You're here to protect *him*."

I realize instantly who he means. "No! It's more complicated than that!"

But he's not listening to me. He laughs harshly. "Of course. How could I have thought it would be any different? Even after he betrayed you, you'll still keep going back to him. You can't save him, Ama! You can't save someone who doesn't want to be saved!"

"I was saving *you*!" I match his volume. My eyes smart with angry tears. He's so wrong.

Tsuko seethes. "Don't mock my intelligence."

I grit my teeth. "I couldn't let you kill him."

"Why?" He scoffs. "Because you love him? That's even more reason for me to murder the selfish bastard. Then you'll be free of this sickening obsession!"

"No! That's not it. You're wrong! You couldn't be more wrong!"

"Then what is it?" Tsuko's chest is heaving, his eyes as red rimmed as my own.

"I couldn't let you kill him because he's your brother!"

Shocked silence follows this outburst. Tsuko stares at me, eyes wide. I meet his stare, resolute in my conviction.

Unlike Alex, Tsuko has known from the beginning that he and Alex were brothers, since the Director first retrieved Tsuko from an orphanage in Neo Taipei, where he'd been sent after his mother passed away. Tsuko hated Alex for so many reasons—Alex's legitimacy, Alex's mother who was alive, their father who called him "son" to the world—and yet, however he might deny the truth, he can't hide his thoughts from me. Not his first-level thoughts that tell him he must hate Alex—for all Alex has, and all that Tsuko doesn't—or his second-level thoughts that manifest in jealousy, judgment, and rage. No, what he can't hide from me are his third-level thoughts, hidden so deep in the mind they reach his heart.

"Your father might have rejected you," I say, "but Alex hasn't. Tell him the truth. Give him a chance."

A sharp pain lances through my skull, and I wince.

"Ama, are you all right? You need medical attention. Does your distress signal work?"

I blink through the pain to find the small switch, flicking it on—it flashes green—then off. "Yes."

"The Shi has a built-in cloaking device to keep it from detection from radar scans," Tsuko says. That explains why no other GMs have interrupted us thus far. "Because of your close proximity, your GM falls beneath the cloak as well. Once I leave, the signal should resume its transmission."

He's leaving.

"Wait." Though Tsuko might have a blood brother in Alex, *my* family has always been Tsuko and Tera. Even in the middle of a battle, I feel safe because he's here. I'm not ready to let him go. "Just tell me one more thing. Why did you interfere in the battle? What were you trying to accomplish?"

Tsuko's expression hardens. "The only way to stop this war," he says slowly, "is to stop the people who are fighting in it. If there are no more people to fight, then there can be no war."

"That's not right, Su! You can't just kill everyone who means to fight."

"It was what I was made for," he says, evenly.

"You were made to fight for the Alliance," I counter, for the Tower's experiments were always in service to the Neo states.

"I was made as a weapon to end war. It just so happens the Alliance and I disagree on the means."

"And the end always justifies the means," I repeat, remembering our conversation in a rainy Neo Beijing alley so many months before.

I expect him to immediately affirm my words, as he did last winter, but he remains silent, his haunted eyes watching me as they used to when we were younger—as if I held a candle and he was in darkness.

"You never told me why you're here," he says finally.

"And I will continue not to tell you, at least for the time being."

"So it goes again." He sighs, resigned. "You get all the answers you seek. And I get . . ." He shakes his head. "A moment of your time."

I can't help teasing. "Would you have it any other way?"

He doesn't answer. Leaning back from the monitor, his hands move off-screen, adjusting controls as he readies to leave. As the Shi's thrusters ignite, he looks once more at the monitor. "Take care of yourself, Ama. Try not to get killed. I'd rather have one moment of your time than none at all."

■ ■ ■

Without the Shi's cloaking device, my distress signal is picked up within minutes. An emergency aircraft arrives, releasing medics who help me down from my GM and onto a stretcher. I'm rolled up the ramp and into a packed interior.

I piece together what I missed from the thoughts swirling around me. While I was on the island, the battle concluded in a truce. The rebels had taken heavy losses, as was predicted. But with the arrival of Tsuko, the Alliance forces had three times more casualties than was forecast for the battles. Admiral Chen ordered a retreat to prevent further loss of life.

My head is stitched up, my arm slapped with a pain-relieving patch, and I'm free to go. I accept a mug of hot tea from a nurse and take a seat in the waiting room, watching the news coming in from Neo International City. The public outcry is fierce. Bereaved families storm City Hall, demanding answers to their questions. Did their son make it? Is their daughter coming home? Council members are stopped outside their apartment complexes, where security attempts to keep back mobs of angry petitioners seeking news, explanations, or recompense.

The aircraft arrives at the nearest warship. I find Giwoo on the bridge looking over a wide monitor display covered with photographs, about one-third of them dark.

"Wang Jangmi!" he says, catching sight of me. He grabs me in an embrace. "Thank God you're all right."

"How is Alex?" I ask. The news on the transport aircraft had said he'd been taken into surgery an hour ago.

Giwoo's expression turns grim. "He's stable. He had a piece of metal in his ribs that needed to be removed." I wince. "And he's broken several bones in his left arm and shoulder. But he came through without any complications. He's resting in the captain's quarters."

I want to go to him; I want to see for myself that he's all right. But as Jangmi, I have no reason or right to. I'm not one of his lieutenants, his friend, or his lover.

"He asked for you before they put him under."

I look up at Giwoo. "What?"

"You were the last person to be seen with that rogue GM. After you knocked him out of the sky, we lost all trace of you. There was one GM that was close enough to follow in pursuit, but it disappeared off the radar." I keep my expression shocked, as if this news is a surprise to me. He must be referring to the GM with the rocket launcher, the one that would have killed me had it not been for Tsuko. "Alex—none of us—knew what had become of you."

Giwoo's voice is calm, neutral, and yet his mind is as wild as my heart. He's . . . *suspicious* of me. His irrational mind that likes and respects me wars with his rational mind that knows the pieces don't fit together. *How could she be alive after an encounter with that pilot? She's a skilled soldier, but he was exceptional.*

He races through possible explanations, most of them damning. *They could both be rebels, but that doesn't add up because why would he kill his own comrades? Maybe the pilot thought she'd died in the crash. Her GM was mostly destroyed when she was picked up. It must be that, unless* . . . Giwoo stares at me, a frown working at his lips. *Unless they know each other.*

I'm exhausted, mentally and physically, but these thoughts are too dangerous to let lie. I slip into his mind and bring one explanation to the forefront—*he left me for dead.* I take advantage of Giwoo's desire to think the best of me. This is the explanation that gives him the justification to trust me. Or at least let me go.

Giwoo blinks slowly. "The commander will have questions for you when he wakes, and you might have to undergo a debriefing from someone off base."

"Of course," I say, though my mind reels with all the possible things that could go wrong.

"As for now, you're dismissed." Giwoo's attention returns to the wall of photographs, his sorrow overtaking all other thoughts. "I'll mark you off as 'found.' Get some rest, Jangmissi. We've a long trip back to base."

I watch as he presses the tablet. On the wall, a grayed-out picture flickers into color. My altered face looks back at me, secrets in her eyes.

■ ■ ■

Later in the night, Alex is stricken with fever. Luckily, the ship is close enough to the NIC base that he's transported to its state-of-the-art medical facility for close monitoring.

Back at base, I'm changing out of my uniform when there's a knock on my door.

"Yuuki," I say with surprise as I open it. Immediately I feel guilty for having not thought about her until this moment. "I'm glad to see you safe. How are Gayoung and Fei Hong?"

"Fei Hong is fine," she reassures me. "Gayoung has multiple injuries she's being treated for, but she should make a full recovery within a few days."

I sigh in relief.

"But that's not why I'm here," Yuuki says. "Alex asked for you."

"He's awake?" I can't hide my relief. Eagerly I reach for my coat, wrapping it around my nightgown. "I thought he had a fever."

"He does." I glance sharply at Yuuki, alerted by the dull-ness of her voice. "But in one of his lucid moments, he asked for you. Demanded it over and over until I volunteered to get you."

Even if I couldn't read minds, I'd suspect the cause of her misery. Because that's what this is—misery masked with indifference. She might have thought to convince me that she's over Alex, but a peek into her turbulent thoughts shows that she's not yet convinced herself.

"It must be that he wishes to question me," I say. "Giwoo said as much."

"Will you come?"

I nod and follow her out the door. Her steps are swift, heading to the medical facility east of the base. The storm has tempered to a light drizzle. We keep to the cement pathways and avoid stepping into puddles.

The rooms inside the facility are crowded with injured soldiers. Yuuki leads me up a flight of stairs to a less congested upper floor, where the senior officers are accommodated. Giwoo paces outside the last room at the end of the hall. Seeing our approach, he motions me forward. "I told Alex that the enemy soldier left you for dead, but he insists upon hearing the account from you himself."

I nod, unsure what to make of this. Had he recognized Tsuko?

I enter the hospital room. Alex must want to question me alone because Giwoo closes the door behind me. I approach the bed. Alex's eyes are closed, and he's hooked up to a monitor that displays his vital signs as well as an IV drip. His heart rate is stable, but his temperature is inordinately high. As I watch the slow rise and fall of his chest, I realize he's . . . asleep. A blanket covers his body, hiding most of his wounds.

There's a chair beside the bed and I perch at the very edge, my hands in my lap. I have a sudden sense of déjà vu. At the Tower, I was often hospitalized in the medical wing due to adverse effects from the Enhancer injections. Sometimes I would wake in the night to find Alex sleeping in a chair beside me, his head pillowed on my leg, his hand grasping mine. What would he be dreaming about that would make him hold on to me so tightly?

Like then, I have an urge to reach out and press my fingers against the crease between his brows.

Alex's eyes flicker, then open. He says, his voice like broken glass, "Ama."

For a moment I can't breathe.

"Are you haunting me?" On the monitor, his temperature has risen another degree. His fever must have broken through the illusion. He sees the real me, but he isn't aware, caught as he is in a fever dream.

I pour water from a pitcher into a bowl of ice set on a table at his bedside. Then, soaking a cloth in the cool liquid, I bring it to his forehead. A beep on the monitor signals a jump in his heart rate. It must be strange, to feel the touch of a ghost. He reaches up and wraps his hand around my wrist. "If you are, don't stop."

I can't hold back the tears that trail down my cheeks.

"You were the loveliest girl I'd ever seen," Alex says quietly. "I wanted to believe that's all you were to me."

"That *is* all I was to you."

"Do you truly believe that?"

A part of me—the greater part—wants to let my pain direct my words, to express the agony I felt at his betrayal. But what would that accomplish? Between the two of us, we are surfeited with pain.

"No," I say truthfully. "I believe you cared for me."

It was difficult, immediately following the betrayal, to see beyond the choice he made to—in my eyes—throw me away. But here, in this quiet room, two years and more after he first broke my heart, I can clear the haze of pain and acknowledge what I had refused to admit at the time. Even if he had chosen to defy his father and stay with me, the Tower and the Council would have never let us be together. To save me, Alex would have fought with the guards and been imprisoned, or worse, been executed. There is no romance in sacrifice.

"Alex," I say, placing the cloth on the bed and taking his hand in my own, "I forgive you. You were faced with an impossible choice. I don't blame you for making the one you thought best in the moment."

"My choice led to your death."

In his eyes, I see a mixture of feelings—guilt, pain, and regret. This is what he can't forgive himself for, not his choice, but the consequences of his choice—none of which he could have known or predicted, none of which actually happened. I can't tell him the truth, but I won't lie to him either.

"Don't think of me as dead," I say, weaving truth and fiction. "Think of me as alive somewhere in the world, far away from here. I survived the crash, and a fisherwoman found me washed up on the shore. She put me in her cart and lugged me back to her village in the mountains, where I healed beneath her care and attention. I live there now. My life is simple and peaceful. I take walks on the village paths. I fish off a boat in the river."

"If you were alive," Alex says slowly, "I would search for you. I wouldn't give up until I found you."

"And what would you do once you found me? In a world

so far removed from battles and glory, where I was content and happy—what would you do then?"

Alex scowls. "I know how to row a boat."

I can't help it. I burst out laughing. Alex blinks, stunned. Then he shakes his head, laughing softly. I haven't heard him laugh in so long, not like this. It makes me want to cry again. His hand tightens on my own. "Ama, you're leaving."

"I am?"

His eyes blink sleepily. A beep on his monitor indicates his fever is receding. The IV must be on a timer to inject medication into his system.

"I think you're the one who is leaving," I say with a sad smile.

"I don't want this dream to be over," he says, slurring his words. His eyes close. "I miss you, Ama."

"I miss you too," I say. A few minutes later, I lean across the bed and kiss his fevered lips. "I miss you even now."

23

RETREAT

Even before the disastrous battle, a party had been planned to celebrate the Alliance's inevitable win. I thought they would cancel it, all things considered, but the following night Giwoo shows up at my door in a tux, his long black hair slicked back, a silver star dangling from his left ear. "Do you have a dress?"

I open my closet to gaze forlornly at the measly pickings. I once owned a whole collection of dresses. But that was before I became a rebel. "What about our uniforms?" I ask.

"Banned for the night. Ironic, considering we're supposedly celebrating the army's victory, hollow though it may be. What about that one?" He points to the red dress I'd worn to the mayor's party.

I'd felt beautiful in that dress, but I was also wearing it

when I saw Alex for the first time in two years. "I've worn it before—" I begin.

"Ah, you're a snob."

I put on the dress.

The storm from the day before has all but disappeared. In a helicopter, Giwoo and I approach the NIC, which appears on the sea in a blend of black, silver, and blue. We take a car from the military landing site to a high-rise in the middle of the city, riding a glass elevator up to the sixty-sixth floor, where the doors open on a luxurious two-story penthouse. People mingle, champagne flutes in hand, as a small orchestra plays a lively symphonic rendition of a theme song from a popular drama. The far side of the room is made entirely of floor-to-ceiling windows, through which a lantern-lit terrace, complete with an infinity pool, can be seen overlooking the city.

"Go Giwoo!" someone calls. A handsome young waiter approaches, engaging him in conversation.

I move closer to a large fountain at the edge of the room, watching as the water cascades from the top pool to the wider middle pool filled with floating candles to the bottom pool replete with water lilies and silver carp.

Opening my clutch, I reach inside to press down on the location tracker. I need to speak with Helen and the others. The battle might have ended without a victor, but the war is not over.

I feel the presence of someone approaching the fountain from the other side. A cold shiver runs down my spine as I sense his mind. Kim Tae Woo.

Through a gap in the falling water, I study the former

Director of Neo Seoul. Alex's father. *Tsuko's* father. And yet I see nothing of them in him. A similarity in features perhaps— pale skin; black hair; a handsome, arrogant face—but not in anything that matters, like the tilt of Tsuko's eyes that sharpens when he's irritated or hurt or the sensuous turn of Alex's lips. Both sons must take after their mothers.

The gap in the water fills, closing him off from view. I turn away, slipping out onto the terrace. It's decorated in a contemporary style with low tables and lounge chairs. The water of the infinity pool is a deep indigo, lit from below by moon-shaped pool lights. A cool breeze sweeps across the Pacific, and the few individuals meandering out here head back inside.

I'm only alone a few minutes before the door at the end of the terrace opens. Helen and Shun approach slowly, two socialites out for a stroll.

We meet inside an empty cabana out of sight of the glass windows. Shun leans down for a quick hug. "Glad to see you're safe."

I return the embrace. "You too."

Helen, noticing my bare shoulders, takes off her coat and wraps it around me. Together we sit on the low couches. "We don't have much time," Helen begins. "Things have gotten a lot more dangerous in the past twenty-four hours. Not only for you, but for the world. However, before we speak further, what can you tell us about the battle?" There's a hard look in both their eyes that hadn't been there when I last saw them.

I tell Helen and Shun everything. They listen carefully, not asking questions until I'm finished.

"*The* Tsuko?" Shun says, eyes wide. "As in, the NSK's greatest soldier? Who was killed during the battle of Neo Seoul?"

I nod. "He's Enhanced, like me, though that information was never released to the public. 'Ama.' 'Tera.' 'Su.' He was the 'Su' component, imbued with both physical and mental enhancements. It was his physical enhancements that enabled him to survive the explosion that destroyed the Tower."

Helen and Shun take a moment to absorb this. I can *feel* Helen's mind whirring. "What was his agenda for yesterday's battle?" she asks. "He wasn't fighting for the Alliance. He destroyed at least a quarter of their troops. And he wasn't on our side. We had fewer losses, but even those few were significant."

"He . . ." I think back to yesterday on the island, his impossible desire to end the war all on his own. "He wants to stop the fighting. He thinks the only way to achieve that end is to kill everyone who chooses to fight."

"So he's not on either side." Helen crosses her arms, her expression contemplative. "I'll only ask this once, Ama. Do you think he can be convinced to fight for the rebels?"

I know what she's really asking. Can *I* convince him to fight for the rebels? I consider her question carefully. No, I don't think I could convince him. To Tsuko, it's not about choosing sides, but eliminating sides.

And yet do I think he would come to my aid if I was in danger? Do I think he would forgo his principles to protect me? The real question is: Would I ask that of him?

I look away. "I can't."

"Ama—" Shun protests.

"That's all I needed to know," Helen cuts him off. "You've done excellent work undercover, but it's gotten too dangerous with the former Director in the city searching for spies." Helen pauses and exchanges a glance with Shun, their thoughts suggesting they have something more to tell me with regards to the Director. "We're taking you out."

I bite my lip and nod. By now, the Alliance will suspect the rebels had prior knowledge of their plans for the battle, which could have only been shared with them through a traitor or a spy. It's the right move to make, though I feel a premonition of the pain to come—leaving Giwoo and Gayoung, Yuuki and Fei Hong. Leaving Alex.

"How will you do it?" I ask softly.

"Tomorrow a missive will arrive at your base. Wang Yunpeng will contract a serious illness and wish to have his daughters attend him. You'll be discharged from the base." Once again, Wang Yunpeng is coming to my aid. I hope to one day thank my "father" in person.

"One last thing," Shun says, with a glance toward Helen. This must have been the information they'd been waiting to tell me. "Since the train, Shiori's been keeping tabs on any news about the other Tera and Ama. She hasn't discovered anything about the other Tera, but the other Ama was spotted in the city, in the company of Kim Tae Woo."

"She's working with him? Of her own free will?"

"Shiori suspects he might have some way to control her, a device to guard him from her powers. He could also be keeping the other Tera somewhere in order to force the other Ama to cooperate."

I wince at the cruelty of this plan, though I recognize its logic. I would have done almost anything if I'd thought Tera was in danger.

"Shiori also managed to hack one of the files on Kim Tae Woo's interface, though only for a few seconds before the security software kicked her out." Shun hands me a slip of paper, with a few phrases written in English and Korean.

Memory Erasure. Multi-Person Hallucinations. Psychoactive Interrogation. Telekinetic Weaponry. Permanent Illusions.

"What is this?" I whisper.

"The file was a list of the other Ama's . . . abilities. Shiori thought it might help you understand your own powers."

I carefully fold the paper and slip it into my pocket. "Thank you."

Helen stands. With the plan for tomorrow set, there's no need to risk lingering longer.

As the two of them take their leave, I remain on the terrace, staring out over the city. A whirring sound draws my attention below to where a small aircraft alights on a landing platform. Several people disembark and head into the building, their laughter drifting up into the sky like smoke. I take out the slip of paper and memorize the few lines before ripping it to shreds and throwing them to the wind.

Back in the penthouse, Giwoo is nowhere to be found, and I assume he either returned to base without me or went off with the waiter.

I move to the glass elevator and press the button for the bottom floor. As the doors shut, a hand slips through at the last moment. Alex steps inside, and the doors close behind him. He's dressed in a blue-black suit immaculately tailored to his lean frame. One sleeve hangs by his side, his arm in a sling.

He looks terrible. There are bruises beneath his eyes that are rimmed in red, as if he's been weeping. The lift begins to descend. I try to probe his mind, but it's the most chaotic it's ever been, churning with some dark emotion.

"I thought you were in the hospital," I say after a short silence, "recovering from your injuries."

"My father wanted to speak with me." There's a flash of recent memory, of a hand raised to strike. I flinch, and the memory dissipates. Alex watches me carefully. "Are you all right?"

"Too much to drink," I lie. "And the vertigo makes me nauseous."

"Here, let me help." Alex reaches out and hits the STOP button, stalling the elevator on the fifty-eighth floor.

"What are you doing?" I whisper.

"Did you speak to him? To that pilot on the island."

He means Tsuko. "No! We crashed, and he must have thought I died upon impact. He left when I made no move to attack."

"Why did you do it?"

"Why did I pretend to be dead? Because it was the only way to live."

"No." Alex presses forward, his good hand gripping the railing to the left of me. "Why did you save me?"

His eyes seem to burn with a dark fever. I look away. "Because you're my commander."

"Am I?" he asks quietly.

Stepping back, he hits the STOP button again, releasing it. The elevator descends once more. Where is this mood coming from?

I attempt another probe of his mind, but it's difficult to make sense of his thoughts, caught as they are in a storm of memories, his father berating him, blaming him for the Alliance's defeat, then leaning down to whisper, *"You've been a fool, son. There's something you don't know."* Abruptly, the memory switches to a dream, of a hospital room and a girl sitting beside him. *Ama.*

The storm in his mind breaks, and I blink, looking up into eyes that are filled with longing, but not for me. "Are you in love with me, Jangmi-ssi?" he asks.

I look away. "How arrogant."

"Then it's just lust," he says. "That's better. Less messy." His voice is empty, without emotion. "If you agree to it, I'd like to start a relationship, purely physical. Unless a torrid affair isn't your style."

A sharp pain lances through my heart. I gasp and almost choke on it. "I hate you."

"Not as much as I hate myself."

The elevator stops, and the doors open to the landing dock I'd seen earlier from above. Alex steps out, and a medic hurries forward to assist him. I witness the truth that Alex has tried so painstakingly to hide: he collapses on the medic's shoulder, leaning on him for support.

The doors close. I sink to the floor, riding the rest of the way to the bottom in tears.

24

THE SPY

I return to base, crying myself to sleep well past midnight, only to wake a few hours later from an awful pounding in my skull. At first, I wonder if I've caught a fever, yet this doesn't feel like sickness. A glance out the window shows that dawn is still hours away, the sky blue and gray with mist.

I stumble outdoors and almost run into a soldier returning to the barracks. She catches my arm as I lose my balance. "Are you all right?"

I force a smile. "Too much to drink last night."

She accepts the excuse, shrugging and slipping past the automatic doors. Whatever this pain is, it's only affecting me.

As I head east away from the barracks, the pain begins to lessen, and yet when I move west, it grows stronger. It's as if there's a source for the pain, like a beacon pulsing outward, intensifying the closer I get to it.

A part of me wants to put distance between it and myself, but Shiori's piece of paper feels heavy in my pocket.

I take the western path toward the medical facility. When I reach the alley behind the cafeteria, I collapse against the wall to catch my breath. So far I haven't seen anyone besides that soldier, though there should be a few patrols making the rounds. The absence of people is unnerving.

An object on the wall catches my eye. It's a metal box. I slide up the panel. Bright numbers gleam back at me: 00:23. I count a few seconds, and the numbers slip to 00:22. A timer.

It's an explosive.

There's movement across the way. In the shadow of the medical facility, a figure stands, having successfully placed another bomb. He wipes his hands on his pant legs. He's dressed in dark colors to blend with the night; his movements are calm and unhurried.

There's something familiar about him. A wave of pain hits me like a ton of bricks. The intruder tenses, placing a hand against the wall to keep his balance, then whips his head around. Our eyes meet.

It's Alex.

But that makes no sense. Why would he place explosives around his own base?

A third person rushes down the path and stops between us. It's . . . Alex.

I gape, my gaze flitting between them both. This Alex is dressed in the suit he'd worn the night before, and unlike the Alex still standing in the shadows, his arm is in a sling.

Realization hits me at the same time as the Alex on the path raises his gun with his good arm.

"Don't!" I scream. The gun blasts through the night. And it's as if it also blasts through the fog in my brain, because the pain disappears, the illusion breaks, and in the shadows of the alley, Tsuko crumples to the ground.

■ ■ ■

I help Alex drag Tsuko's unconscious body into the medical facility. The emergency staff rushes forward, but Alex motions them away, issuing orders. The entire base must be alerted of a bomb threat and all non-military personnel evacuated.

We lay Tsuko on a bed in the emergency room, and Alex slaps a pair of electro-braces onto Tsuko's wrist, securing him to the bed. The cuffs activate with an electric hiss. Even Tsuko, with his Enhanced strength, will have difficulty breaking an electro-chain.

"Leave us," Alex says, and the orderlies hurry from the room, closing the door behind them.

Tsuko lies on his back, his eyes closed. One tear trickles down his cheek, the body's reaction to the gunshot wound bleeding from below his rib cage. I remind myself that, like Tera, Tsuko has advanced healing capabilities. Still, it's not as if the pain of a bullet wound is less for him.

"You tried to stop me," Alex says quietly. "When I raised my gun to shoot him."

"I thought he was you." It's a reasonable answer for anyone who isn't me.

"He's an Enhanced human," Alex says, "part of a super soldier program my father led back in Neo Seoul. Not only does he have super strength and speed, as evidenced in the recent battle, but he's also a telepath. He can manipulate your mind, make you believe things that aren't there, that aren't true." It's odd to hear Alex speak of the project, to explain it to *me*, of all people.

"Did you know who he was when you shot him?" I ask. If my understanding is correct, then Alex would have seen *himself* when he looked at Tsuko. That would have alerted him to the truth of mind manipulation at work. Perhaps he thought it was the other Ama, if he knows of her existence. He wouldn't have thought it was me.

"I could see him."

I frown. "What do you mean?"

He sweeps his hair back from his forehead. Beneath is a thin circular band of metal. "Last night, my father gave this to me. It protects my mind from being manipulated."

And yet the illusion *I* placed in his mind still holds. I recall one of the abilities written on the piece of paper Shun had given me. *Permanent Illusions*. Until I fully release the illusion, he'll see me as Wang Jangmi.

Cautiously, I test my powers against the band and get . . . nothing. No thoughts. No emotions. Just silence.

"Damn it." Alex reaches into his pocket.

"What's wrong?" I ask.

"Last night, my father gave me not just the protective device, but also entrusted me with a file that shows the location of the rebel bases. I must have dropped it in my rush to get over here."

My heart sinks. Which of the rebel bases are now compromised? "Where did you see it last?"

"In my room. In the officers' quarters."

Tsuko is awake. He may appear as if he's sleeping, the fall and rise of his chest giving no indication of a change, but I can feel his mind flicker with awareness.

There's a knock on the door of the hospital room. A soldier in the uniform of a junior grade lieutenant enters and bows. "Commander, the bomb squad has located eight explosives, positioned on all the major buildings. They're all on a timer, and the system for each is varied. We might be able to defuse two—three at the most—but not all of them. Per regulations, the GM hangars as well as this medical facility are being prioritized."

"And the evacuation?"

"All nonmilitary personnel are headed toward the docks as we speak."

"Good." When the soldier doesn't leave, Alex frowns. "There's more."

"The control tower spotted an unidentified aircraft several kilometers off base to the east. We think it might be a rebel GM carrier. The colors match those of the United Korean League."

Alex curses beneath his breath. "How much time do we have before the explosives detonate?"

"Fifteen minutes."

"I want all soldiers in their GMs and mobilized for battle."

"Yes, sir." The soldier leaves.

When we turn back to the bed, Tsuko's eyes are open. His gaze slides from Alex, lingering on me.

"You're awake," Alex says. "I should have aimed higher."

"Did I hear that correctly?" Tsuko says, ignoring him, his eyes still trained on me. "The bomb outside the medical facility will be defused?"

"Don't worry," Alex growls. "You'll survive. Or perhaps I'll move you to the barracks, and we'll see how many lives an Enhanced soldier really has."

Tsuko's gaze remains on me. "For me, many, but not for all."

Alex frowns. "Why do you keep looking at her?"

For a moment, Tsuko says nothing, confusion coloring his thoughts.

Then I watch as he puts everything together—the fact that Alex hasn't called me by name, that I've stood silent throughout this encounter, as if I don't know Tsuko, as if Alex doesn't know *me*.

Tsuko bursts out laughing.

My cheeks flame with anger. How dare he laugh in a situation like this, captured as he is, with explosives that *he* placed set to go off in less than fifteen minutes? But then, as I watch him wipe tears of joy from his eyes, I have a single thought: When was the last time I'd seen him laughing? He looks a little mean and cruel, laughing at my expense, but still, the rare sound takes my breath away. He looks as he's never looked before—young and happy.

The smile vanishes from his face. He's read my mind.

"You think this is funny?" Alex asks softly. "Is this a game to you? You have the skill and power to change the course of a battle, the mental strength to manipulate a whole base into seeing a shared illusion, and yet for two years, you've hidden like a coward, joining the fight only now because of some false sense of justice. You think you're taking on a heavy burden to fight both the Alliance and the rebels, but a vigilante is not a hero but a thorn in the side of change. It's easy to risk your own life. It's much harder to risk the life of another."

"I've heard this speech before," Tsuko says. "I've given it myself. The difference between us is that you still believe in the dream, that you're fighting for what you believe in, for a cause, a side, a person, for glory, for some far-distant future where you're not hurting, where the people you care about aren't dying, while I—" He lifts his gaze. "I've woken up."

Alex sneers. "Have you woken up, or have you given up?"

Tsuko's eyes narrow. "You're one to speak."

"What does that mean?"

"You gave up on Ama."

"Don't—" Alex growls.

I step forward, though neither brother notices, so intent upon hurting each other.

"She never belonged in the project. Tera and I, we were soldiers. We understood our purpose—to fight, to kill. Not her. She was good. She was kind. Her dreams were always bright and warm. I could feel them when she was nearby. For someone like me, who always lived in darkness, she was like the sun."

I press a hand to my mouth, tears slipping down my cheeks. *I never knew.*

"And then you came." Tsuko's eyes go hard, his voice bitter. "And she invited you into her beautiful dream, and what did you do? You destroyed it. You tore it apart and left her drowning in a nightmare."

Alex lunges.

Tsuko raises his hand, moving with an inhuman speed.

"Su, no!" I scream.

At the last moment, he pulls back his strength, and a blow that would have killed Alex only knocks him unconscious. He slumps to the floor.

I rush to Alex's side, pressing my hand to the side of his head where a lump is forming.

"I had to get him close," Tsuko says. "Hurry and check to see if he has a key to the electro-braces on him."

I stare at Tsuko. "You were provoking him on *purpose?*"

He says, deadpan, "I don't need powers to mess with his mind."

"Are you—" I gape at him. "Are you *joking?*"

"Ama, get the keys."

I find a device in Alex's pocket, releasing the lock. Tsuko stands up from the bed, rubbing his wrists. "I've been counting in my head. We've got about ten minutes before the first of the explosives go off. I have my GM cloaked a kilometer off base.

If we commandeer a vehicle, we can get there and make our escape."

"I'm not going."

Tsuko speaks slowly. "He'll be fine. You heard them before. The bomb outside the medical facility was defused."

"No, it's not that. I never told you the real reason I was there during the battle. I'm an undercover operative, working with PHNX."

This shouldn't come as a surprise to him. He was the one who told me about PHNX, all those months ago.

When Tsuko says nothing, I continue. "Alex mentioned he has a file that lists the location of all the rebel bases. I need to retrieve that file and find out which of them are compromised."

"I'll go with you."

"No, it's too dangerous."

"I'm not going to let you walk across an Alliance base unprotected and alone."

"You're going to *let* me because I'm older than you, and you have to listen to me."

Tsuko blanches. "That doesn't work. And you're older than me by a year!"

"Su, please. Your face has been circulated all over by now. You can't manipulate all the minds on the base, and you've used up so much power as it is." Even he can't deny my logic. "No one will suspect me. They know me as Wang Jangmi, not a rebel spy. If I hurry, I can get to the officers' quarters, retrieve the file, and escape in a GM, no one the wiser. Please, Su. Trust me."

I know I've won when he sighs. "If you die, I'll never forgive you."

■ ■ ■

The officers' quarters are located at the edge of the base, facing the sea. I have to take a roundabout way to get there, since the area is crawling with soldiers. Though most know me as Wang Jangmi, many would still question why I was rushing toward the officers' quarters when all soldiers have been given the order to mobilize for battle.

I lose precious minutes, but it's worth it because when I finally arrive, the area is abandoned, the grass upturned from running feet. A colossal shadow falls over me as a God Machine flies out over the ocean to meet its waiting brethren. There's no visible sign of the UKL rebels.

Dawn gilds the horizon. The front doors to the quarters whisper open at my approach.

I've never been inside this building, but I've studied the layout in preparation for the mission. Alex's rooms are on the top floor, on the westernmost side. I take the stairs, as the elevator requires an authentication protocol. I face a similar problem outside the door to Alex's rooms, contemplating the keypad. I try Alex's birth date: 0818. The light on the pad blinks red, processing an error. The digital clock on the keypad shows that it's ten minutes past six, which means I have five minutes to retrieve the device and escape out of reach of the bomb.

I raise my hand and place it on the keypad, then close my

eyes and concentrate. I've never done this before. I'm not even sure if it'll work. I focus my energy on the keypad, imagining my mind is a fist wrapped around it, squeezing tight. My head begins to throb from the pressure. The keypad hisses with smoke, and the door slides open with a click.

Inside is a spacious one-room apartment with a kitchenette, a bathroom, and a few pieces of furniture. It's similar to my own room in the barracks, except for the extra space and the floor-to-ceiling windows that take up the side of the room facing the ocean. I race over to the desk at the center of the room, where a single data chip rests upon the surface. I reach out to grab it.

The slide of a shoe across linoleum alerts me to danger, but it's already too late. The cold metal of a gun presses against the back of my neck.

"Even knowing this was coming," Alex says softly, "doesn't make the betrayal any less painful."

I reach out for his thoughts, but they're blocked by the protective band.

"For how long?" he asks.

"Since the start."

"Did you work alone, or did you have help? Was Giwoo—?" His voice breaks.

"We met in Neo Beijing," I say hurriedly, "before I joined the army. He has no idea of my involvement. He is innocent in all this."

"If Giwoo wasn't involved, how did you get the information about the battle? The strategy was only shared with the senior officers."

I try to turn, but his gun digs deeper into my neck. "Stay where you are. If you move, I *will* shoot."

My heart beats wildly. "Alex, don't do this!"

"I'm disappointed," he says cruelly. "I hadn't thought you would beg. I thought you'd tell me to pull the trigger. Or are you that afraid to die?"

"I'm more afraid that you'll regret it."

Alex adjusts his grip on the gun. I tense as the metal of the barrel moves slightly to the left. "You place too much worth on your life. You're nothing to me."

"If only that were true!"

He curses. "I know you were working for the rebels, but what about Tsuko? How do you know him? I don't understand how it all connects."

"Alex, please!"

"And why me? Why did you choose my base, my *people*? Did you think I was weak? Did you read the reports of my past and think I could be swayed, manipulated, seduced?"

I can't speak against the tears slipping down my cheeks.

"Because it worked. You can congratulate yourself on that."

Again, I reach out with my mind, but the band is like a wall, blocking me out.

"Who's the bigger fool," Alex says softly, "me for wanting to believe in you, or you for destroying the illusion?"

"There is no illusion! Not anymore. Take off the band. Look me in the eyes and ask me for the truth."

"What difference will it make? I won't be swayed by tears. You're an enemy of the Alliance, a spy, a traitor. You'd be executed for less than the crime you've committed."

"Alex, you don't understand. It's *me*. It's—"

A colossal boom shakes the building, and the glass in the windows shatters. Alex and I are thrown apart. A screaming wind blows inward, accompanied by the sounds of machine gunfire, the UKL rebels and NIC soldiers engaging in combat. I have no time to think. There's a low groan, and the room begins to tilt. I slide toward the gaping window of broken glass.

"Jangmi!" Alex catches my hand. I'm dangling outside the window, blood slipping down my wrist where I cut myself on the glass.

On Alex's face is a powerful range of emotions—pain, anger, and fear.

Another groan and the room shifts even more. The veins in Alex's good arm are taut, straining to hold on to me. He's balanced, one foot on the sill, one foot on the pane of glass that had shattered with the bomb. Cracks in the glass begin to form. It won't hold beneath our combined weight.

"Alex!" I shout. "You need to let go or we'll both fall!"

"I won't abandon you!" There's real terror in his voice. "There has to be a way," he says, looking around desperately.

I don't want to give up either, but I can see no other options. It's either I die or we both die. I'm angry and upset and scared. My head throbs from Tsuko's earlier mind manipulation and the use of my telekinetic power. I only have enough energy for one final, desperate move. Alex must see my determination because he cries, panicked. "Don't, Jangmi!"

Everything happens in a moment.

I jerk my hand from his grip, releasing the force in my mind to knock him back. In the process, our hands are ripped apart.

I fall, my consciousness blacking out at the edges.

Across the sky, a GM races toward me, one hand outstretched. A person stands in the palm of the GM, her hair in the wind, a fierce expression on her beautiful face. An achingly familiar voice shouts, "Ama!"

She's here.

The only person who could save me now.

Tera.

I let oblivion overtake me.

ACT 3

25

REUNION

I notice two things upon waking: the first, a song plays on the radio, one I've heard before—a smooth-voiced soprano croons about missed opportunities and rekindled love—and the second, someone holds my hand.

I open my eyes, adjusting to the low light. I'm in a cave, or what appears to be a cave. The walls are made of rock. The person who holds my hand stares at me with wide, worried eyes.

She leans forward; her serious expression turns to one of abject joy, and her mind fills with light and love for me. "Ama, you're awake!"

"Tera, your hair!"

She immediately palms the shoulder-length strands. At the Tower, her hair was always the same length, long and straight. Now, not only is it short and styled in waves, but I can make out streaks of red and blue in the naturally dark brown strands.

"Jaewon says he liked it longer," Tera says, wrinkling her nose, "but I don't care. I like it this way."

I laugh at her surly expression. When they met two years ago, they were always bickering. That's how I knew she liked him. No one can annoy Tera like Jaewon can.

"Where is he?" I ask. I'm excited to see Jaewon. Not only is he amiable, good-natured, and very nice to look at, but he has a mind that always puts me at ease, warm and attentive as it is. It was one of the reasons I took to him so quickly. Not like Tera, who'd needed some coaxing. "What?" I press when she hesitates. "What is it?"

"He's . . . well . . ." She scratches her neck.

I sigh. "Spit it out, Tera."

"He's with Alex."

I blink. "You took Alex?" Relief washes through me, then . . . "Why? He's not a rebel. Why did you take him?" Tera's distressed thoughts slip through—distress due to how I might react when I find out the truth. "You're interrogating him!" I sit up higher in the bed. "Are you—Are you hurting him?"

"No! Of course not. We're just asking him a few questions. Jaewon is overseeing everything. He won't let anyone hurt Alex. You know how Jaewon is—loyal to a fault—and remember, they used to be friends."

I calm down. She's right. Jaewon will protect Alex. He's logical and dependable, often thinking before acting. Not like Tera.

"What happened?" I squeeze her hand. "Start from the beginning."

Over the next thirty minutes, Tera fills me in on what happened in the past twenty-four hours, how while flying north over the NIC en route to the UKL's base in the mountains, they received a distress signal from an unexpected source.

"Tsuko," I breathe.

She nods. "He told me that you were on base, that you were in danger. I hurried as fast as I could, arriving just in time to see you fall."

I stare at her in awe. "How did you do it?"

"I switched the GM to autopilot, climbed out onto the hand, and caught you around the waist, jamming my fist into the wall to slow down our momentum."

I laugh, overjoyed to see Tera confident in her abilities, when at the Tower, she'd been so afraid of her own strength.

How these past two years have changed her. I wonder, have the years changed me?

"Tera," I say, "I have so much to tell you, all that's happened to me since we've been apart, all that I've done. It began with the transport carrier crash. Did you know—?"

"I didn't know for sure, but I couldn't accept that you'd died in the crash. Your body was never found. Jaewon swore to me that once the war was over, we would look for you."

"After the crash, I was badly injured. A fisherwoman found me and brought me back to her village." In the story I told Alex, that part hadn't been a lie. "I eventually left because I was afraid of endangering the villagers. I made my way to the closest metropolis, Neo Beijing, because I thought I could hide in anonymity." I tell her about joining PHNX and going undercover. "Can you believe it? The things I've done. Me, of all people. It must be shocking."

"I'm not surprised at all," Tera says matter-of-factly.

I laugh. "You're just saying that."

"No!" She leans forward, fervent. "You're the strongest person I know." I begin to protest again, but she insists. "It's true! Well, you *and* Jaewon."

"Tera," I drawl, "you can bend a metal bar."

She rolls her eyes. "Strength isn't just physical. You should know that better than anyone."

I bite my lip. She's right again.

"The real difference between you and Jaewon and Alex and me is that Alex and I seem strong on the outside, but on the inside, we're fragile as glass, while you and Jaewon appear to be breakable, but you bend with the wind."

Her words slip over me like a balm, her certainty and faith in me empowering. I take her hands in my own. "I will acknowledge my own strength as long as you acknowledge yours. And together we will balance each other, two halves of one whole."

Tera's hands lightly squeeze mine. "With every second you're here, I feel stronger."

There's a knock on the door. I turn, expecting to see Jaewon's friendly face, but a young soldier enters instead. "Captain," she says, addressing Tera, "Lee Jaewon requests your presence in the holding cell."

"Understood. Thank you, soldier."

The woman bows before leaving. Tera squeezes my hand one final time, then stands. "I have to go. Will you be all right here alone? I can have someone sit with you."

"I'm fine. Is this—?" I hesitate. "Are you going to see Alex?"

She nods, her expression grim. "Like I said, we won't hurt him, but he is the commander of an Alliance base and has information that can help the rebellion." She pauses, watching me with a worried expression. "If I'm not mistaken, he doesn't know that you've been with him this whole time, that you're ... you. Since waking, he's been asking for someone named Wang Jangmi."

"That was my alias." I'd told her about going undercover, but not everything that I had to do, that I had to do to *Alex*.

Tera whistles low. "I don't envy either of your positions right now." She stands. "In any case, our leader, Oh Kangto, wants to keep Alex under guard while he's here for security purposes. I don't think you'll be able to see him for a while yet."

I swallow thickly. "I understand."

She doesn't look convinced, but she nods. Leaning across the bed, she brushes a kiss across my cheek. I breathe in the scent of her—lilac and clove. "I'm so glad you're here."

I wait a few minutes after she leaves before peeling back the blanket.

Not that I don't trust Tera and Jaewon, but Alex is an enemy leader. He's responsible, indirectly or otherwise, for the deaths of many of their comrades, some of whom might choose to seek revenge.

My hip is a little sore from where Tera must have caught me around the waist, and when I pull back the waistband of my pants, I see a bruise has formed. Making my way to the door, I exit into an industrial-looking hallway.

It's deserted, which is fortunate, as I don't know what I'd say to someone should I run into them. I'm dressed in a pajama-like pants and a shirt—clothes Tera presumably dressed me in—and I'm not wearing shoes. I reason for a moment that I could always use my powers, then quickly stop that train of thought. I'm no longer in an enemy encampment, but among allies. My powers should only be used to defend myself.

The base is a sprawling network of interconnected hallways constructed of steel, cement, and natural rock. More people appear the farther I walk, and though a few stare at my disheveled appearance, no one stops me. I make my way past living quarters much like the one I'd woken up in, alongside large open areas with hydroponic gardens, people tending the leafy plants growing on vertical stands. I pass by a bustling canteen, where I hear mostly Korean, though I pick out other languages in the crowd, and an indoor fitness center. I'm impressed at the organization and technology; this base must be self-sustainable.

Rounding a corner, I arrive at a glass bridge suspended over a canyon, and that's when I see I'm not underground, as I'd previously thought, but high up, somewhere in a great mountain range. Below is a misty valley, almost obscuring the large battleship docked beneath the clouds—the same battleship that destroyed Neo Seoul's Tower during the battle of Neo Seoul with its infamous Ko Cannon. Right now it appears harmless, like a sleeping giant, mountain birds winging around its elevated bridge.

I walk into an atrium that branches in multiple directions. I've been mostly following the flow of the path, but now I need a hint of where to go. I close my eyes and concentrate. Trying to keep my powers as uninvasive as possible, I flit from thought to thought, brushing upon the minds of those around me.

There.

In someone's mind, I catch an image of Tera as she hurries across the space. I follow the memory of her.

It takes me down a side corridor with one door with a security lock through which a man in uniform is exiting. As the man passes by, I pull a numbered code from his mind. At the door, I key it in. The door slides open to reveal a small upper floor chamber with a balcony. Stairs on either side lead down to a lower chamber where Jaewon, Tera, and a few other rebels stand in a circle around Alex, who's tied to a chair.

They're currently in a heated argument, and no one looks up at my entrance. I quickly move to the balcony wall, ducking down and peeking over the top.

Because of his broken arm, only Alex's legs and good arm are tied down.

"Alex," Jaewon is saying. He looks exhausted. I wonder if this whole time I've been resting, they've been going through the motions of an interrogation. Though, at this point, Alex looks the most at ease, leaning back in the chair, while Jaewon paces before him, clearly frustrated. "I'm trying to help you. Oh

Kangto won't be as patient when he arrives tomorrow morning. You have to give me something."

"I already told you. I won't give you information that might risk the welfare of my soldiers."

Jaewon groans. "Then make something up."

Alex laughs, shaking his head. "You're either terrible at interrogations, or brilliant."

"Lee Jaewon," one of the rebels says, a sneer in his voice, "maybe if you stopped flirting with the bastard, we could actually get some answers out of him."

Tera's head whips to the side. "Why don't you say that one more time?" she growls.

The man actually takes a step back.

She returns her attention to Alex with a scowl. "I promised I wouldn't use force on you. But you don't make it easy with that attitude."

Alex blinks. "Promised who?" Tera bites her lip. But Alex jumps to a different conclusion. "There's nothing you can do that would hurt me more than Wang Jangmi already has." I wince. The pain he feels now is nothing to what he'd feel if he knew the truth. "Besides, you already know everything there is to know. Your spy should be commended."

"I think we should tell him," Jaewon says.

Alex frowns. "Tell me what?"

Crouching in this position makes the bruise on my stomach hurt, so I move a bit and hit my knee on the balcony wall. Immediately Tera's head swerves in my direction, catching the sound.

"I've had enough of this," the rebel from earlier says. "For my comrades." He pulls out a gun and points it directly at Alex's chest.

Tera twists around, lightning quick, and tackles him, but not before he releases the trigger. The violent noise echoes through the chamber, then silence.

Everyone swivels their heads to Alex, who's looking down at his own white-shirted chest. No bloom of red. No wound, and yet the man's aim had been true.

"Is that—?" Jaewon points to a small object suspended in the air—the bullet.

Tera recovers quickly, jumping off the would-be assassin and pushing Alex out of the bullet's trajectory. With a jerk of my mind, I release the bullet. Loosed, it hurtles the rest of the way, exploding against the stone floor.

I blink away the haze in my mind to find everyone staring at me. I meet Alex's eyes. "Ama," he breathes.

He's not wearing the band.

His eyes snap to Jaewon. "Hurry, untie me."

I do the only thing I can—I run.

26
CONFESSION

He knows. Oh god, he knows.

Back in the atrium, I search wildly for a place to go, unsure of which direction will take me to the living quarters. I choose a hall at random. It leads to an indoor garden with a natural stream. I dash along the length of it, following the water as it curves around a bend and flows into a small pool surrounded by a bamboo thicket with a low stone bench. It's a dead end.

I turn, only to hear footsteps upon the path, running swiftly. I take a step back, then another, until I'm pressed against the bamboo wall. Alex appears around the corner. He stops when he catches sight of me. Tera and Jaewon must have bought us a moment alone because neither of them has followed.

His mind rages with emotion—confusion, anger, pain, and a knowing of who I am, of what I've done. I close off the reach of his thoughts, unable to bear them in the face of my own.

In two years, this is the first time he's seen *me*. I imagine how I must look, battered, unwashed, and dressed in old pajamas. Even with the ordeal Alex has suffered, he looks incredible, his face cleanly shaven, his white shirt somehow in pristine condition even after being kidnapped and shot at.

Nerves pool in the pit of my stomach as silence stretches between us. I open my mouth to speak, but nothing comes out. Tears of frustration lodge in my throat.

"My actions are unforgivable," I begin. "I— I can't say I'm sorry for them. I thought they were necessary for the cause I believe in. But I *am* sorry for the grievous wound I've dealt you. I should have never taken this mission knowing you were involved, knowing how I felt about you, knowing how you once might have felt about me . . ."

Alex's eyes narrow slightly, though he doesn't speak.

I push on. "The truth is, though I was sent to your base as a spy, I had my own agenda. I won't deny it! I wanted to see you again, to prove to myself that you once loved me, that you regretted having betrayed me. And witnessing you in pain, I felt satisfaction. A sliver of it—but enough!"

"Ama," Alex says slowly, unbelievably, "I don't care."

"You don't understand!" I shout. "I wanted to hurt you! I wanted to hurt you for hurting me!"

In three long strides, Alex closes the distance between us, his good arm circling me. Then his mouth is on mine, and he kisses me as if the echo of my confession rings in his ears.

He breaks the kiss, only to lift one hand to cradle my face, his thumb reverently brushing the curve of my cheek. "There's nothing to forgive. You're alive. That's all that matters to me."

I bask in his words and attention, then frown when I realize what he's saying. "It doesn't matter to you that I hurt you on purpose?"

"First, I don't think you did. I think circumstances as they were might have led to some pain on my end, but you didn't actively think up plans to make me suffer. And second . . ." He shrugs. "Even if you did, I wouldn't care. That just shows me that you give a damn."

"Alex," I say softly, "people who love you shouldn't want to hurt you."

He must know I'm thinking of his father because he grimaces. Then abruptly he asks, "Did you revel in my pain?"

"No!"

"When you saw I was suffering, did you seek to prolong it?"

"No, of course not!"

"You just felt a twinge of satisfaction when I got what I deserved."

"Well, yes."

He shrugs. "You're not a saint, Ama."

His words echo Tsuko's in an alley in Neo Beijing what feels like a lifetime ago, except Tsuko had said the opposite. I sniff. "Some people think I am."

Alex shakes his head. "First you're adamant you're not perfect. Now you're offended that I agree with you."

"You used to think I was an angel." In the Tower he was always careful with me, patient and sweet.

"I never thought you were an angel."

I stiffen in his arms, and he almost drops me.

"God, Ama. We're standing on gravel!" With his good arm, he helps me to the stone bench. There isn't enough room to sit side by side, so he kneels before me, his bad arm resting on his knee.

"Wait, Alex, we can both stand."

"No. I think you'll want to be sitting for what I'm about to say."

I bite my lip, nervous. He looks away. The hand that rests on the bench beside me is curled in a fist. I gently cover it with my own, and he relents, interlocking our fingers.

He brings our joined hands to his lips. "When I think of angels, I think of creatures that are flawless and untouchable. I don't think you're flawless. I don't put you on some damn pedestal. And I clearly don't think you're untouchable."

My face heats up, but he continues. "Two years ago, I was going through a lot. My father was putting pressure on me. I was watched constantly—by my father's hired thugs, by my classmates, by the media. I acted out partly to drown out the noises in my head, partly because I wanted to see how far I could push my father before he killed me. When I entered the Tower, I was told you were off-limits. By multiple people. Dr. Koga. Practically every scientist working on the project. My father. You were forbidden, and therefore, I had to have you."

I listen to his confession, hardly breathing.

"But you were nothing like I thought you'd be. More significantly, my reaction to you was unexpected. When I was with you, I felt joy. When we were apart, I longed for you. But most incredible to me was that when we were together, the noises in my mind were quiet. I don't think it was because of your powers. I think it was because I felt safe with you, in my mind and in my heart."

I squeeze his hands, feeling safe in my heart, if not wholly in my mind—not yet. There are so many obstacles for us to overcome before we can truly be together, perhaps more than we *can* overcome, considering all the forces working against us.

"Ama," Alex says after a brief silence, "there's something I want to ask you. Earlier you said, 'You knew how I once *might* have felt about you.' What did you mean by that?"

I hasten to brush it off. "It was nothing."

"I don't want any more obstacles between us, especially of our own making. Did you doubt my feelings for you?"

When I don't immediately respond, he scowls. "What is it? Tell me."

Slowly I disentangle my fingers from his. He tenses, instinctively tightening his hand, but then he lets go. I sit farther back on the bench, giving myself space to breathe and think.

"Ama?" Alex says, his expression clearly confused and hurt.

"The morning before the battle. At the school, when we were separated . . ." I trail off as he grimaces. That day is painful for him to remember too. I gather my breath. "When the guards were taking you away, I was desperate. I thought that we had a chance if we fought together. When you told me it was over, I didn't believe you. I thought you were lying in order to protect me. But then you—you *showed* me your thoughts, as clear as the sky was that morning."

Alex waits for me to finish, though his eyes burn with emotion.

"The mind doesn't lie, Alex. You weren't in love with me. For a time, you tricked yourself into believing you were because you wanted so much for it to be true. But in the end, it just—it just wasn't."

Even now, the memory of that morning hurts, when he'd swept back the storm clouds in his mind and I saw through them to the truth. I think it was the shock that hurt the most, of having all my dreams swept away. He didn't love me, his mind had come to realize. Desire wasn't love. Obsession wasn't love.

"Ama," Alex says, "the mind *does* lie. At least mine does. Even I don't know what I'm thinking every moment of the day. That morning, I was a wreck. My father had personally gone to the school to make an example of me. You were in danger. I had to get you away. I knew the only way I could convince you to leave me was to convince you that I didn't love you. And the only way to convince you that I didn't love you was to convince myself of it. Apparently it worked for you. It didn't work for me."

"Alex—" I reach for him, but he shakes his head.

"Hear me out a little longer." He takes a deep breath. "Sometimes I have some pretty terrible thoughts, but that doesn't mean I act on them, or that they last for more than a few seconds, drawn from some deep part of my mind rooted in darkness and some Freudian shit. I'm no angel, Ama. Far from it. My love for you will always be flawed. I'm jealous. I'm insecure. I'm selfish. I need you more than you'll ever need me. I know you have powers. But trust my word on this; trust *me* who is telling you now. I love you. I have always loved you. I will always love you."

I can't stop the tears from streaming down my face. I'm glad for the thick cotton shirt now, using the sleeve of it to wipe my eyes.

"Wait." Alex reaches into his back pocket and pulls out a silk handkerchief. "Here."

We both stare at the piece of cloth, suspended in the air between us.

"You've been kidnapped, you're a prisoner in an enemy encampment, and you have a handkerchief."

Alex frowns. "It's mulberry silk."

"We thought of taking it off him," a cheerful voice says from behind us, "but we allowed him some dignity." I look up to see Lee Jaewon approaching with a wide grin on his face. I jump to my feet, and his smile softens. "It's good to see you, Ama."

I've always liked Jaewon. Two years ago, he was the last person I spoke with before my transport carrier crashed in the Bohai Sea. He'd been aboard with me for a short while before disembarking at Neo Seoul's Tower, under arrest as a rebel. To think this handsome, gentle-souled boy was integral in the destruction of the Tower, and because of that, is high up on the list of the NSK's most wanted criminals. Of course to the rebels, he's proportionately as beloved as one of the rebellion's greatest freedom fighters.

"You did it," I marvel. "You managed to escape the Tower, and with Tera, too."

"I had help," he says warmly.

I blush. He's referring to how, before he'd left the transport carrier, I showed him the location of Tera's imprisonment through a telepathic link.

"I wouldn't have made it far without your help," Jaewon says. "Or yours, Alex. I always hoped to repay that debt in the future."

"I'm grateful for it," Alex says. "Thank you, Jaewon-ah." Jaewon scratches the back of his head, blushing like a schoolboy.

"Where's Tera?" I ask, looking past his shoulder.

He sighs, his smile replaced with a look of resignation. "Speaking with some visitors. In fact, that's why I came to get you. Do you know anyone by the name of Helen Li?"

"Yes," I say, sitting up. "Is she here? Where is she?"

"You better come quick. I think Tera might murder her in a fit of jealousy."

27

AMA & TERA

We leave the small garden and take an elevator to an upper floor that opens to a wide room with a huge glass window overlooking the mountain range.

The peaceful space is undercut by the tension in the room. Shun and Shiori look on as Helen faces off against a very irate Tera. Jaewon might have been exaggerating, but not by a lot.

"You should have known the risks of putting her back into the field," Tera is saying, her stance furious. Shun and Shiori have their hands at their waists, hovering over their concealed weapons. Helen appears calm. She meets Tera's gaze without flinching. "Kim Tae Woo was looking for a spy. More than that, he suspected the spy was Ama, whom he never could confirm died in the crash. He followed her trail to Neo Beijing and sent an assassin to finish her off."

I blink in surprise. This is news to me. Tsuko must have discovered who sent the assassin in Neo Beijing. What else did Tsuko and Tera speak of yesterday before she came to rescue me? Two years ago, they fought so bitterly.

"If it wasn't for Tsuko," Tera continues, "the former Director might have succeeded that night, as he would have yesterday." Alex tenses at the mention of Tsuko. "And don't lie and say you had a contingency plan in place to rescue her. If we weren't conveniently passing by, she would have never gotten out!"

Helen takes this criticism of her decisions in stride. Then, nodding, she says, "For that, I'm indebted to you. As the leader of my team, I feel responsible for Ama's safety and well-being. I am grateful to you for saving her. Please tell me if there's anything I can do to reward you for your service."

Tera sputters. "That's not—" She scowls. "I don't want anything!" Jaewon chokes with laughter he attempts to hide with a cough.

Helen notices my presence. "Ama!" She embraces me. "I'm so glad you're safe." Then she holds me at length, eyeing me up and down. "What are you wearing? You poor thing. I brought you your clothes as well as the rest of your belongings."

I blink at Helen, wondering at this change in her personality. She has always been kind, but never affectionate. Tera stands to the side, biting her lip, clearly jealous. Jaewon smiles ruefully, now looking sympathetic. I catch Helen's eye, and she smirks, and I realize she's fully aware of the stir she's causing.

"Ama," a low, flirtatious voice interjects. Shun steps forward with a grin. "I guess the wedding's called off." I'd almost forgotten about our covers. Before I can ask, Shun reassures me. "If you're worried about Wang Yunpeng, he's safe. He's claiming you brainwashed him. " He adds, with a wink, "Too bad I can't claim you brainwashed *me*."

I fear Jaewon will perish from laughter. Suddenly Alex is there, inserting his body between Shun and me. "That's right," he says, his voice at its most arrogant. "Part of your cover was that you were engaged. So this is the fiancé? You could do better."

Shun arches a brow. "Why aren't you in a cell somewhere?"

Jaewon looks around, eager. "Who's my counterpart?" He points at Shiori, who's been watching the proceedings with a gleeful expression. "You?"

"Now that everyone's relationships are established and clear to all," Helen says, "may we proceed with the more serious topic on our agenda, namely, the war?" Everyone nods, chastened. Even Tera seems to accept Helen's authority. After all, she is older, and well, she is Helen.

"Also . . ." Helen glances significantly at Alex, then at the rest of us. "I understand there's some trust and shared history between the four of you, but I'm afraid I don't have such assurances."

Jaewon nods, catching on quick. "I'll escort him back to the holding cell." To Alex he says in a lower voice, though all of us can hear, "You promised you'd cooperate if I allowed you to speak to Ama."

I can see the struggle playing out on Alex's face as his gaze moves from Shun to me, deciding whether his jealousy is worth breaking a promise. "Alex," I say, "I'll come find you later."

This seems to placate him, and the tension drains from his shoulders. "Follow me," Jaewon says. Alex hesitates, as if deciding something. Then, reaching out with one hand, he tugs me toward him and presses a kiss to my lips, quick but firm. He releases me and strides back toward the elevator alongside Jaewon.

Beet red, I turn to find Shiori and Shun gaping at me. "I totally underestimated your skills at seduction," Shiori says.

"I'd be jealous if I wasn't so impressed," Shun adds.

I'd forgotten this would be one of the complications that would arise when Alex's and my relationship was revealed, though perhaps more embarrassing for me and confusing to others than an actual problem, like the fact that Alex and I are on opposite sides of a war.

Helen appears unfazed. In fact, there's a little knowing smile at the edge of her lips that she quickly conceals when she notices me looking.

"I don't think it can get any clearer than that," Tera drawls, breaking the silence. She leads us to a long wooden conference table, and we take seats with PHNX opposite Tera and me, with an empty seat beside Tera left for Jaewon.

"Will others be joining us?" Helen asks.

"Oh Kangto is not on base at the moment," Tera answers. "He's meeting with the other rebel factions as we speak, including agents from PHNX. Jaewon and I represent the commander's interests when he's away."

Helen nods, then places her hands together on the table, her expression serious. "I'm afraid I didn't come here just to see you, Ama. Last night, PHNX operatives intercepted an alert from the NIC, where the members of the Neo Council were said to have met in an emergency session. The alert wasn't meant to be kept a secret for long—such a large movement of military vehicles, GMs, and personnel would not escape notice. They're mobilizing for war in an attempt to crush the rebellion, targeting all our bases along the coast as well as the villages known to harbor fugitives."

"But that transgresses the terms of the treaty!" Tera says. "How long do we have?"

"Two days."

"That doesn't give us time to evacuate the villages. I have to contact Oh Kangto immediately."

"My colleagues should have already informed him. The meeting of the rebel factions was in part to discuss what we should do if this very thing were to happen. I wouldn't expect Oh Kangto any time soon, not until all the rebel coalitions have reached an agreement."

Jaewon returns. As he pulls out a seat, Tera fills him in.

"Damn it," he says, leaning back in the chair. "We were afraid this might happen, but thought that the Alliance's fear of public backlash would prevent them from going through with it."

"There's more." Helen grimaces. "And it concerns you, Tera. And Ama. That is, it concerns all of us, but I believe you two would have particular insight." Her gaze fixes on Tera. "While en route to the NIC, we encountered two super soldiers on the train. The Alliance is planning to deploy them in the next battle."

Tera and Jaewon exchange a glance.

"One with Tera's capabilities, the other with Ama's. According to a trusted source involved in their development, they haven't completed the full trial; however, because of the unforeseen circumstances of the last battle . . ."

"Tsuko," I say. Of course. Now that Tsuko has, more or less, shown his hand in the game, the Alliance will want to neutralize him as a potential threat.

Helen nods. "The Alliance decided on their deployment despite the risks, the instability in their powers, their lack of discipline."

This changes everything. Tsuko appearing altered the course of the battle. Having two super soldiers, however untrained, fighting for the Alliance would be fatal to the rebellion.

Tera takes a deep breath. "The truth is, I wanted to fight in the June Solstice battle, but Oh Kangto and the other rebel leaders voted against it. Like with Tsuko, we knew that once the Alliance discovered that I was alive, that I was working for the rebellion against them, they'd stop at nothing to destroy me, regardless of the treaty. The Alliance's actions—breaking the treaty, mobilizing for a targeted attack against civilian towns and villages—show our fears were not unjustified."

It's ironic that the weapons the Alliance created to strike fear in the hearts of its enemies became that which it fears the most.

"For the past year, Jaewon and I have been searching for girls like Ama and me, those with powers, who are either still enmeshed in the project or have escaped it at some point and are in hiding. We were in the middle of returning from following one of these leads when we received Tsuko's distress call. We want to help these girls, give them shelter, freedom, *choices*. Whatever it takes to make them feel safe again."

Tera sits back in her seat, flushed. She looks to Jaewon, who gently squeezes her hand, then at me. I smile in return. My heart beats with pride for her.

She turns to Helen. "My involvement, however, no longer needs to be secret now that the Alliance has chosen to deploy super soldiers. I will confront them on the battlefield."

"We'll go together," I say. "Two of ours against two of theirs."

"No," Tera says immediately. "It's too dangerous."

I frown. "But Tera—"

"You'll stay here at the base where it's safest."

Helen looks between Tera and me but wisely chooses not to express her opinion. Pushing back from the table, she stands. "If you'll excuse me, I'd like to get some fresh air."

Jaewon quickly moves to escort her.

I stare at Tera's profile as she refuses to look at me. I understand that her protest comes not from a lack of faith in me, but from her fear of losing me.

"I survived for two years without you," I tell her quietly. "I've also faced off with both of these super soldiers before, alongside Shiori." Shiori gives a little salute. "I can handle myself."

"We're not speaking of this anymore," Tera says, her words clipped. "It's for your own good. Oh Kangto left me in charge, and my decision is final."

■ ■ ■

I love Tera, but right now, some distance between us is needed. Leaving her with Shiori and Shun, I follow in the direction Jaewon had taken Helen earlier, opening a heavy exit door into an outdoor stairwell, built into the side of the mountain. It overlooks the mist-filled valley, partially obscured beneath the colossal shadow of Oh Kangto's battleship currently docked against the side of the mountain.

As I walk outdoors, I hear Jaewon's low voice and Helen's throaty laughter in the landing below. "And then get this, Noona," Jaewon is saying, and somehow I'm not surprised he's already on such easy terms with Helen; Jaewon is honest and charming, and Helen falls into the role of older sister well. "She picked up the table and threw it across the room!"

It's rather easy to deduce he's telling a story about Tera. I cough to let my presence be known, and Jaewon looks up, a boyish grin spreading across his face. He bows slightly to Helen, then climbs the few steps to meet me. "I'll leave you two alone," he says.

As he leaves, a memory stirs, of the time I met Go Giwoo at the base. He said Alex chose him as a lieutenant because he "reminded him of someone he once knew." Now that I'm looking, the similarities are unmistakable. Like Giwoo, Jaewon was a part of Red Moon. They're both of Korean descent, dependable and inherently good-hearted. I wonder if Jaewon would be amused to know that he really does have a counterpart.

I walk the few steps down to the landing where Helen is waiting for me. The sun setting over the mountains limns her dark hair with shades of gold. I remember that first time I saw her up close, in my small apartment in Neo Beijing. She was standing by the window, and when I entered, she had turned to me. I wonder if I had sensed then how she would change my life.

Helen smiles with sympathy, misinterpreting the train of my thoughts. "Give Tera time, Ama. It's difficult to watch a younger sibling grow up and experience heartbreak and danger. As an older sibling, you want to protect them from the world. You want to carry their burdens upon your own shoulders."

She's speaking from experience. How difficult it must be for her, to knowingly put her younger brother into dangerous situations.

"But sometimes," she says with a sigh, "an older sibling has to step back, to let go." She smiles sadly. "I was actually never supposed to come here. The information I had was already being shared with the rebel leaders, Oh Kangto included, but I made excuses and came anyway because I wanted to see you. Unfortunately, we've stayed too long as it is."

"You're leaving?" I can't hide the dismay in my voice. "But you've only just gotten here."

"We're being recalled to PHNX headquarters. Our covers

were compromised when Wang Yunpeng's involvement was discovered. We all can't claim to be brainwashed," she says, gentling her words with a smile. "In any case, the mission for which we were sent to the NIC is complete, thanks to you. It's time to return and regroup. PHNX was never a combat unit, and so we won't be participating in the actual fighting. *When* the war is won, there will still be corruption to expose, people to save, small battles to be fought. That's where our future lies."

She takes my hand. "This is my official invitation to join us, should you wish to. There is always a place on our team for you."

I hold back a sob. "There's so much I want to tell you," I say, "how grateful I am that you invited me into your world, that you believed in me, that you trusted me." I blanch, realizing there is one thing I kept from her. "I never told you the truth about Alex, that I knew him even before he became our target."

I kept the truth from her because I didn't think she'd let me act as point if she knew, afraid she'd believe my past with Alex would cloud my judgment. Now I see it was selfish of me to risk the group like that. Had I not been able to manipulate Alex's perception of me, everything would have been ruined.

"Ama," Helen says quietly, "I knew."

I blink. "What?"

Sighing, she leans against the railing. "I was given your profile before we met. Your past relationships were included, with Tera and Tsuko. With Alex. When the identity of our target was revealed, I wondered myself if headquarters was aware of the position it was placing us in. I debated whether to tell you what I knew, but when you woke from your illness, you had this fire in your gaze, a fierce determination. I decided to see where it would take you."

"Did Shiori and Shun . . . ?"

"Only I knew. I trusted that you would do what you must to complete your mission. My only concern was the emotional toll. I can imagine it was difficult."

I sigh. An understatement if I've ever heard one.

"Though I must admit a reckless hope on my part that, should you ever reconcile, you would turn him to our side."

I remember the way the recruits looked to Alex in awe that first night on base, the way he led his troops into battle, the way he'd searched for Go Giwoo all night long and accepted money from Giwoo's grandmother. "Alex is honorable. He won't betray his soldiers."

"And you won't ask it of him. Ah, selfless love. The true enemy of the rebellion."

We both remain quiet as the sun, which has been peeking between the mountains, descends. Dusk settles over the valley. Helen gives me one last hug. "The items I brought you should have been delivered to your room. This is goodbye." She smiles. "For now."

"Give my love to Shun and Shiori."

"You'll see them again."

■ ■ ■

I gather my thoughts. For the first time since joining PHNX, I'm alone, obligated to no one. If I wanted, I could continue down that path Helen and the others had disrupted so long ago, fleeing to another city or village, hiding in anonymity. Or I can stay here on base, as Tera suggested, safe and protected.

I remember Tsuko asking me what I wanted—that rainy night in Neo Beijing. His question was the catalyst for joining PHNX. Do I know the answer now? I thought maybe it was Alex I wanted, and I did, I *do*, but in working alongside Helen, Shun, and Shiori, I found something I didn't even know I needed—purpose. I remember overhearing the shopkeepers in the old street market in Neo Beijing, who, after watching the footage that we'd broadcast from the labs, gathered to voice their opinions.

Spreading the truth, shedding light—I felt like I was making a difference.

It's ironic that I was created for a purpose similar to the one I pursue now. But that purpose was forced upon me. I didn't choose it—it wasn't *mine*.

I want to help people on my own terms. I want to help the people I love—Tera and Jaewon, Helen, Shun, and Shiori, even my supposed enemies at the base, Giwoo, Gayoung, Yuuki, and Fei Hong.

I want to protect Alex. I want to protect Tsuko.

I want to build a better world for all of them. For those shopkeepers on the street, those children in the Tower, and for myself, past and present; for my future, perhaps hazy and distant at the moment, with so many branching pathways—yet *certain* and full of hope for the first time in my life.

■ ■ ■

I return to the meeting room to find Tera and Jaewon sitting alone at the long conference table, their shadowy forms illuminated by the last rays of the setting sun. They sit on the same side, their chairs turned to face each other, Jaewon's knees on either side of Tera's.

I watch as Tera presses her hands to her face. "I just—I just don't want her to get hurt."

When Jaewon doesn't respond, Tera frowns. "You're not going to say anything? Usually this is the moment when you say one of your Jaewon-isms that are more annoying than wise."

Jaewon leans forward slightly, brushing aside a stray hair that had fallen across Tera's cheek. "Not tonight. I don't really have any insight. She's your sister. I just want you to be happy, so I'll listen and accept whatever decision you make."

There's a pause. "You're doing it again!"

Jaewon laughs, the sound open and light. The shadows make it so I can't see Tera's expression, but I can feel her mind grow warm, filled with bright, luminous colors—yellow, pink, and red. She leans in for a kiss.

I clear my throat. In a moment, Tera is out of the chair and in front of me. I blink at the sudden movement. "You could give someone whiplash."

Jaewon laughs. "Welcome to my world."

"I'm sorry for how I acted earlier." Blushing, Tera scratches her chin, a tell that she's nervous.

"You said you believed I was strong," I remind her gently.

318

"I do!" she says fervently. "I do believe you're strong. The idea of you in danger just frightens me. It always will." She sighs. "See? This is how you're strong, and I'm not. I am a mess thinking of all the things that could go wrong in battle, and you have faith in both of us."

"I'm not so strong," I say. "I worry about you. The decisions you must make as a soldier. The fact that, though your body is nigh unbreakable, the people you love aren't—Jaewon and me. I worry what would happen to you if anything should happen to us."

She grins. "I worry about your body, and you worry about my mind. We're quite a pair."

"We *are* a pair," I say. Then I remember that's not exactly true. "Tera, that morning when you saved me, was that the first time you'd spoken to Tsuko since the battle of Neo Seoul?"

She nods. "I was so shocked to hear from him. We didn't speak long. He told me how you were in danger, that he suspected his father knew you survived the crash and was behind the assassination attempt. What has he been doing for two years?"

I tell her everything Tsuko hopes to accomplish by interfering in the battles.

"He was always so reckless," she says when I've finished. "I could never predict what he'll do next."

Tera and I both stew in our thoughts. Later we walk over to the table to find Jaewon, his arms pillowing his head, fast asleep.

28

AMA AND ALEX

Though Tera and Jaewon both vouch for Alex's willingness to cooperate, a direct order from Oh Kangto arrives that can't be overruled: Alex is to be jailed until his return and kept under constant supervision, as is required of any high-level hostage. I fall asleep in Tera's bed, only to wake in the morning with a vicious headache. Tera is gone. When I knock on Jaewon's door across the hall, no one answers.

My head pounds as if there is a vise around my mind, clamping shut. I've felt pain like this before, back on the base.

Tsuko is here.

Like before, I follow the pain to its source, racing through the halls and out into the atrium. It's crowded with more people than were present the day before. Oh Kangto must have returned, the rebel factions having finally reached a decision on how to counteract the Alliance's threat.

I enter the elevator and close my eyes, the pressure behind them mounting the higher I go. When it seems to reach a pinnacle, I press the emergency STOP button. The doors to the elevator open to an aircraft bay. Tera is standing right outside, poised to get on.

"Ama!" she shouts, her voice muted from the wind whistling through the opening in the mountain.

I try to make sense of what I'm seeing. Oh Kangto has arrived. I recognize the leader of the UKL from the news reports, a handsome man in his late sixties. Two years ago he'd been captured and tortured in the Tower, and he now wears the mark of that time in a scar across his face. Beside him are Kim Tae Woo and two armed guards. The former Director of the NSK peers at his surroundings, not attempting to hide his disdain.

"They just arrived," Tera informs me. "I was coming directly to get you."

"What's going on?" I ask.

Tera bites her lip, clearly worried. "I don't know. I haven't had a chance to talk to Oh Kangto. He was supposed to return from the meeting of the rebel coalitions this morning, but *alone*, not with the former Director of the NSK. Something isn't right."

The elevator pings behind me. Alex strides forward, his hands tied behind his back, with Jaewon escorting him.

"What are you doing here?" Tera hisses.

Jaewon frowns. "Oh Kangto called in five minutes ago. He ordered me to bring Alex to the bay."

"Is this a hostage negotiation?" Tera asks. But that can't be right. If Kim Tae Woo was promising money in exchange for Alex, then the negotiations should have taken place on neutral ground, not in the heart of the UKL base.

Alex catches sight of me, his eyes widening slightly. Then his gaze strays over my shoulder to where his father stands. Maybe it's the waves of energy eroding the barriers in my mind, but I'm struck with a flurry of thoughts—surprise at his father's appearance, worry for me, frustration that he's so powerless, and beneath it all, panic and fury. If Tera can give me whiplash with her movements, Alex can give it to me with his mind.

There's no time to speak. Having noticed Alex's arrival, Oh Kangto calls Jaewon over.

I look around the room for Tsuko, but the energy is so thick here, it's difficult to pinpoint the source. Tera takes my hand with a squeeze, and together we follow behind Alex and Jaewon.

The Director's eyes narrow at Alex's approach. "Are you all right, son?" he asks. "Did they harm you?" His concern is genuine, though ironic. The rebels have treated Alex far more gently than he ever did.

Then his eyes alight on Tera and me. His voice grows chilly. "We spent billions on a project, only to hand the results over to the rebels for free."

Jaewon tenses, but Tera steps forward, all grace and fury. "I congratulate you on a job well done." She opens one fist, then closes it. "Would you like a demonstration of what I can do?"

The Director scowls. "You should keep your children on a tighter leash, Kangto-ssi. Independence breeds disobedience."

Tera and Jaewon wait expectantly for Oh Kangto's response, but he remains silent. They exchange a look. Apparently Oh Kangto is not one to take unwarranted criticism of his "children."

"What's going on, Commander?" Jaewon asks. "Why is Kim Tae Woo here?"

Oh Kangto appears slack-jawed. Then he glances at the people gathering around us in the hangar—engineers and other rebels. He smiles, nervous, like a child.

"Ajeossi?" Jaewon presses softly.

Another psychic wave hits me. Through the pain, I can sense a thread of power winding around Oh Kangto's mind like a cage.

"It's a trap," I gasp. "Oh Kangto's mind is being controlled."

Tera turns feral, eyes sparking green.

The Director grabs Oh Kangto's arm. "You sign his death warrant by killing me." He glances over his shoulder. "Ama?"

Everyone blinks, confused for a moment. One of the two guards steps forward. Then the pressure in my mind recedes, and where once a woman stood now stands the girl from the train.

The other Ama wears the Helm, which explains the reach of her powers. Yet even though she's dropped the illusion, my head still throbs with pain.

Beneath the Helm, the other Ama's eyes meet mine, and a flash of triumph spreads across her features.

She believes she's won the competition between us, which is regrettable. Wouldn't it be more to our benefit to be friends and allies, rather than supporting the agenda of a selfish man?

"I was content to discover the location of the rebel base and retrieve my son," the Director says. His gaze snaps to me. "But you've been a thorn in my side for the past two years. If an assassin can't kill you, then I'll do it myself." Reaching out, he snatches the gun from Ama.

Before anyone can react, the remaining guard moves in behind him, raising their gun to the back of the Director's neck. The pressure I'd been feeling finally disappears entirely.

"You might tighten the leash, Father," Tsuko says quietly, "but I assure you, I will break it."

The other Ama gapes at Tsuko. She must have not have noticed his presence, concentrating as she was on maintaining her own illusion and controlling Oh Kangto's mind.

"You won't kill your own father," the Director seethes.

"Perhaps not, but you can't say that for sure."

"I call your bluff."

It all happens in the blink of an eye. The Director's gun goes off, and the bullet meant for me hits Tera, who jumps in front of it, taking it in the shoulder. Jaewon tackles the Director, but not before the Director twists around to release another bullet, this time aimed at Oh Kangto. Alex, anticipating his father's move, knocks the commander to the ground, and the bullet whizzes above them.

I approach the other Ama, waiting for an attack, remembering the list of skills from her file. But nothing comes, and I notice she is trembling. With gentleness, I lift the Helm from her head. She looks up at me with tears in her large brown eyes. She can't be older than fifteen. "You're not my enemy," I tell her.

I feel a body crouching beside me. For a moment, I completely forget about the other Ama. "Tera! You're bleeding."

She shrugs.

"You saved my life *again*."

"Of course I did. I'm the Tera to your Ama." She grins, and I smile at her in return.

When we look back at the other Ama, she's staring at us. "My— My Tera," she whispers. "I don't know where she is."

Tera holds out her hand, and the other Ama takes it. "We'll find her. I promise."

Behind us, Jaewon has finished securing the Director with electro-braces. Oh Kangto shakes his head as if to clear out the last dregs of befuddlement. "Somebody better fill me in quick," he says. "We have a war to fight."

Then I realize that not everyone is here.

Tsuko and Alex are gone.

■ ■ ■

Oh Kangto's words spur everyone into action. The pilots and engineers in the bay who have been watching from a distance hurry forward to escort the Director away. Jaewon and Tera supervise the transport of the other Ama.

I slip away in the chaos, following the trail of muddled minds.

I don't know what Alex will do now that he finally knows the truth—that not only does he have a brother, but that his brother is *Tsuko*, someone who has tried to kill him in the past, someone whom he has tried to kill. At the back of the hangar, I catch the sound of their voices. Tsuko is halfway up the boarding steps of a small military aircraft, with Alex standing below.

"I didn't know," Alex says.

Tsuko shakes his head. "It doesn't matter. It changes nothing."

"It changes everything!" Alex places one foot on the step, and Tsuko tenses. "What were you doing here? Were you planning on—" Alex swallows. "Were you planning on killing our father?"

"He's not my father."

"Why are you making this so difficult?" Tsuko and I both flinch at the intensity of Alex's emotions—confusion, hurt, and regret.

"Because," Tsuko says, "sharing a father like ours doesn't make us family, it just makes us cursed."

Alex says nothing for so long, I don't think he'll speak. Then, "I'm sorry."

Tsuko turns, eyes flashing. "Don't be. There's no reason for you to be. Nothing has changed!"

"For you, perhaps. But for me, I didn't know our father had another child. I didn't *know* that I had a brother who is younger than me, who was being abused like me, though in a different way. I should have been there to protect you."

"I can protect myself."

"That's true," Alex says with a self-mocking grin. "But it's strange. You say that you don't want a brother and that nothing has changed, and yet I can't say the same." With these parting words, Alex takes his leave. When he's far enough away, I step into view.

Tsuko practically groans. "I have to go."

"Su, please."

"I don't want to be tragic, Ama. I don't want you to think I'm sad or hurt or angry, and I don't want to be comforted. Sometimes I just want to be alone."

It's the closest Tsuko has ever come to expressing his feelings to me. I swallow my need to *talk* and move back. He closes the hatch, and the boarding steps retract into the aircraft. There's a shout as the small aircraft rolls onto the flight deck, gaining speed and taking off through the opening in the mountain. A few rebels sprint to their aircrafts, intent on following, but by then, Tsuko is already too far gone.

■ ■ ■

I return to find Oh Kangto has called the entire rebel base to the atrium. I search the crowd for Alex, but he's nowhere in sight. Standing on an elevated platform at the back, with Tera and Jaewon flanking him on either side, Oh Kangto addresses the gathering. "Tomorrow morning the Alliance forces are planning an all-out strike against our bases on the coast of South China."

There are a few gasps in the crowd—those who hadn't yet heard—and murmurs of anger and fear.

"We're evacuating the surrounding villages as we speak," Oh Kangto continues, "but the area is vast. And the truth is, to run now is to lose the war. We need to move the stage of the battle to one of our own choosing."

"How?" someone shouts from the crowd.

"By using the Ko Cannon. During the battle of Neo Seoul, the Ko Cannon destroyed the Tower, which inversely destroyed the system of the cannon. It has taken two years to repair. It's stronger than it was before. In effect, it has the power to wipe out an entire city."

"You're going to threaten a city to stop the battle," Jaewon says in understanding. "Have you decided which city to target? It has to be a city the Neo Council values."

The names of cities are put forth. Neo Tokyo. Neo Beijing. Neo Shanghai.

Oh Kangto shakes his head wearily. "I won't ever threaten a historic city again. It almost killed me to hurt my beloved Seoul, though I felt the destruction of the Tower was necessary. No, I will not target any city built for the people."

"The NIC," Tera says, her bold voice carrying. "You're going to target the city built for the Council."

"I'm afraid so. Because of the power needed to expend that amount of energy, it needs to be situated over its intended target with a charge time of sixty minutes. And it can't be stopped once it's begun."

The atrium is quiet as this information sinks in. Like the Alliance, we'll be destroying a city with a high civilian population.

"Will there be a warning given?" Jaewon asks into the silence.

"Two hours before we arrive, we will warn the Alliance that unless it withdraws its attack upon civilian villages, we'll unleash the cannon upon the city. That gives it a total of three hours to evacuate, should it fail to accept our terms."

"So if the warning is given at 0600 hours," Jaewon says, "then at 0900, if the worst should happen, the NIC will be destroyed."

Oh Kangto nods grimly.

"They'll send all their forces against the battleship," Tera says. "It's possible that the Alliance will destroy the ship before it can release the cannon."

"It's a risk I'm willing to take. We'll have to defend the battleship for the hour it takes to charge the cannon, and it's uncertain whether our rebel brothers- and sisters-in-arms will join us. This is a bold move, and the UKL will carry most of the weight. But this is not an autocracy, and I would have you express your opinions now."

No one says a word, and curious, I brush over their thoughts to see that though some rebels doubt and some worry, their minds match Oh Kangto's decision.

"You've all worked hard. I am proud to call you comrades and friends. Make your final preparations for battle. We leave tomorrow morning at 0500."

■ ■ ■

I discover from Jaewon that Alex was brought to a separate chamber by order of Oh Kangto. He might not completely trust Alex, but he's still thankful to Alex for having helped save his life.

A sleepy-eyed guard lets me through the door into a small chamber with a single bed and a door leading into a bathroom. I can hear the sound of the shower running.

A window at the far wall looks out over the valley, now wreathed in twilight. In less than eight hours, this entire base, every soldier willing to fight, will fly south to defend the battleship against the forces of the Alliance. The conclusion is not foregone. Even if the Alliance should accept the terms of the cease-fire, what's to stop them from attacking the next day or the next? Regardless, the rebels will keep on fighting, even for a tomorrow that was never promised.

I hear the door to the bathroom open and close. A few seconds later, Alex's arm circles around me. I lean back into his embrace. We stand like that, gazing out as the sun sets over the mountains.

"I'm sorry I didn't tell you about Su," I say softly. "I found out years ago through a brief glimpse into his mind. It was not something he ever intended for me to see. I didn't think it was my place to tell you. I hoped he would tell you himself."

Alex is quiet for a moment, and I'm careful not to peek into his thoughts. "I don't blame you or . . . him. I blame my father for not telling me, for subjecting Tsuko to the project, and then for brainwashing him at a young age to kill. No, I don't blame him or you." His hand tightens on my waist, and I turn to face him. "He might not be a brother to me, not yet, but I'm willing to try."

I wrap my arms around his neck. "I'm so glad to hear that, because he *is* like a brother to me."

"You should tell him that," Alex mutters.

I pretend not to hear.

"I was there for Oh Kangto's speech," Alex says, changing the subject. "It's a good plan, though unlikely to work. The Alliance won't accept those terms."

"Are you all right?" I ask softly. "You won't be there to fight beside your soldiers."

"They'll be fine." He looks away. "I trust them to act on what they believe is right."

I nod, though I feel tightness in my chest at the thought of facing Giwoo or Gayoung on the battlefield.

"Ama," Alex asks, "are you reading my mind?"

I blink. "No! While I was undercover, I did read your mind, I even manipulated it, but I swear—"

"That's not why I was asking. I just wanted to tell you something. Not with my thoughts, which admittedly are chaotic right now, but with my words."

I bite my lip. "All right."

"I love you, but more than that, I trust you."

"And I trust you!" I say. "I've changed in these past two years. I don't need to look into your mind to know your heart. Moreover, I don't have to look into your mind to know *my* heart." I lean into him. "You were right what you said before, that the mind doesn't always express the heart, nor is the mind static, but ever changing—that's what makes each individual so unique. We can learn, we can grow, and we can change.

'What I wish for most after tomorrow's battle is that people can open their minds, seek new avenues for old problems, ask questions; that they can look at their friends *and* their enemies and realize that every person in the world has a mind that dreams and a heart that aches."

I realize my passion has carried me away a bit. I blush.

But Alex's expression is serious. "I've never heard you speak about the future. The world needs a leader like you."

I shake my head. "*You're* the leader. You command the respect of everyone on your base. You've led them to victory in battle."

"I'm a good soldier," Alex admits. "But a world striving for peace doesn't need soldiers. And the truth is, I don't have your conviction." He gently takes my face in his hand, his thumb brushing over the arc of my cheek. "The difference between you and me, besides the obvious, is that I don't care if a person has a world inside them. I don't care about the stranger on the street, or even my own father. I don't give a damn. My heart aches only for you."

Alex kisses me as if he wants to have a hundred thousand tomorrows, and for tonight, it's enough.

29

THE FINAL BATTLE

I wake to an empty bed and a sinking feeling of where Alex might have gone. My suspicions are confirmed when I find the guard outside slumped on the floor, unconscious. Luckily, I don't have to break the news to Tera and Jaewon. In the dim light of the aircraft bay, the night peeking through the opening of the mountain, both of them appear exhausted.

"He stole a service GM not a half hour ago," Jaewon informs me. "It's been so hectic here, no one realized what was happening until it was too late."

"Shouldn't we leave now?" Tera asks. "It won't be much longer before he alerts the Alliance of our plan."

Jaewon frowns. "Alex wouldn't do that. He's probably gone back to warn his people."

Tera bites her lip and looks at me, and I can feel the doubt in her mind.

I feel it too, like a coal lodged deep inside me, sickening my heart. Then I remember Alex's words. *I love you, but more than that, I trust you.* Was he trying to tell me then that he would do something that would make me need to believe in him, to trust him?

Oh Kangto's voice rumbles through the speaker system above: ***All military personnel to battle stations. We depart in fifteen minutes at 0500.***

"Come," Tera says, grabbing my hand. "I want to show you something." She leads me back down the elevator, through the atrium crowded with friends and families saying goodbye, perhaps for the last time. I tighten my grip on her hand. We maneuver down a packed tunnel that opens into a wide valley where GMs are lined up in rows beneath the shadow of the UKL's colossal battleship. More GMs are being rolled up a ramp into the GM hangar beneath the ship. Temporary lifts for boarding are set at the side of the ship, and Tera and I take one of these. I rest my head on her shoulder as we make our way up.

Inside, the ship bustles with activity, crew members running down the long halls to their stations. We pass a short corridor leading to the bridge, where Oh Kangto will command the ship during the battle, as well as a medical bay and engine room. The hall opens to the central core of the ship where the nuclear reactor of the Ko Cannon is located, currently dark with inactivity. In a few hours it will be sparking with enough atomic energy to wipe out an entire city.

From the central core of the ship, we enter another long hallway lined with hundreds of escape pods. Tera presses open a door to a small chamber, where she grabs a piloting suit off a rack and hands it to me.

I put it on over the clothing I wore the night before. "Once we take off, how long until arrival at the NIC?"

"Three hours, give or take a few minutes."

I swallow thickly. Alex won't have made it back to base by the time Oh Kangto issues the warning, unless he used the communication system in his GM to contact Giwoo and the others.

I trust you.

I shake away the doubt.

Now suited up, we take a lift down into the bowels of the ship to a massive hangar. GMs are lined up in rows, metal walkways positioned at chest level for easy boarding.

"Tera!" a woman calls from above, leaning over the railing of a metal walkway. We quickly climb the stairs and join her in front of a massive barrel-chested GM.

"This is Dr. Kim," Tera says, introducing me to the smart-looking woman with brown skin and graceful white hair. "She's the engineer and machinist who designed the Ko Cannon as well as the one who trained Dr. Chung, the lead machinist at Neo Seoul's Tower."

I bow, and Dr. Kim smiles approvingly. "Let me show you both what I've been working on all night."

She pulls a latch on the side of the GM, and the chest opens, revealing the piloting cockpit. She ushers us inside. I'm surprised to find two seats in the narrow space, situated back-to-back.

"Yesterday Tera came to me with a challenge," Dr. Kim

explains. "A way for you to use your powers amid a GM battle. Taking inspiration from Tera's own GM, the Extension, which hooks up with her brain waves to act as an extension of her body, I managed to implement a similar system here with the use of the recently acquired Helm."

I gape at Tera, who grins. "The other Ama won't be needing it. I thought, what better way to put it to use than for *you* to use it in battle?"

With the other Ama secure for the moment, watched by a guard wearing Alex's borrowed protective band, I had thought Tera might push home her point from earlier, that I shouldn't fight in the battle, as my specific skills are no longer needed. Instead, Tera has not only accepted that I'll fight, but figured out a way to *help* me utilize my powers.

Tears spark in my eyes. I'm overwhelmed by her belief in me.

"This GM is an old model," Dr. Kim continues, ever the mechanic, more interested in the GM than my emotional outpouring. "It never made it out of the prototype stage because it was too expensive to mass-produce. However, in implementing the Helm, I realized I needed a GM with a large enough computer to account for the massive output of power. This GM was the only one we had on base that could offer that support."

"Thank you," I gush. "You've given me the wings to fly."

Dr. Kim laughs, pointing at me. "I like her."

"And I'll be in the Extension," Tera says. "Watching your back. Honestly, I feel bad for the Alliance." She grins. "They won't know what hit 'em."

■ ■ ■

The forces of the UKL take off at exactly 0500. An hour later, at 0600, Oh Kangto issues a warning to the Alliance from the bridge: ***Adhere to the treaty and cease the attack on the rebel bases. Failing to do so will result in a launch by the Ko Cannon over the NIC at 0900.***

Now we wait.

"Alex didn't tip off the Alliance," Jaewon says, sitting back in his seat in the commanders' lounge. "Otherwise their retaliatory force would have reached us by now."

"That could be because the communication system in his GM was broken," Tera says, careful not to look at me. "We can't put our trust in him yet."

I scowl, but she has every right to doubt Alex. She doesn't have the history that Jaewon and I have with him.

In tense silence, we monitor the screens set up in the lounge, those showing the real-time view from the bridge, but also the reports coming in from all the major cities of the Pacific—Neo Beijing, Neo Tokyo, Neo Seoul, and even the NIC. They all paint the UKL as a group without honor, not exposing the full story—that the Alliance was the first to break the treaty.

Then, a half hour before arrival, we make our way back to the GM hangar.

Oh Kangto issues a command from the bridge: ***All GMs stand down until arrival at Neo International City.***

"The ship has combat capability," Tera explains, "and the shields themselves were constructed to withstand heavy gunfire."

Fifteen minutes out, the first of the Alliance's retaliatory force reaches us. I buckle into my GM, holding on tight as the assault begins. Loud shakes and booms reverberate through the hangar, though as Oh Kangto assured us, the shields hold. Inside my GM, I switch on the monitors; as expected, it's linked to the bridge of the battleship, where through the main view I can see the force the Alliance sent to stop us. About five hundred GMs approach, supported by fighter jets and bombers that swoop in, pummeling the ship with short-range missiles.

I recognize the black-and-white colors of the main Alliance forces with a few dots of color to denote special GMs. If Alex, Gayoung, or Giwoo are within their ranks, I see no sign of them.

The battleship pushes forward.

Tera switches on the video link between our GMs. She appears on my bottom right screen, seated in the cockpit of the Extension, fingers thrumming the control board. Another loud boom shakes the hangar, and she winces. "I don't know if we'll last at this rate."

"Our outer shields are down," Jaewon says, appearing on my bottom left screen. "We'll feel the bombs more now."

As if to demonstrate his words, a second explosion causes pieces of the hangar to detach from above, smattering metal shards across the GMs below.

"I've had enough of waiting," Tera says. "Flight control, ready the hatch for launch."

"Affirmative," the flight deck officer responds.

"Wait," Jaewon calls out, "the Alliance's formation just broke up. They're being attacked."

I quickly revert back to the main camera. A black GM cuts through the squadron, leaving destruction in its wake.

"Su!" Tera and I shout together. We don't have time to rejoice. The Alliance must have been prepared for his interference. They quickly regroup, surrounding him from all directions and unleashing a storm of artillery. When he attempts to escape, he's stopped by the sudden barrage of an unidentified GM, moving at an incredible speed, its design familiar, sleek, almost skeletal compared to the more massive mobile machines.

"It's an Extension," Tera breathes. "It's exactly the same as mine."

The other Tera pounds the Shi with bullets, moving at a speed faster than humanly possible.

"Tera," I say. She doesn't react at first, too caught up in witnessing her powers in another human being. "Tera! Su needs us."

She blinks, startled, then nods, a look of determination, of anticipation, in her eyes.

Oh Kangto's voice bellows from the bridge: *All units ready for launch!*

I ignite my thrusters and lower the Helm.

The floor drops from beneath me. For a moment it's free fall, my stomach lurching as the GM pitches through the air, but then my thrusters beat back the wind, steadying my flight. Tera appears in front of me, her Extension all sharp edges, glittering and dangerous. "Let's go."

Together we speed through the sky. Enemy GMs attempt to block our path, but Tera easily dispatches them. The GMs drop from the sky, the pilots ejecting and parachuting to the sea below, to the city below. We're directly above the NIC.

The Alliance has failed to accept the terms of the cease-fire. A loud groan erupts from the battleship as the Ko Cannon begins to charge. 0800. The countdown clock has begun.

All around us the UKL forces meet the Alliance forces in battle. Tera pivots and zooms around the side of the ship, with me following in pursuit. During the Solstice battle, I'd mostly watched from afar with the snipers, but now I'm in the thick of it, dodging melee attacks and taking bullets against my outer shield. A few GMs come within range, targeting me, and I reach out with my mind, the Helm augmenting the reach of my powers tenfold. Grabbing hold of the pilots, I slip them into unconsciousness.

When I refocus, I realize I'm barreling toward the city, having lost control of my GM while under. Before I hit the Dome over the city, a GM zooms in, catching me by the arm.

"And that was a problem we failed to consider," Jaewon says from the GM, breathless.

"What was that?" Tera asks, appearing on my screen. "Ama, are you all right?"

"I'm fine," I answer. "Just not used to piloting and using the Helm at the same time. Did you find Su?"

"He and the other Tera have left the main battlefield. They're right above the NIC base."

Jaewon and I fly east of the city to join Tera. Tsuko and the other Tera are engaged in a furious battle, at speeds impossible to follow. They would be evenly matched if it weren't for the damage the Shi had taken in the initial assault. The other Tera manages to sweep in close, jamming a blade though the Shi's chest.

"No!" Tera screams. The other Tera removes the blade, and the Shi drops into the sea, sinking beneath the waves. I quickly reach out with my mind and latch onto Su's. He's alive, though his GM is nonfunctional.

Tera races into the fight, with Jaewon providing backup, and soon the other Tera is falling back to the base, unable to withstand their joint assault. She barely lands before Tera slams her into the ground. A dust cloud erupts from the base, which seems abandoned on closer inspection. Where has everyone gone—Alex, Giwoo, Gayoung, Yuuki, and Fei Hong? I didn't see their GMs in the initial assault.

Tera manages to finally pin the other Tera down, jamming her blade into the Extension's engine.

"I'll die before I surrender!" the other Tera shouts, her young face appearing on my screen, the same I'd seen on the train all those months ago.

We don't have time for this. A glance at the clock shows that only a half hour remains before the Ko Cannon is set to destroy the city and everything within a five-kilometer radius.

I fly in close and reach for her thoughts, hitting her with an image that she can't deny—the other Ama looking up at us with hope. *My Tera*, she had said. And our Tera answering back, *We'll find her*. Still, due to what might be a personality trait of *all* Teras, this one won't give up, stubbornly resisting me. Through the screen, I can see her hand darting toward the self-destruct button. Like the pilots before, I grab her mind and slip her into unconsciousness.

"God." Tera scowls. "She's so headstrong. Am *I* like that?"

Jaewon and I both say, "Yes."

Together, Tera and I manage to get the other Tera's GM on the back of Jaewon's. "I'll take her to the other Ama," Jaewon says. "She'll start to heal once she sees we haven't harmed her." He looks as if he'll say more, but holds his tongue. It's not good-bye if you don't say it.

Once they're gone, Tera and I take to the sky, intent on joining the battle.

My heat sensor beeps a warning just as a beam of light erupts from the western side of the base.

Tera is quick to react, pushing me to the side as the beam slices between us, mere centimeters from making contact.

There's a drop of silence, and then . . .

"Ah," a familiar voice drawls through my comm. "I missed."

Giwoo.

A second GM whirls into view, bright red and patched with recent repairs. "Another super soldier?" Gayoung scoffs. "I earned my skill through hard work and training. What did you do for yours?"

Tera responds, deadpan, "I endured years of torture and the deaths of most everyone I knew."

"Damn," Gayoung says. "Sorry I asked."

"Giwoo-yah, Gayoung-ah," I call. "It's me. Jangmi."

"The traitor, you mean?" Gayoung mocks, though she can't hide the hurt in her voice.

Giwoo is slow to respond, but then his face appears on my screen, studying me through the monitor. "I'm glad you're all right," he says finally. "I was worried."

"And Alex?"

"You don't know? It's all over the news."

I quickly switch on the coverage of the battle, unsure of what I'm seeing.

Giwoo fills me in. "An hour ago, Alex arrived back on base and ordered all units to the NIC to help get the citizens out of range of the cannon. We were in the middle of evacuations when the Dome closed prematurely, leaving thousands of people still trapped inside, including Alex."

My heart leaps into my throat.

"But the Dome isn't strong enough to withstand a direct hit from the cannon," Tera says. "The Council won't risk their own lives. They witnessed the cannon's destruction during the Battle of Neo Seoul. It's even more powerful now than it was then."

"The Council members are not in the city," Giwoo says. "They were the first to flee."

Shocked silence follows this statement. "They left everyone behind to die?" I whisper.

"In the narrative they'll spin afterward," Tera says grimly, "Oh Kangto will be the villain. It'll draw us even deeper into war."

"But the worst of it is," Gayoung says, a sob in her throat, "they've branded Alex a traitor. He went against the direct orders of the Council by commanding his soldiers to abandon their posts to evacuate the civilians. He's a hero, but instead, he'll be remembered as a traitor."

"Ama," Tera says, "I need to warn Oh Kangto of these developments. He wouldn't have imagined the Alliance would abandon its people like this. Maybe there's a way he can stop the cannon."

"Go. Hurry," I say. She flies off in the Extension at break-neck speed.

"Is there anything we can do?" Giwoo asks, staring at me from the bottom left screen. "We want to help." On the right screen, Gayoung nods in agreement, wiping the tears from her eyes.

"Your commander gave you orders to evacuate the people," I say. "There are soldiers in the water, those who ejected from their God Machines. When the cannon hits, it'll have a blast radius of five kilometers. Make sure everyone is outside the vicinity."

"Roger that," Gayoung says, saluting me.

"Mission accepted." Giwoo grins. They take off in separate directions.

As for me, I am going to save Alex and the city, and there's only one person in the world who can help me.

30

AMA

For the second time in a week, I find Tsuko on an island. I'm relieved to find no visible wounds on him, though his eyes are closed and his head rests gently against the trunk of a palm tree.

He looks up at my approach. "Ama."

"I need your help, Su."

He shakes his head slowly. "I'm tired, Ama. Let me rest for a bit."

"Alex is in danger." He scowls. "That woke you up."

"What do you want from me?" He blinks against the sunlight. "If you hadn't noticed, my GM is at the bottom of the Pacific."

"I have a GM. You can use mine."

"You'd trust me not to just leave the battlefield?"

"I would," I say. "But don't worry, you won't be tested. I'm going to go with you."

He frowns. "I don't understand."

"Let me show you."

Tsuko's eyes narrow with suspicion, but he relents and follows me to the GM.

"Look," I say, stepping inside. "You sit here." I point to the front seat. "And I sit at your back. You'll do the fighting and the piloting, and I'll . . . think really hard." I tap the Helm. "We have to go, Su. There's not much time. Alex needs us."

"You keep saying his name as if it'll make a difference." Tsuko belies his words when he takes a seat, his movements assured. The GM lifts into the sky. Above us, the Ko Cannon sighting light appears over the city like a heavenly pillar. Tsuko and I fly through its glittering illumination.

An Alliance GM approaches fast, and Tsuko takes aim and shoots—right through its engine. Before it crashes into the sea, the pilot ejects from the GM.

Sweeping the gun in a practiced motion, Tsuko shoots four, five, six more GMs out of the sky, always careful to destroy the engines, not the pilots. Taking notice, several Alliance GMs break away from the Dome in pursuit. Tsuko dispatches them all.

I hold my breath. He hasn't killed a single one.

"I do believe the end still justifies the means," he says, a little defensively. "Though since I am strong enough to save a life when it would be easier to kill, maybe that should mean something."

08:55.

"Bring us above the Dome, Su."

The Ko cannon begins to crackle with energy, signaling its imminent release. The Alliance troops have mostly dispersed, except for those flying the colors of the NIC base, who are still retrieving pilots from the water at Giwoo's and Gayoung's direction. I see the bright colors of Fei Hong's and Yuuki's GMs. The Dome has gone opaque, a sign of strengthening its barrier. Alex is inside somewhere. As are so many others, innocent people abandoned by the Council.

Our screens flicker, and a broadcast begins, transmitting to all the telecommunication devices in the vicinity, possibly all of Asia.

Oh Kangto appears on the bridge of his battleship. He's alone, no sign of Tera. Has he figured out a way to stop the cannon?

Slowly, he bends his back in a deep bow. "Words cannot express my sorrow. My intent today was never to threaten civilian life but to destroy an empty city. There were other factors at play, as there always are . . ." He's referring to the Alliance orders to attack all the rebel bases. "But the fact of the matter is that I hold a very terrible weapon in my power, which I've severely mishandled. I won't ask for your forgiveness."

08:58.

"I've realized that destruction is not always the answer. While it is glorious to be a phoenix and rise from the ashes, it is perhaps more practical to be a magpie that gathers sticks and string to make a home for its children. It has taken me sixty-eight years to reach this revelation. I share it with you now in hope of a better future for all."

"Why he is speaking as if he's going to die?" I ask.

"There's not enough time to stop the reactor," Tsuko says. "There's only one way to slow it down that has enough of a force to mitigate the energy of the cannon."

"He's going to self-detonate," I whisper.

"Indulge an old man before he goes. Remember the past, strive for a better future, and embrace the moment. I look forward to witnessing all that you are capable of."

He bows one last time. There's a brief moment of silence, and then the entire battleship implodes.

■ ■ ■

Even with the internal explosion, the energy of the beam still breaks through the ship, hitting the Dome. Though severely weakened, the beam is still powerful enough that cracks form across the Dome's surface.

I pull the Helm down over my head, following the heat of the beam to the place where it connects with the Dome. The energy shield has almost lost all power beneath the onslaught. Bracing myself, I add my own energy, augmented by the Helm, to the shield. Blazing heat consumes my mind. I scream and grip the arms of my seat, but I don't let go. I just need to hold on until the cannon's power depletes.

How long that might take, I don't know. Or if I can last until then.

The pain is unbearable. But so is the thought of failure. So many people I love are below me, still ceaseless in their efforts to save even a single life. I won't let them be hurt, and I won't let Oh Kangto's sacrifice go to waste.

Still, I feel my mind fading, my power breaking against the heat of the cannon. Then Tsuko takes my hand, sharing the burden. His thoughts flood into me, soothing and cool like summer rain. Together we withstand the heat until at last the beam fades. Pieces of the battleship fall in flaming shards from the sky, turning to ash as they make contact with the Dome.

They look like falling stars.

It's the last thought I have as Tsuko and I fall unconscious, our hands clasped together, never letting go.

EPILOGUE:

DREAMS OF
TOMORROW

6 months later

It's almost midnight by the time I reach Neo Beijing's starlight district, though I have no fear of the police—one of the first acts of the new Council was to abolish curfew. I pause on the stairs of the lounge and listen to the piano drifting up from the smoky depths.

I'm glad I slept on the eight-hour flight from the American Neo States, where I've been for the past three weeks working on a mission with PHNX. We're tasked with getting back cultural artifacts that were sold overseas illegally during the war. Helen was right. Even with the end of the war and the signing of a new Neo Charter giving autonomous rule to the states, corruption still exists, and injustices that were committed during the war must be put right.

Still, it's not a process that will happen overnight. After

completing our mission, Helen gave me a few weeks to myself before we start all over again with the next one.

I step lightly down the stairs. My heart soars with the knowledge that I'll be onstage again, with a microphone in my hand and a song in my heart.

Ren, the bartender, wipes down the counter at my approach. "You look like you're in need of a drink."

I laugh and press my hands to my cheeks, still chilled from the wind. "A champagne cocktail, please. Something tasty."

I move my gaze over the crowd, catching sight of Auntie, Mrs. Chen, and TingTing by the bar. They wave to me, but don't stand up out of politeness to the singer onstage, an elderly gentleman with a beautiful baritone.

Ren slides my drink across the counter. "It's on the house."

"Thank you!" He's placed a strawberry on the top. I dip the bright red fruit into the sparkling glass and bring it to my lips. It tastes sweet and fresh.

"What would I give to have half your enjoyment of things?"

I look down the counter to where Alex leans against the bar. He looks handsome in a black coat and jeans with his hair swept back, still wet from the snow. I realize I've never seen him in casual clothing before, only in uniforms or suits. He looks wonderful. I hide my admiration by taking a sip of champagne. His eyes follow the motion. "You should get a drink yourself," I say.

"Alas," he laments dramatically, "I have no money, having absconded from my duties to catch a last-minute flight to Neo Beijing." He smiles, a slow smile. "Anything for the music."

"For the music, sure," Ren scoffs.

I shift a little closer down the bar. "Well, as someone who recently received her paycheck, I could buy you a drink. What'll you have?"

"Whiskey, neat." He nods at Ren. "Thank you."

"If you kids are finished flirting," the bartender says, "I believe the lady has a song to sing."

Alex closes the distance between us. "You look beautiful." He places a kiss on my cheek. "I've missed you."

While I've been all over the world the past few months, he's been in Neo Seoul. After the events of the last battle, the Council's actions—abandoning the people and sacrificing them to prove an example—were condemned by the public; inversely, Alex's popularity grew after it was released that he'd disobeyed orders to protect the people. The newly elected Director of Neo Seoul offered Alex a position on her advisory board, and since then, he's been helping her pass new and progressive policies. As for the old Director, he and the rest of the Council members were forcibly removed from office.

I return Alex's kiss. "I missed you too." I pay for his drink and reach for my glass. "Sit where I can see you."

He nods at a table right in front of the stage with a single chair and bouquet of yellow roses.

I approach the stage and place my glass on the piano. Jimmy, the piano man, nods his head in greeting, trailing a scale in F major. "What'll it be tonight? A song of love, a song of hope . . . Ah!" He catches my expression. "A song of new beginnings."

I step up to the microphone and bring it to my lips. My gaze follows Alex as he makes his way from the bar to settle in the seat before the stage. I begin the song and let my feelings—of joy, of homecoming, of peace and hope—carry me through.

I had never thought a year ago as I sang on this same stage and longed for so many things that I would be back here again with so many of those dreams fulfilled.

I think of Tera and her own dream, how she and Jaewon are looking for more children who've been affected by the Amaterasu Project, helping them to escape and teaching them to control their powers. They're offering them the safety and security that Tera, Tsuko, and I never had.

Of course, even as some dreams are fulfilled, more arrive to take their place, the possibilities of the future infinite. There's still so much work to do with PHNX, in modifying and improving the Neo Charter, in bringing peace and unity to the Alliance. But also in seeing new things and exploring this world, experiencing all that it has to offer, with the people I love the most.

Here in the lounge, I can see their minds like stars in the night sky—TingTing's bright with joy for me, Alex's burning with love, and in the vast darkness, a muted yet constant star seated in the corner.

I sing for all of them because though I do believe every person in the world has a mind that dreams and a soul that aches, I can admit that perhaps a few mean more to me than the rest.

To all my friends who've changed my life for the better, who've taught me so much and held my hand in the darkness, who've given me hope and dreams of a better tomorrow, this song is for you.

ACKNOWLEDGMENTS

Though I wrote *Rebel Seoul* as a novel that could stand alone, I found myself wishing, as I neared the end, that I could tell Ama's story. I am so grateful that my publisher, Tu Books, gave me that chance. *Rogue Heart* is for every reader who ever wished their favorite side character got their own story.

To my brilliant editor, Stacy Whitman, friend and mentor: You have shaped this book into one I am incredibly proud of. To Lee & Low and the rest of the Tu Books team, with special thanks to Jalissa Corrie, Keilin Huang, and Hannah Ehrlich: I am forever grateful to have won the New Visions Award and been welcomed into this badass family of trailblazers.

To Elise McMullen-Ciotti and Shveta Thakrar, for making me look good.

The cover gods blessed me with artist Shane Rebenschied and designer Sheila Smallwood. Thank you for creating a front and back cover that captures perfectly the spirit of *Rogue Heart*.

To my agent, Patricia Nelson, champion and wisest of witches: Thank you for guiding my path and giving me the confidence to reach for the stars.

I remember first starting out on this journey and wishing, more than anything, for writer friends who could be true friends of the heart. I honestly thought it was an impossible dream. To the cult, for making this dream a reality: Alex Castellanos, Amanda Foody, Amanda Haas, Ashley Burdin, Christine Lynn Herman, Claribel Ortega, Erin Bay, Katy Rose Pool, Maddy Colis, Mara Fitzgerald, Melody Simpson, and Tara Sim. Akshaya Raman— It's hard for me to imagine a time without you, you've become such an important person in my life. Check your phone, I'm sure I sent you a text message. Meg RK—To find someone who truly understands me is a rare gift, and I found that in you. Janella Angeles—You are one of my favorite people in the world. Your words (and voice!) are music to my ears. Team Rocket for life. Kat Cho—cousin and friend. The title of Alex's #1 fangirl goes to you. Love you, cuz.

To the Sailor Scouts, Nafiza Azad and Karuna Riazi, incredible wordsmiths and sisters of my heart and soul: I admire and love you both. So many thanks to my friends from Lesley: Gabrielle Brabazon, Michelle Calero, Candice Iloh (my boo!), Devon Van Essen, and Stephanie Willing (my voice of calm and reason in the storm). As well as to my editor siblings: Supriya Kelkar and Olivia Abtahi.

Thank you to all my Las Vegas friends for the chats and café dates: Ashley Kim, Michelle Kim, Sonja Swanson, Veeda Bybee, Chelsea Sedoti, Elizabeth Kite, Daria Peoples-Riley, Lauren Rha, and Cynthia Mun. To the wedding crowd: Lucy Cheng, Michelle Thinh Santiago, Rosie Chen (thanks for the name!), Jenny Quach, Megan Hurtz, and Jennifer Lee. And to the many friends and peers who inspire me: Julie C. Dao, C. B. Lee, Lori M. Lee, Ellen Oh, Cindy Pon, David Slayton, Swati Teerdhala, and Andrea Wang.

A huge thanks to the librarians, bloggers, and booksellers who shared *Rebel Seoul* with readers. I am honored to be a part of this community that loves books.

And lastly, so much love and thanks to my amazingly supportive and loving family: Halmeoni (I love you thiiiis much), my wonderful aunts and uncles, to Bokyung, Adam, Xander, Jennifer, Sara, Wyatt, Bosung, Katherine, Wusung, Boosung, Christine, Sandy, Susie, Kevin, Bryan, Josh, Scott, Seojun, and Noah. And to Toro, my constant companion.

To Jason, my hero: I love you and I miss you.
To Mom, Dad, and Camille: You are my heart.